Summerhills

Summerhills

D. E. STEVENSON

ISIS
LARGE PRINT
Oxford

First published in Great Britain 1955
by
Collins

Published in Large Print 2005 by ISIS Publishing Ltd,
7 Centremead, Osney Mead, Oxford OX2 0ES
by arrangement with
the Author's Estate

British Library Cataloguing in Publication Data
Stevenson, D. E. (Dorothy Emily), 1892–1973
Summerhills. – Large print ed.
1. Domestic fiction
2. Large type books
I. Title
823.9'12 [F]

ISBN 0–7531–7371–9 (hb)
ISBN 0–7531–7372–7 (pb)

Printed and bound in Great Britain by
T. J. International Ltd., Padstow, Cornwall

Foreword

Major Roger Ayrton M.C. was a very energetic young man. He was interested in his military career and full of plans for his family and his friends. Roger was "the head of the family" (it was an old family with fine traditions and had been settled for many years in a pleasant valley in South-West Scotland) and since he took his position seriously Roger felt it was his duty to look after his relations and put their affairs in order. His plans for his brother and his three young half-sisters were sensible and benevolent and as he was a wealthy young man no financial difficulties were involved.

In Roger's case money was not the root of all evil, it had come to him without his volition and he used it to improve his property and to help others less fortunate than himself. Some of his plans flourished exceedingly and bore fruit, others did not. Roger found that you could not arrange people's lives for them, he could not even arrange his own life in a satisfactory manner. Things happened unexpectedly.

Although complete in itself the story of *Summerhills* and the Ayrton's family affairs is really a sequel and the history of the five young Ayrtons growing up and facing life can be found in *Amberwell*.

The Ayrton Family and their Friends

MARION AYRTON, *widow of William Ayrton (his second wife)*

ROGER AYRTON, *son of William Ayrton and his first wife*

THOMAS AYRTON, *Roger's brother*

NELL AYRTON, *Roger's half-sister* ⎫ *Daughters of*
ANNE SELBY, *Roger's half-sister* ⎬ *William Ayrton*
CONNIE LAMBERT, *Roger's half-sister* ⎭ *and Marion*

STEPHEN AYRTON, *Roger's little son*

EMMIE SELBY, *Anne's little daughter*

GERALD LAMBERT, *Connie's husband*

YOUNG GERRY, JOAN AND LITTLE MARION, *children of Connie and Gerald*

BEATRICE AYRTON, *sister of William Ayrton*

MR. AND MRS. LAMBERT, *Gerald's parents*

MR. ORME, *Rector of St. Stephen's Church at Westkirk*

CHAPTER
ONE

1

The aeroplane was flying over green rolling hills; they were beautiful hills, bathed in summer sunshine, with the shadows of small clouds trailing across them. Here and there was the flash of a little burn or a sky-blue tarn and there were dozens of tiny white dots — which were sheep. Major Roger Ayrton, looking down over the silvery wing of the aircraft, recognised the hills as the Cheviots. He had seen many hills of all sorts and sizes (during the war he had served in Africa, in Italy and in Germany) but no scenery however magnificent gave him the same pleasure as the rolling hills of his own country.

Roger had left Hamburg that morning, had changed planes at London Airport and was now on his way to Renfrew. The flight had been somewhat uncomfortable for they had run into bad weather and been forced out of course, but that was over now and best forgotten. Looking round at his fellow passengers Roger saw that they were recovering from their unpleasant experience and their faces were resuming a natural expression and hue. This recovery was completed by the second pilot who came into the cabin with a breezy air and promised clear skies and a happy landing.

"We're a bit late, aren't we?" asked Roger.

"About half an hour, that's all," replied the man. He hesitated and then added a trifle diffidently: "I don't suppose you remember me, sir?"

Roger prided himself upon his memory for faces, but although he had a vague feeling that he had seen the man before he was unable to place him. Was it in the Desert Campaign? Was it in Italy? Could it have been before that when he was training recruits on Salisbury Plain?

"My name is Fraser," said the second pilot. "I worked for a bit in Amberwell Gardens before the war."

"Did you!" exclaimed Roger. "Well, of course I ought to remember you, but I expect you've changed a good deal since those days."

Even now Roger could not place him, for there had been so many garden-boys at Amberwell (boys in earth-stained overalls who had dug and barrowed and mowed under the eagle eye of Mr. Gray) and this man was smart and dapper in his pilot's uniform.

"I've changed a good deal," agreed Fraser smiling. "I was a dirty little tyke in those days and Mr. Gray was always after me, but all the same I was very happy at Amberwell and I often used to think of the gardens — the green stretches of grass and the fine old trees — when we were in the Desert with the sun glaring down and miles of nothing but sand."

Roger had had the same experience. He had often thought of his home when he was in the Desert. It had been like an oasis — far off and unobtainable, haunting his dreams.

2

"I knew you at once, sir," continued Fraser eagerly. "You came home on leave from Sandhurst while I was there. I was at Amberwell when you had a big Christmas Party and I helped to carry in the tree — and I saw it when you and Mr. Tom and the three young ladies had decorated it with tinsel and fairy-lights and coloured balls. I thought it was beautiful. And I found a sprig of mistletoe in the woods for Mr. Tom. He was the one for jokes!"

"He still is," declared Roger smiling.

"Perhaps you don't remember . . ."

Roger remembered the Christmas Party very well indeed. It was the winter when his parents had gone to South Africa and Aunt Beatrice had come to Amberwell to keep an eye on things. Aunt Beatrice was a queer mixture, sometimes moody and irritable, sometimes cheerful, so you never knew where you were; but it was she who had ordained the party and organised it, and the party had been a tremendous success.

"And the young ladies," said Fraser. "I hope they're all right. Miss Connie was the pretty one and Miss Nell was the shy one. I don't think she ever spoke to me once, all the time I was there, but she had a very nice smile . . . and Miss Anne was the laughing one. How she used to laugh! There was one afternoon when I was cutting the bowling-green and you were all having tea out of doors. There was some joke on and you were all laughing. Miss Anne was rolling about on the ground — helpless."

3

"Yes," said Roger, smiling. "She used to laugh like that."

"I hope —" began Fraser.

"Oh, she's all right, but of course she's grown up now," Roger explained.

"Oh, of course."

"She married when she was very young and her husband died. She's got a little daughter. Connie is married too; she's got three children."

"Fancy that!" exclaimed Fraser. "It doesn't seem all that time ago since I was at Amberwell."

Roger did not reply; to him it seemed a very long time ago since the five of them had played so happily in Amberwell Gardens.

"I hope you don't mind me speaking to you, sir," continued Fraser. "I wouldn't have bothered you but we'll be passing over the Ayrshire Coast in a few minutes and I thought you'd be interested to see Amberwell from the air." He lowered his voice and added, "I told the pilot about you being in the plane and he said we'd come down a bit lower and give you a good view."

"But will that be all right?" asked Roger in surprise. "I mean I don't want him to — to —"

"Absolutely O.K.," replied Fraser cheerfully. "Don't you worry about that. It's a pity we can't drop you off as we pass. I suppose that's where you're going, isn't it?"

"Yes, I'm going home to Amberwell."

The mere saying of these words gave Roger's heart a lift. He was going home to Amberwell. He had been looking forward to his leave for months, he had arranged things so that he could take his leave in June. Amberwell was always lovely, but in June it was at its best — breathtakingly beautiful.

2

The pilot was even better than his word for not only did the plane "come down a bit lower" on reaching Amberwell but it banked and circled once, so Roger experienced the curious sensation of seeing his property rise up from the ground. He had flown a great deal, so he was aware that it was merely an illusion — the plane was leaning sideways that was all — but to see Amberwell rising up like a tilted plate and looking in through the window was quite extraordinary. Roger gazed at it, entranced. The old grey house lay in a fold of the hills and all round it were the gardens, gay with flowers and blossom, green with lawns and trees. There was the bowling-green, surrounded by its high hedge of yew, and beyond was the kitchen-garden, sheltered within sturdy stone walls. Roger could see the avenue winding down to the gates and he could see the slender spire of St. Stephen's Episcopal Church which had been built by his great-grandfather . . . The town of Westkirk looked like a toy-town with its harbour full of toyboats; the tide was out, revealing stretches of pale brown sands and rocks covered with sea-weed.

Roger's delight in this unusual view of his home was slightly marred by the feeling that this should not be happening. He had no idea how much latitude the pilot of a civil aircraft was allowed but he was pretty certain that a tour round a private passenger's private estate was out of order. Perhaps he should have refused — but how could he? The reactions of the other passengers added to his uneasiness; they laid aside their books and papers and looked out of the windows in surprise.

"Are we there?" somebody inquired.

"We're coming down, aren't we?"

"But this isn't Renfrew!"

The plane, having accomplished a circle, rose higher and flew on.

"What was that in aid of?" asked another passenger casually.

Nobody replied.

Fraser had said jokingly, "It's a pity we can't drop you off as we pass." This was the obvious thing to say, so obvious as to be rather foolish, but now that Roger had seen Amberwell and was watching it disappear rapidly into the distance he would have given a good deal to step out of the plane and float down to the ground. It was almost unbearable to be carried on to Renfrew. What an ass I am! said Roger to himself. I've waited months and months quite patiently. Why should I begin to fuss *now*? That was the curious thing about Amberwell: when one was far away one remembered it off and on, as one remembered one's childhood with a vague nostalgia which was not unpleasant, but the moment one started home one was filled with impatience. Amberwell pulled like a magnet; the nearer one approached the harder it pulled.

However there was nothing to be done but to curb his impatience. He could hire a car at Renfrew and be home in time for tea and as they were not expecting him until Friday (for it was only at the last minute he had made up his mind to fly) he would walk in and surprise them. They would be having tea on the terrace as they always did in fine warm weather. Nell would be sitting at the table behind the silver tea-pot and beside her, tucking into scones and honey, would be Stephen. These two were all the world to Roger: Nell, his half-sister and Stephen his little son. They had been all the world to Roger ever since his young wife had been killed in London in an air-raid when Stephen was a few weeks old. Clare's death had been such a terrible shock that Roger's heart had withered within him and he had felt that he would never care for anybody again. That was eight years ago now, and Roger still thought of Clare but the memory was no longer unbearable.

The third member of Roger's household was his stepmother. She would be having tea on the terrace too — reclining upon her chaise-longue with a rug over her knees and a little table beside her. Mrs. Ayrton had been an autocrat in her day (when he was a boy Roger had been frightened of her) but now she was ageing, her reactions were slow and she had lost her grip. It was Nell who held the reins and guided Amberwell. Nell managed everything — and yet she was not a managing sort of person. Nell was still "the shy one" as Fraser had said. She was so quiet and retiring that people scarcely noticed her and despite all that she accomplished she was unsure of herself and doubtful of her own capabilities. Dear Nell, thought Roger, it would be lovely to see her and have a good chat. There were all sorts of things — some important and some not — that Roger wanted to discuss with Nell.

The plane was now approaching Renfrew. Roger's thoughts were interrupted and a problem presented itself to his mind. What ought I to do? he wondered. Shall I thank the pilot for giving me a tour round Amberwell — or not? Could I possibly give him something — or couldn't I? It was rather a difficult problem but fortunately it was resolved quite easily for when the plane had landed and the door was opened the pilot was standing at the bottom of the steps . . . and Roger knew, the moment he laid eyes on the man, that he could not offer him money. Besides, the other passengers were crowding round and there was only time to shake the pilot's hand and to murmur, "Thanks awfully, I enjoyed it," before passing on.

CHAPTER
TWO

1

Roger had decided to approach the terrace by a flight of stone steps leading from the garden. It would be fun to surprise his family by running up the steps and saying, "Hallo!" He left his luggage at the front door, paid the taxi and went round the side of the house. The gardens looked beautiful in the afternoon sunshine; the lawns smooth and green, the borders a mass of colour. During the war the gardens had been neglected and the whole place had got into a frightful condition, but Mr. Gray had managed to get it into proper order again. Of course Mr. Gray was not satisfied and grumbled that the grass would never be the same and the hedges were ruined for want of pruning and the weeds which had flourished unchecked were still coming up every year, but to Roger the place looked beautiful; he could find no flaw in it.

He passed beneath a trellis of roses and paused for a few moments beside the lily-pool. There was a rock in the middle of the water and on the rock sat the bronze-mermaid with a shell in her hand. Roger remembered when the pool was made and the fountain placed in position, and he remembered the first time he had seen the fountain playing and how the water had sprung up from the shell like a silver pillar in the moonlight with opalescent rainbows in the falling drops. How long ago it seemed!

But it was no use dawdling here. Roger wanted to see his family and have a cup of tea, so he turned and ran up the steps to the terrace; but he did not say "Hallo!" because nobody was there.

For a few moments Roger stood there gazing at the empty terrace. He had imagined the scene so vividly that he could hardly believe his eyes . . . but perhaps they were having tea in the morning-room this afternoon. Roger opened the french windows and looked in. No, they were not there. He was ridiculously disappointed — even a trifle annoyed — for Roger had never in all his life returned to Amberwell and not found Nell to welcome him. It was quite an unreasonable feeling of course because they were not expecting him until Friday.

Having looked all over the house and failed to find his relatives Roger made a bee-line for the kitchen and, pushing open the door, discovered Mrs. Duff and Nannie sitting at the table having tea. They did not see him at first and Roger stood and looked at them affectionately. These two were part of Amberwell. Roger could not remember a time when they had not been here. Mrs. Duff had been born on the estate — her father had been his grandfather's coachman — Nannie had been with the Ayrtons since Roger was an infant in arms. They were old now. Roger, who had not seen them for some time, realised that they were both very old and it made him feel sad. Amberwell would not be the same when —

"Maircy, it's Mr. Roger!" exclaimed Mrs. Duff.

"Yes, it's me," said Roger smiling.

They both rose with remarkable alacrity and began to talk at once, welcoming the wanderer with delight, declaring that he was not expected till Friday and explaining that the family had all gone to tea at the Rectory.

"My goodness!" exclaimed Nannie. "Nell *will* be upset! Fancy you arriving and her not here!"

"Well, never mind," said Roger. "You'll give me a cup of tea, won't you?"

"I'll make a fresh pot and take it through to the morning-room," suggested Nannie.

"But I'd much rather have it here with you," said Roger, smiling.

Nannie and Mrs. Duff were very pleased and presently the three of them were sitting round the table and Roger was hearing all the news.

"Mrs. Ayrton's not too grand," said Nannie. "Very wandery, she is."

"But not always," objected Mrs. Duff. "Just off and on — and if you ask me she knows a good deal more about what's going on than you think."

"How does she get on with Anne?" asked Roger.

This was one of the problems which Roger wanted to solve, and he had no qualms at all in asking Mrs. Duff and Nannie about it, for these two were loyal to the core and knew as much about the Ayrton family as Roger himself — perhaps more, if truth be told. Anne was Roger's youngest step-sister, she had married when scarcely more than a child and without her parents' consent. They had been very angry, of course — any parents would have been angry — but instead of making the best of a bad job they had literally cast her off and forbidden her to write to her family. Perhaps they had not intended to cast her off completely; perhaps in time they would have relented — Roger did not know — but the War had come and Anne had vanished. Anne and her husband had moved from their little flat in London leaving no address. When Roger returned from France he had tried to trace them, but without avail, and it was years before Anne was found. By this time her husband, Martin Selby, had died and Anne was working in a market-garden near London and was having a hard struggle to keep herself and her little girl.

Roger often wondered what had happened to Anne during those lost years; she said very little about them but they had changed her from a happy-hearted child into a serious-minded woman with a passion for independence. It was the passion for independence that bothered Roger, for instead of coming home and living comfortably at Amberwell — which seemed to him the obvious thing for her to do — she had insisted on "doing a job" and in Roger's opinion Anne's job was most unsuitable. She was keeping house for old Mr. Orme, the rector of St. Stephen's at Westkirk. She and little Emmie were living in the Rectory at the gates of Amberwell and in spite of Roger's efforts to induce them to come home Anne refused to budge. The only concession Anne had made in response to Roger's persuasions was the acceptance of his offer that little Emmie should come to Amberwell daily and do her lessons with Stephen.

All this was in Roger's mind when he put his question to Mrs. Duff and Nannie; he wanted to see Anne again, and renew his persuasions, but before doing so it was important for him to know how she was getting on with her mother. Nell would tell him of course (he would ask Nell about it) but it would be useful to hear what these two had to say on the subject.

"It's funny," said Nannie, stirring her tea with a thoughtful air. "It's funny how Mrs. Ayrton's taken to Anne. All those years when she wouldn't speak of Anne — and now Anne can twist her round her finger. Sometimes I wonder if she's forgotten the row altogether."

"She's not forgotten the row," declared Mrs. Duff. "She's just put it all out of her mind."

"It's the same thing, Kate," said Nannie in surprise.

"It's not. It's quite different."

"If you forget a thing —"

"But she's not forgotten. She's just put it out of her mind."

Roger listened to them arguing. Mrs. Duff was right, thought Roger. He knew exactly what she meant and agreed with her.

"Och well," said Mrs. Duff at last. "I know what I mean and I know I'm right, but it's no good arguing with you. I'd as soon start an argument with Ailsa Craig — it would be more useful."

"What about Stephen?" asked Roger tactfully.

The red herring was successful as he knew it would be. They both adored Stephen and could talk about him endlessly without the slightest disagreement.

2

When they had finished discussing Stephen and his doings there was a short silence.

"And the new governess is a nice enough creature," said Mrs. Duff.

"Not bad at all," agreed Nannie.

"Oh yes, the new governess," nodded Roger. He remembered now. Nell's last letter had informed him of Miss Paterson's departure and the arrival of a substitute. "*She's like a horse,*" Nell had written. "*A very nice-looking horse — if you know what I mean! She's got very long legs and she wears trousers.*" Roger had smiled over the description (he had never seen a horse wearing trousers). As a matter of fact the description had not predisposed Roger to the new governess for he was allergic to trousers upon a female. It was Roger's firm conviction that no female looked well in trousers. He was surprised to find Mrs. Duff and Nannie so enthusiastic about the woman — "nice enough creature" and "not bad at all" were the height of praise.

"She's no bother," continued Nannie. "I *will* say that. We've given her the nursery-flat to herself. I've come down to the dressing-room to keep an eye on Mrs. Ayrton. It seemed queer at first not to be in the nursery, but I'm getting used to it — and it saves me the stairs. My legs are not as young as they were and that's the truth."

Mrs. Duff gave Roger a look that was almost a wink.

"That sounds a splendid arrangement," said Roger solemnly. He was aware that Nell had been trying for years to coax Nannie down from the nursery-flat.

"I'm getting used to it," repeated Nannie. "At first I was always finding myself half-way up the nursery-stairs."

"She's teaching them well," put in Mrs. Duff as she poured out another cup of tea and pressed another large slice of cake upon her guest. "There's not a doubt she's teaching them better than Miss Paterson."

"I'm not so keen on the running," Nannie declared. "It seems daft to me. I never knew a child yet that couldn't run of its own accord."

"Running?" asked Roger in surprise.

"She's mad about it —" began Nannie.

"Wheesht, this'll be her!" exclaimed Mrs. Duff, holding up her finger.

The kitchen-door opened and a young woman came in with a tray in her hands. "Oh, I'm sorry!" she said, putting down the tray and turning hastily. "I wouldn't have come in if I'd known you had a visitor."

Roger got up. He could not think of anything to say; but Mrs. Duff rose to the occasion.

"It's not a visitor, it's the major," said Mrs. Duff with admirable poise. "It's Major Ayrton, Miss Glassford."

Roger had time to think of several things as the young woman hesitated at the door. He thought: Good old Duffy! No society hostess could have done it better! And of course Nell is right — she *is* like a horse!

But all the same Nell's description had given Roger an entirely wrong idea of the new governess, for although she was like a horse, had unusually long legs and wore trousers she was very attractive indeed with smooth dark hair and a beautiful complexion. She was tall and slender . . . and as Roger looked at her he was obliged to revise his life-long conviction and to admit that there was at least one exception to the rule about females in trousers.

"I've just arrived," said Roger. "Mrs. Duff is giving me a cup of tea."

"We were expecting you on Friday —"

"I flew," explained Roger smiling.

They shook hands. Miss Glassford's hand was cool and firm. There was no nonsense about her hand-shake.

"It's Amberwell's fault," continued Roger. "I didn't mean to fly, but when I begin to think about Amberwell it makes me impatient to get home."

"I don't wonder."

"You like Amberwell?"

"Who wouldn't?"

Miss Glassford said no more than that, but it was enough. Panegyrics about the beauty of Amberwell would have spoilt the effect completely.

By this time Nannie and Mrs. Duff had begun to clear the table so it was easy for Roger and Miss Glassford to talk. They began by discussing the weather but soon got on to Stephen's scholastic progress.

"Stephen is precocious in some ways, but a little backward in others," said his new instructress. "I think Miss Paterson's methods must have been old-fashioned. Emmie is different of course. Emmie has had a proper grounding."

Roger was not so interested in Emmie. "Will you be able to push him on?" asked Roger anxiously.

"Oh yes, but not all at once. You can't cram children of eight years old."

Roger explained that he did not want Stephen crammed but he did want him to be up to standard before he went to school.

"School?" asked Miss Glassford in surprise. "Miss Ayrton didn't say Stephen was going to school."

"Oh, not till next year at the very earliest," Roger assured her.

Miss Glassford sighed. "Of course it would be splendid for Stephen but I can't help feeling a little sad. You won't want me when Stephen goes to school, will you?"

What could Roger say? Of course they would not want her, but how brutal it would be to say so! It was quite impossible to say so with Miss Glassford's soft brown eyes gazing at him appealingly. Miss Glassford's soft brown eyes had a sort of hypnotic effect upon Roger and he did not know whether to be glad or sorry when the conversation was broken off by Nannie exclaiming that she heard voices in the hall.

"It's them!" cried Nannie. "Oh my, won't they be excited when they see you!"

Stephen sat upon Roger's bed and watched him
unpack. There were presents for Stephen in the suitcase
— he had known there would be presents and he would
not have been human if he had not watched eagerly for
them to come to light — but the presents were nothing
compared with the joy of seeing his father and knowing
that he would be here at Amberwell for three whole
weeks.

"We'll bathe, won't we?" said Stephen. "I can swim
now — very nearly. Can we have a picnic to-morrow at
the Smugglers' Cave?"

"I don't know about to-morrow. I'm going to be
pretty busy with one thing and another . . . here,
Stephen, catch!" A brown-paper parcel came flying
across the room and landed on the bed.

"Ooh, what can it be!" cried Stephen, falling upon it
and tearing off the string. It was a mechanical toy, a
little acrobat who turned somersaults. Stephen was
enchanted with the gift.

It was amazing to Roger to see Stephen growing up,
to watch the development of his personality. Every time
Roger returned to Amberwell he discovered a new and
more mature Stephen. This time Stephen had grown
from a child into a little boy and somehow in the
process had become more like Clare. He was very like
Clare, thought Roger; the small pointed face, so full of
affection and intelligence, and the bright eager eyes.
Even the unruly lock of hair which strayed on to
Stephen's forehead reminded Roger of Clare.

"Can I have a holiday while you're here, Daddy?" asked Stephen. "Aunt Nell said she thought I could, but I was to ask you."

"Not all the time, I'm afraid. You see you've got to buck up like anything with lessons. You don't want to be behind the other boys when you go to school."

"Am I going to school?"

"All boys go to school."

"But Daddy, that would mean going away from Amberwell!" cried Stephen in dismay.

Roger looked at his son thoughtfully. Here was another Ayrton who already, at eight years old, had got Amberwell in his blood.

"Well, we'll see," said Roger. "I've got a plan about that . . . but anyhow it won't be for ages, so there's no need to worry. Look, Stephen, here's another parcel."

This time the parcel did not come flying across the room. Roger brought it over to the bed and helped to open it. This time it was a very small parcel with a box inside . . . and, inside the box, there was a little silver watch wrapped in tissue paper.

"Oh Daddy, a watch!" shrieked Stephen. "A real watch of my very own! Oh Daddy, how gorgeous!"

The watch was strapped firmly on to the small thin wrist to the joy and delight of its new owner. Roger's pleasure in the gift was somewhat dimmed by the thinness of the wrist.

Stephen was not as robust as other boys. It was no wonder, for he had come through a dreadful experience when he was a few weeks old. When the bomb fell upon the house in London, and Clare was killed, the baby had been buried in the ruins. It had been thought by the salvage men that there were no survivors but Roger, who had arrived on the scene shortly after the explosion, had heard the baby crying. Clare was gone — there was no hope of saving her — but the baby was alive. Clare's baby, the precious little creature that she had loved so dearly, was somewhere in the midst of that ghastly pile of rubble. Roger crawled in beneath the twisted girders and tottering masonry and found him.

The baby had been sent to Amberwell and had arrived there very ill indeed. He had been at death's door and if it had not been for Nell and Nannie, who had nursed him tenderly and coaxed him back to life, he certainly would not have recovered.

All this passed through Roger's mind as he strapped the watch on to the thin little wrist — and that awful night of agony seemed real and near, as if it had happened last week instead of eight years ago.

"What's the matter, Daddy?" asked Stephen.

"Nothing," said Roger hastily. "Nothing's the matter. We're going to have a fine time. We're going to have picnics and we're going to bathe and we must go round Amberwell — you and I together — and look at all the old haunts, but we've got work to do as well. I've got various things to arrange and you've got your lessons, so we can't just enjoy ourselves all the time."

CHAPTER
THREE

1

"What do you think of Georgina?" Nell inquired.

Dinner was over and she and Roger had settled down comfortably in the morning-room for a talk. Nell had her mending-basket beside her and Roger had lighted his pipe.

"Georgina!" echoed Roger in surprise.

"Miss Glassford," explained Nell. "She asked me to call her Georgina. I'm finding it rather difficult but it would be rude not to — when she's asked me."

Roger smiled; it was so like Nell.

"Georgina is a difficult name," continued Nell. "I believe I could manage it better if her name was — was Margaret, or Helen. I mean something fairly ordinary. The only thing to do is to practise saying it to myself over and over again."

"Have you managed it yet?"

"Not to her face. It's awfully silly, isn't it?"

"Not really," said Roger comfortingly. "In fact I think it was silly of her to ask you. Either you feel like calling a person by her Christian name — or else you don't."

Roger was quite pleased at the red herring which saved him from the necessity of answering Nell's question. He was not ready to say what he thought of Georgina Glassford.

"She's a good teacher," said Nell. "She makes lessons more interesting than Miss Paterson."

"That's good," said Roger. "Lessons ought to be interesting and we want Stephen to be up to the right standard before he goes to school."

"Oh Roger, don't send him to school!" exclaimed Nell in dismay.

"Nell, listen —"

"Oh Roger — please! You know how delicate Stephen is. He might be miserable, miles away from home. He might get ill! There isn't a good school anywhere near. It would mean sending him to Edinburgh — and he isn't used to boys —"

"That's just it. Listen, Nell —"

"But he's got Emmie to play with — it would be different if he were alone — and they get on splendidly —"

"Will you listen to me for a moment!" cried Roger. "I want to tell you something. I've been thinking about this for months and I've got a Big Idea."

Roger had been thinking about the problem for months, in fact ever since he had gone back to Germany after his Christmas leave. On the one hand he felt that Stephen really ought to go to school, and have the companionship of other boys and learn to look after himself, and on the other hand he felt that Nell had a right to her say in the matter and that he had no right to seize Stephen away and pack him off to school.

Roger was still shilly-shallying when he received a letter from Arnold Maddon presenting him with another problem to solve; Arnold's affairs were not really Roger's responsibility of course, but all the same he was very anxious to help him. Arnold's father was the doctor at Westkirk, and had attended the Ayrton family for years. Arnold himself was a year younger than Roger, he had played in the Amberwell Gardens when they were all children together and in fact had been one of Roger's closest friends. Later, when they grew up, their ways had parted; Arnold had gone to Cambridge and Roger to the Army, so they had not met for years, but they wrote to one another occasionally and Roger heard news of his friend through Nell. He had heard that Arnold had been wounded in the war — so badly wounded that he had spent several years in hospital — and he had heard that at long last Arnold had been released from hospital with an artificial foot and was living with his father in Westkirk. Roger felt a little guilty when he saw Arnold's letter amongst his other correspondence for he had intended to write to Arnold.

The letter started in a ribald manner which made Roger smile but his smile faded as he read on:

"I felt a bit like Rip van Winkle when I got out of hospital," wrote Arnold. "It's rather an alarming experience to tumble suddenly into a big bustling world and rather humiliating to find oneself *de trop*. I have been trying to get a job and have been answering advertisements and pursuing possible openings all over the country but nobody seems to want me. A post as junior master in a boys' school is the sort of thing that would suit me best, but unfortunately most schools would rather have a hefty fellow with two feet who could coach rugger and take the boys for cross-country runs. I don't blame them really. What use is a cripple even if he does happen to have a First in History. Now, at last, I have heard of a post in a small private school in North London. It is a dim sort of place and I did not like the headmaster — he was rather Squeerish I thought — but I have got to the stage when I would take any sort of job. You see I can't go on living at home and doing nothing. Dad has been wonderful to me but quite honestly he can't afford to keep me here eating my head off and not earning a penny piece. The point of all this drivel is that the headmaster wants a reference and I thought perhaps you would not mind writing a thing to say I am honest and respectable and moderate in my habits! You could also say you had known me since my boyhood without stretching the truth. Sorry to bother you, old top, but it would be helpful.

Yours ever,

ARNOLD

Roger had immediately sat down and written a glowing testimonial which he could do quite easily "without stretching the truth," for Arnold was a fine fellow and extremely clever. In fact Roger was of the opinion that any school would be very lucky indeed to get Arnold as a master — despite his handicap. It would be nice to enclose a fat cheque in the envelope, thought Roger, but of course he could not do so; Arnold would be furious. He sat and thought about it sadly. What a waste! Arnold as a junior master at Dotheboys Hall!

Then quite suddenly Roger's two problems clicked together in his mind and he saw that they solved each other. The Big Idea was born. He would buy a large house in the vicinity of Amberwell and start a school himself; thus Arnold would have a worth-while job and Stephen could be educated within comfortable reach of his home.

Fortunately Roger was in a position to back his plan financially, for he had inherited a fortune from his wife, and although he looked upon the money as belonging to Stephen he need have no qualms about using some of it for this purpose. It would benefit Stephen, and other people as well, and it was a project which would have appealed to Clare — he was sure of that.

This was one of the occasions when money was useful; it was not always an asset, Roger had found. Most of his brother officers had little beyond their pay and those with families had difficulty in making ends meet. It was embarrassing to sit and listen to their conversation upon the subject — and to say nothing yourself. You would willingly have helped them but it was not easy, for those you would have liked to help were too proud to accept a penny and the other kind were apt to sponge, knowing that you could afford to pay for their entertainment and seeing no reason why you should not do so.

The more Roger thought about his plan the more he liked it and instead of dispatching the glowing testimonial to his friend he tore it into small pieces and sent a cable saying: RETURNING AMBERWELL FRIDAY KEEP YOURSELF FREE UNTIL I SEE YOU

2

All this had happened only a few days ago, and so far Roger had said nothing to anybody about his Big Idea; before the thing was settled he wanted to discuss it with Nell.

"Look here, Nell," said Roger. "Stephen really must go to school. We don't want him to grow up a Cissie. You wouldn't worry about him if he could go to a school near Amberwell, would you?"

"There isn't one," said Nell.

"We'll make one," said Roger . . . and he proceeded to lay bare his plans. "You see, don't you?" said Roger earnestly. "It would solve the whole problem. If Stephen could go to a school near Amberwell you could keep an eye on him and see he was all right."

"Yes," said Nell a little doubtfully. "Yes, that wouldn't be quite so bad. There's no hurry of course."

Roger left it at that. Nell would think about it and gradually she would realise what a splendid idea it was. Meantime Roger intended to get on with his plan for there was a great deal to do: he must see Arnold about it; he must find a suitable house and put in hand the necessary alterations.

"There's another thing I wanted to talk to you about," said Roger after a short silence. "I wondered whether there was any chance of persuading Anne to come home."

"Oh Roger, I wish you could!"

"You're sure it would work?"

"Of course it would work. It would be splendid. You see Anne understands Mother. I've never understood Mother," said Nell rather sadly. "I've tried my best, but it's hopeless. I simply can't understand what she's thinking or feeling. For instance when Anne came to see her after all those years there was no reconciliation; Mother never even kissed her. Mother just accepted her as if she had been away for the week-end and sent me to make the tea. Wasn't that strange?"

Roger nodded. As a matter of fact Nell had told him this before, and he had thought it very strange indeed, but Mrs. Duff's explanation threw light upon the subject. "She's just put it all out of her mind," Mrs. Duff had said.

It occurred to Roger that his step-mother was fortunate. Most people have uncomfortable memories which they would like to banish, but few can banish them completely. The brain plays queer tricks upon us. We can wrap up an uncomfortable memory and put it away on the top shelf of the cupboard and lock the door upon it; there it stays until a chance sight or sound or smell unlocks the door and the thing tumbles out at our feet — the nasty ugly thing that we had forgotten!

There were not many ugly things in Roger's cupboard, but he would not have been human if he had never done anything to be ashamed of. There was the ugly thing which had happened soon after Clare's death, when Roger had been feeling utterly miserable and full of bitterness, and there was the ugly thing which had happened at Sandhurst when he and another fellow had got tight and made fools of themselves; but one of the worst things in the cupboard was a childhood memory, quite a small and ridiculous incident to haunt a grown man. The occasion was a party given by his father and his step-mother to celebrate the opening of the fountain in Amberwell Gardens. It was a very hot day and Roger and Tom, dressed up in their kilts and doublets, had felt boiled and sticky with heat. They had been thoroughly bored with the proceedings and had sneaked away to bathe. The tide was in and the sea was cool and clean. It was a gorgeous bathe, they had enjoyed it enormously and had prided themselves upon their cleverness in escaping from authority and spending the fine summer afternoon in such a sensible way.

Then, on their return, they had met their father and their conduct had been shown in a new light. He had been furious with them and had told them they had neglected their duty as hosts. "Amberwell is offering hospitality," Mr. Ayrton had declared. "You belong to Amberwell — these people are your guests as well as mine! You ought to be ashamed of yourselves . . ." He had said a good deal more, for Mr. Ayrton had never been one to mince his words, but the rest did not matter. What mattered was that Roger had failed in his duty to Amberwell. The idea haunted Roger; it would haunt Roger until he died. Sometimes he wondered if Tom remembered the incident with discomfort — probably not, for Tom was different. Tom loved Amberwell in his own way, but he lived in the present, enjoying life and taking things as they came.

Nell's voice broke into Roger's memories. "What are you thinking about?" she asked.

"About Tom — really," replied Roger (which was true enough). "Tom takes things as they come. He's far too good a doctor to go wandering round the world on pleasure cruises; he ought to settle down and take his profession seriously."

"What a lot of trouble you have with your family!" said Nell smiling. "Stephen is to have a school specially made for him; Anne is to come home and live like a lady; Tom is to put up a brass plate in Harley Street. Haven't you any plans for Connie and me?"

"Connie is all right," replied Roger with a grin. "She spoils her children of course — I'd like to send young Gerry to a tough school where he would get bullied into shape — but I shan't lose any sleep over it. As for you, I'd like to send you for a long sea-voyage. You've been mewed up in Amberwell all your life, toiling and moiling for other people. You ought to get away from all the worries and enjoy yourself and see the world. That's my plan for you."

Nell laughed. She said, "You had better find somebody else to look after Amberwell — and Stephen — before you buy my ticket."

CHAPTER
FOUR

1

Roger had so many jobs on hand, arranging the affairs of his family, that he felt he had better start upon them at once, so the very next morning after his arrival he walked down to the Rectory to see Anne. It was a cloudy morning but there was a brightness behind the clouds which promised a fine day, probably a very warm day. A wicket-gate led from the grounds of Amberwell into the little churchyard and beyond that was the small garden belonging to the Rectory surrounded by a fine beech hedge.

It was essential for Roger to get Anne alone — without Mr. Orme — so he was pleased when he saw her kneeling upon the ground planting out lettuces. She was wearing an old blue overall, her hands were dirty and her soft brown hair was untidy — and altogether she looked like the little Anne of long ago who was always getting into trouble with Nannie on account of her unruly hair. Roger had come with the intention of speaking to Anne firmly — he was annoyed with Anne — but he felt his annoyance vanishing as he looked at her.

"Hallo, Roger, how nice to see you!" she exclaimed, sitting back on her heels and smiling at him. "Nell said you weren't coming till Friday —"

"I flew," said Roger. He was getting rather tired of explaining how and why he had arrived before he was expected. He had explained the matter to Nannie and Mrs. Duff, to Miss Glassford, to Nell and Stephen and Mrs. Ayrton and also to Mr. Gray whom he had seen for a few moments in the gardens.

"Well anyway it's lovely to see you," declared Anne. "You don't mind if I go on with this job, do you? Sit down on the barrow."

He sat down on the barrow and watched her. She did the job quickly and neatly, singling out the seedlings and tucking them cosily into their little holes.

"You do that well," remarked Roger.

"It's one of my favourite jobs. You know I worked in a market-garden during the war."

"Did you like working in the garden?"

"Yes, but I like my present job better. I think I do it better, too. I'm an old-fashioned sort of person; making a home and looking after people is my line. It satisfies me completely."

"I wish you'd come home to Amberwell."

"I know. You said that before, and it's very kind of you, but I'm not coming home, Roger."

"Why?" he asked. "You've never explained why. Is it because you still feel bitter about the way you were treated? It wasn't our fault, you know. We did our best to find you."

"I never felt bitter!" cried Anne in surprise. "You've got it all wrong, Roger. Everything that happened to me was my own fault and nobody else's. I was an absolute fool to marry Martin."

Roger gazed at her in surprise. "But Nell told me —"

"Nell thinks I loved Martin and was happy with him. I wasn't happy — I don't think anybody could have been happy with Martin — but I made my bed and I had to lie on it. I don't know why I'm telling you this. I haven't told anybody else except Mr. Orme."

"I won't tell anybody —"

"I'll kill you if you do," declared Anne fiercely.

There was a short silence.

"Forgive me, Roger," said Anne at last. "It was horrid of me to say that, but — but I don't want anybody to know."

"I'm terribly sorry you had such a rotten time," said Roger. He hesitated and then added, "But I don't see why that should prevent you from coming home."

"There are dozens of reasons," she declared. "Every one of them is enough to prevent me from coming home."

"Tell me one."

Anne sighed. She said, "I'm awfully bad at explaining things and I don't know which reason comes first. Perhaps Mr. Orme comes first. He needs me. He really needs somebody to take care of him and I can do it well. I'm very, very fond of him, you see. He needs me — and I like to be needed. Nobody has ever needed me before. That's a whole reason in itself, isn't it?" urged Anne, looking up at Roger appealingly.

"Yes . . . I suppose it is."

"And then there's Mother, of course. That's another reason."

"But your mother wants you! Nell says you get on with her splendidly."

"It isn't fair," declared Anne.

"What isn't fair?" asked Roger in surprise.

"Oh dear!" exclaimed Anne. "Don't you understand! I thought Mother would be difficult; I thought she might refuse to have anything to do with me. Nell thought so too."

"But it wasn't like that at all. Your mother was delighted to see you."

"That's what's so unfair."

"I don't see it," said Roger hopelessly.

"Don't you see it isn't fair to Nell? Nell has been here all these years, looking after Mother, running Amberwell, coping with everything — and Mother treats Nell like a black slave! Then the prodigal daughter walks in and gets roast chicken and new peas and a ring on her finger. Is that fair?"

Roger could not help laughing, and Anne, who never could resist a joke, began to laugh too (but not, Roger noticed, with her usual abandon).

"I don't know why we're laughing," said Anne at last. "It's all perfectly true — even the ring is true. Mother insisted on giving it to me (it's a sapphire, set with diamonds, which belonged to Grandmother) and she always orders chicken and peas when Emmie and I go there to lunch. As a matter of fact I've always thought the story of the Prodigal Son was awfully unfair. Mr. Orme has explained it to me, but I still think the Elder Brother had every right to be annoyed. Nell isn't annoyed of course — she's an absolute saint, there isn't a grain of jealousy in her — but I'm annoyed on her account. The chicken and peas make me sick. I'd rather have shepherd's pie."

Roger did not laugh this time. "Yes, I see," he said. "Well, in that case I suppose we must leave things as they are in the meantime . . . but remember you can always come home to Amberwell if and when you want."

Roger was thinking that things might change. Anne's mother was frail; she would not live for ever; Mr. Orme was old and not very strong. Yes, circumstances were bound to alter, perhaps sooner, perhaps later. One had to face facts. The day might come when Anne's two reasons would disappear. Of course one could not say this to Anne; one could only say — as he had said — that she could always come home if and when she wanted.

Roger would have been surprised if he had known what Anne was thinking as she looked up at him from her kneeling position on the ground. She had told him that she had dozens of reasons for not coming home to live at Amberwell . . . perhaps she had not as many, but she had more than two. He's very good-looking, Anne was thinking. He's very attractive indeed; so big and strong and vital, with his nice brown face and his fair hair and blue eyes. I wonder if he has got over the tragedy of losing Clare. I don't believe he has — quite — but some day he'll get over it and have eyes for other women and I do hope he'll find the right woman. Roger deserves a very special sort of wife.

It was Roger's future wife — that shadowy but very special sort of woman — who was the absolutely insuperable obstacle to Anne's return home. For, however special she might be, she would not want a sister-in-law to share Amberwell (to sit at her table and take up a place at her fireside) and Anne loved Amberwell so dearly that she could not go back and live there and then be banished again. No, she could not bear it . . . but of course one could not say this to Roger.

"Are you coming in to talk to Mr. Orme?" asked Anne, rising from her knees.

"Not to-day," replied Roger. "I've got to go and see Arnold — about something."

"Poor Arnold, I wish he could get a job," said Anne with a sigh.

2

The Maddons' house was in Westkirk High Street. Dr. Maddon was a widower and lived in a flat above the surgeries, and except for a woman who came in for a few hours daily he lived alone. His daughter, Harriet, had a job in Glasgow and came home only very occasionally for a week-end. Since Arnold had been discharged from hospital he had been living with his father. Dr. Maddon was an old man now; he had retired two years ago leaving his partner, Dr. Brown, to carry on the practice, but there were a few patients in the district who insisted upon having their old friend to see them when they were ill, and this gave Dr. Maddon an interest in life and kept him from stagnating.

Roger knew the house well. He had often visited it when he was a child, and to-day as he approached it he remembered happy times. The door of the Maddons' private apartments was at the back of the house, so Roger went round and was about to ring the bell when he heard a shout from the garden and Arnold came towards him up the path. They had not met for years and Roger was shocked at his friend's appearance — shocked and distressed — for not only was Arnold lame, but he looked so much older; his hair was grey at the sides and his face was thin and lined.

"Hallo, Arnold!" said Roger more cheerfully than he felt. "Don't say you thought I wasn't coming until Friday."

"All right I won't," replied Arnold smiling (and the smile lighted up his face and made him look more like the Arnold of bygone times). "As a matter of fact you couldn't come soon enough for me. I've been wondering ever since I got your cable whether I was destined to be secretary of the Prime Minister or assistant dustman in the Westkirk Cleansing Department."

The words were jesting but Arnold's eyes were anxious and Roger was so upset by their expression that for a moment he could not speak.

"Don't worry old boy," said Arnold quickly. "I expect the job has fallen through — they always do. It was decent of you to bother. I turned down Squeers but I can easily write to him and I'm pretty sure he'll take me. He's not likely to get anybody else for the money he's offering."

"The job's all right," said Roger.

"The job's all right!" echoed Arnold incredulously.

"Yes, it's yours if you want it."

"But Roger, they'll want to *see* me before they take me! I mean — I mean did you tell them I'd lost a foot and — and —"

"It's all right, I tell you," said Roger gruffly. "Let's sit down and I'll tell you about it."

They sat down on the wooden bench beneath the chestnut tree. The bench was an old friend. Roger remembered one very warm summer afternoon when he and Arnold had played with it for hours. They had been reading *The Last of the Mohicans* and the bench had been a canoe in which they had navigated rivers and shot rapids . . . but Arnold was waiting to hear about the job and it was difficult to know how to begin to tell him.

"I want to start a school," said Roger bluntly.

"You want to start a school!"

"Yes, will you take it on?"

"What on earth do you mean?"

"Headmaster," said Roger.

For a few moments there was silence. Then Arnold said, "You're not really thinking of it seriously?"

"Yes, I am," declared Roger, seizing Arnold's stick and beginning to poke a hole in the grass. "I want to buy a big house near Westkirk and start a school for little boys."

"Look here, what's this in aid of? I mean I shall get a job all right. I don't want —"

"It's in aid of Stephen," said Roger firmly. "Stephen must go to school and Nell wants to have him within reasonable distance of home."

"You don't mean you're going to start a school on purpose for Stephen!"

"Stephen — and others."

"My dear old boy, you're mad! Do you realise the snags? Have you the slightest idea what it would cost? Where would you get the boys?"

"We'd get lots of boys," said Roger confidently. He was beginning to get into his stride now that the subject was opened. "I've got plans about that. There isn't a Prep. School in the district — so we'd get some of the locals — and my idea is to have reduced fees for the sons of serving officers. There are dozens of fellows nowadays who can't afford enormous school fees and would be only too glad to send their sons. You can't help people by giving them money, but they could be helped indirectly — like this — and we could have special arrangements for keeping the boys in the holidays if their fathers were serving abroad . . ."

Roger continued to enlarge upon his ideas and Arnold listened. At first he listened with disbelief, as if to a fairy-tale but after a few minutes he began to realise that his friend was in earnest . . . and he began to hope. For months and months Arnold had tried to get a job; he had answered advertisements for junior masters; he had answered advertisements for assistant librarians, for secretaries and for clerks; he had even answered advertisements for floorwalkers (though how he proposed to walk about and stand upon his feet all day long nobody knew — least of all Arnold). Nobody had wanted him. Most of the advertisers never even answered his letters. If Roger's idea came to anything it would be a miracle — no less. Arnold had never even dreamed of anything so marvellous as a school of his own. It would be something to make, something to build — a worth-while task. He could carry out his own ideas of education; he could . . . but of course it was too good to be true. It could not happen.

"Look here, Roger!" he exclaimed, interrupting the flow of his friend's imagination. "It all sounds marvellous but where do you propose to get the money?"

"I shall sell some stock," replied Roger promptly.

"You mean you have the capital to — to —"

"Yes, that's what I mean. I know it seems queer; but you see Clare's grandfather left her all his money and she made a Will leaving it to me. I didn't know about it till afterwards. Of course the Death Duties cut it down a lot and the Chancellor of the Exchequer takes most of the income, but even so I don't spend half of it. There's a man called Creech who looks after it. He looked after it when Lord Richmore was alive so I just left it in his hands. He buys and sells shares, and everything he touches seems to turn up trumps and the stuff goes on piling up in the most extraordinary way."

Arnold was speechless.

"Money is like that," continued Roger thoughtfully. "It's awfully queer sort of stuff. If you've got lots you're practically bound to get more unless you're a perfect fool. At first I hated the money. I mean I'd lost Clare and the money seemed a sort of — a sort of insult."

"A sort of insult!"

"Yes, what use was the beastly money to me — without Clare? But now I just accept it as a responsibility and do my best with it . . ." and Roger continued to give Arnold his ideas about money in general, and his own fortune in particular, and the curious problems it involved.

To say that all this was an eye-opener to Arnold, who scarcely had two pennies to rub together, was to understate the case. Arnold had been of the opinion that if you had "lots of money" all your troubles were over but when Roger had finished his little lecture he realised that he had been totally mistaken.

"Well, there it is," said Roger at last. "I can't give it away because it isn't mine. I look upon it as belonging to Stephen. That's why the school is such a good plan, don't you see?"

"Yes, it isn't as mad as it sounds."

"It isn't mad at all."

"But what about Creech — or whatever his name is?"

"Creech will be pleased," declared Roger confidently. "It doesn't matter if he isn't pleased — but he will be. I had a letter from him the other day saying we ought to find an investment which doesn't pay much interest but has good future prospects."

"There would be no interest at all for years."

"But there would be — ultimately?"

"Oh yes, if it were a success. Unless of course you intend to take the sons of your friends for nothing."

"Not for nothing," said Roger hastily. "Reduced fees is my idea — and it needn't pay. That's the beauty of it. We can plough back any profits; we can put them into a properly equipped lab. and a swimming-pool and that sort of thing. We can run the place as a school should be run — no silly luxuries of course but everything up to date. You shall have *carte blanche*, Arnold."

Arnold was almost swept off his feet but he made one more protest: "Look here, do you realise what it would cost? You'd have to buy the house and alter it and furnish it and engage staff — all that before you could start the school at all. Honestly it might be five years before we could get enough boys to make it pay."

Roger noticed he had said "we." "I know of several boys already," declared Roger. "Sons of fellows in the Regiment — seven for certain — and Stephen makes eight."

"I believe I could raise three," said Arnold thoughtfully.

"Well, there we are! There's our cricket eleven!"

Arnold began to laugh; his laughter was somewhat hysterical.

"Shut up!" cried Roger, shaking his arm roughly. "This is serious, Arnold. There are all sorts of things to arrange. We've got to find a house and get an architect on the job before I go back to Germany. After that you have to manage everything yourself."

"I could get a temporary job until —"

"You're engaged from now," said Roger firmly. "I must have a man on the spot to see to things."

"But Roger —"

"Take it or leave it," said Roger airily.

"You are an ass, aren't you?" said Arnold in a shaky voice.

CHAPTER
FIVE

1

On one side of Amberwell the Ayrtons' nearest neighbours were the Lamberts, whose only son Gerald had married Connie Ayrton. Mr. Lambert was the director of a big shipbuilding firm on the Clyde; he had built Merlewood himself, had laid out a very pleasant garden and had settled down with his pretty wife. He had now partially retired and Gerald was carrying on the business with zeal and efficiency. The Lamberts were the sort of people who had sailed through life without many troubles; they were fond of each other, they had enough money to be comfortable and their son was thoroughly satisfactory in every way.

On the other side of Amberwell across the moors was a fine old mansion called Stark Place which had belonged to the Findlater family for generations. There had been Findlaters at Stark Place long before Amberwell was built; and that was not yesterday. Now, like all big houses, Stark Place had become far too big for its owners. Most of the rooms were shut up; the furniture was swathed in dust-sheets and the long empty corridors were silent. Sir Andrew and Lady Findlater still lived in one of the wings. It was not very comfortable but it was easier to live there than to move.

Unlike the Lamberts their lives had not been plain sailing, troubles had crowded upon them and had made them old before their time. In these days of heavy taxation it was impossible to make ends meet and to keep the old house in reasonable condition.

The Findlaters' two sons had joined the Army at the beginning of the war and Ian — the elder — had been killed. This was a crushing blow for Ian was devoted to his parents, and they to him. Andy was different, an independent character who had always gone his own way and was not particularly interested in his family. He had made the Army his career and was at present serving abroad. The Findlaters' third child was a daughter — they were fortunate in her if in nothing else. Mary Findlater had served in the Wrens during the war but had now come home to look after her parents.

Mary found Stark Place extremely dull after her war-time activities, but she was very fond of her parents and it was obvious that they needed her badly, so she settled down and cooked meals and washed dishes with admirable cheerfulness. She and Nell Ayrton were friends, they had played together when they were children and had a good deal in common on that account, so when Mary felt things were getting her down she walked across the moors and through the Amberwell policies to see Nell — and talk.

Two days after Roger's arrival Mary suddenly felt in need of a chat with Nell, so she scurried through all her necessary duties and set off quite early.

Amberwell Gardens had always been beautiful (except during the War when it was impossible to get labour). They were beautiful now, and to Mary's eyes they were as neat and tidy as they had ever been. The hedges were trimmed to perfection, the lawns were smooth and there were orderly rows of vegetables flourishing in the kitchen-garden. The greenhouses were painted white, and their glass panes glittered merrily in the sunshine, the doors and gates and occasional seats were all in excellent condition and Amberwell House itself looked well-cared-for and comfortable. In fact it looked almost — smug. Of course Mary knew the place well (she had seen it all before, hundreds of times), but somehow this morning she saw it afresh: the difference between Amberwell and poor old Stark Place!

Admittedly Amberwell was smaller, and therefore less expensive to maintain, but it must take a good deal of money to keep it like this, thought Mary enviously.

She went in and shouted for Nell, and Nell appeared.

"Hallo!" said Mary. "I won't say I hope I'm not interrupting you because I know I am — but I don't care. I wanted to see you."

"It's nice to be interrupted," replied Nell. "I was making up the laundry — it's a dull job. Besides I was just going to have a cup of coffee in the morning-room."

"I hoped you were," said Mary smiling.

The morning-room was the prettiest room in the house. It was small and cosy and it got all the morning sunshine; the french windows opened on to the terrace. The Ayrtons used it as a sitting-room in preference to the big drawing-room for it was so much easier to keep.

The two girls sat down and talked. Nell wondered if her friend had come for any special purpose — or just to see her — but it did not matter one way or the other for Nell always had time to talk to a friend. However busy she happened to be she could sit down and give her visitor the impression that she had leisure to enjoy a chat. Nell was the perfect listener for she was sincerely interested in people.

"Your gardens are lovely," said Mary. "I can't bear to look at our gardens; we simply can't afford enough gardeners to keep them properly. Everything is awfully difficult nowadays." She sighed and added, "We've got to paint all the outside woodwork of Stark Place. It's going to cost the earth. Who did you get to do yours?"

Nell mentioned a firm in Ayr. "They're rather expensive, but they're frightfully good and Roger doesn't mind spending money on Amberwell."

"Oh!" said Mary, slightly taken aback.

"Roger has plenty of money," Nell explained.

This information might easily have sounded boastful but on Nell's lips it did not. Coming from Nell it was merely a simple statement — and Mary recognised it as such. Naturally she was surprised, for few people have "plenty of money" nowadays and even if they are fairly comfortably off they rarely mention the fact.

"You see," continued Nell as she poured out the coffee and offered her friend a biscuit. "You see Clare had a great deal of money and she left it all to Roger."

"I see," said Mary.

"You knew Clare, didn't you?" asked Nell.

"Oh yes, very well indeed. We were at school together at Roedean. Clare was the sort of person who did everything well and yet she wasn't a bit stuck-up. Everybody loved Clare. She really was a wonderful person."

"I never saw her," said Nell sadly. "We were always going to meet, but we never did . . . and then she was killed. I often wished I had seen her — even once — so that I could have talked to Stephen about her."

They discussed other things after that and the subject of "money" was not mentioned, but Mary thought about it as she walked home. She had a feeling that it was unfair. Why should some people have heaps of money and other people not enough to make ends meet? It was an unreasonable feeling; it was even rather a nasty feeling — she knew perfectly well — but she could not banish it completely however hard she tried. She could not help feeling annoyed with Roger.

Nell had told her amongst other things that Roger was home on leave, and had said she must come over to lunch and meet him, but Mary did not want to meet Roger — at least she was not particularly keen to meet him — so she had refused to fix a day. I'm a pig, thought Mary. I really am a pig. I don't know what's the matter with me.

2

By this time Mary had reached the gate of the walled-garden, she pushed it open and entered . . . and there was Roger himself talking to Mr. Gray. It was his own garden and he had every right to be there but Mary was not pleased. In fact Mary would have turned and gone round the other way, but she was too late; Roger had seen her.

"Hi, Mary!" he shouted, waving his arms and running towards her down the path (more like a boy of twenty than a "moneyed gentleman"). "Hi, Mary! Wait for me! It's ages since I saw you . . . but you haven't changed a bit," he added as he took her hand. "No, you haven't changed the tiniest bit. You still look about sixteen."

Mary was pleased in spite of herself; it is not unpleasant for a young woman who has had a great deal of sadness and worry in her life, to hear that she looks many years younger than her age.

"Sixteen, not a day older," declared Roger with conviction.

"Nonsense," said Mary.

It was not really nonsense. There was a good deal of truth in Roger's compliment, for Mary was a very attractive creature, small and well-made with a round rosy face and dark curls. She had a slight tendency to plumpness which worried her considerably but which in her case was becoming.

"I suppose you've been over to see Nell," said Roger. "Did she tell you about our plans for a school?"

"For a school!" echoed Mary in surprise.

"I see she didn't tell you — perhaps she thought it was a secret — but I'd like to tell you if you wouldn't be bored."

By this time Mary had forgiven Roger — and indeed she felt ashamed of her bad humour — so she smiled at him in a very friendly way and said that she wanted to hear all about Roger's plans.

They walked on together and Roger explained his ideas: a preparatory school for little boys run on modern lines; a school with moderate fees to suit the pockets of professional men with small incomes . . . and so on and so forth.

Roger was so tremendously enthusiastic about his project that Mary was swept away. "It's a wonderful idea," she declared.

"You think so — really?"

"Yes, it's simply marvellous."

This was good hearing for Roger. The other recipients of his confidence had required a great deal of persuasion before they had seen the beauty of the plan. Arnold had come round, of course, and was now as keen as mustard, but Nell was still half-hearted.

"You'll want a really good headmaster, won't you?" said Mary thoughtfully.

"I've got one. Arnold Maddon."

"Oh Roger, he's the very man!"

"Yes, that's what I thought. It's all fixed and he's agreed to take it on. All we want now is a suitable house and then we can get cracking. I suppose you couldn't suggest a house, could you?"

Mary was silent for a few moments. They had left the gardens and were walking up the steep path which led to the woods.

"Can you think of a house that would do?" repeated Roger. "I mean you know all the houses round about Westkirk. Merklands is for sale, but we want something bigger. Merklands hasn't enough ground."

"What about Stark Place?" asked Mary in a low voice. It was such a low voice that Roger was not sure he had heard aright and in any case he could hardly believe his ears.

"Did you — did you say — Stark Place?" he asked incredulously.

"Yes. You may not want it, but if you thought it would do —"

"Do! Of course it would do! Nothing could be better! Does Sir Andrew want to sell it?"

"I think he might — sell it. I'm not sure but — but I think he would."

"Oh Mary — but you would hate the old place to be sold!"

"In a way, yes; in a way, no," she replied with a little sigh. "I love Stark Place — we all love it — and it would be horrid to sell it, but not any worse than seeing it fall to pieces before our eyes."

Roger was silent.

"It's so big," continued Mary. "It's so enormous that nobody will ever be able to live in it comfortably again.

Certainly Andy will never be able to live there and keep it as it should be kept."

"Mary, it seems quite dreadful!"

"I know. But honestly the place has become a sort of Moloch — wasn't that the creature that demanded human sacrifices and swallowed them whole? Well, anyhow, that's what Stark Place is doing. Everything and everybody has to be sacrificed. It swallows every penny of money we possess. It's wearing out the parents and worrying them to death. A house like that, which isn't properly lived in, needs constant repairs. No sooner do we get the roof mended than the drains go wrong and there's woodwork to be renewed and painted. There's always something."

"I can understand that," said Roger. "Even Amberwell runs away with a good deal of money and it's half the size of Stark Place."

They had reached the woods by this time and stopped for a few moments beside a huge mossy stone which was one of Roger's favourite haunts. He had often sat upon the soft turf with his back against the stone and looked down at Amberwell. To-day, pausing here as usual, Roger looked down and decided that this view was very like the view he had had from the plane . . . the whole place, house and gardens and lawns, was spread before one's eyes. How awful if one had to sell Amberwell!

"Mary," said Roger awkwardly. "You had better think about it carefully before you say anything to Sir Andrew. It might upset him."

"I wonder," said Mary thoughtfully. "I don't believe the parents would mind — awfully much. They sort of stopped minding about things when Ian was killed."

They walked on in silence for a few moments and then Mary continued, "No, I don't believe they'd mind. I could move them into a small house in Westkirk. It would be much better for them and far more comfortable than camping in a corner of the Place."

"Would Andy mind?"

"No," replied Mary with conviction. "All Andy minds about is his career."

Roger hesitated and then he said, "Oh dear, I don't know whether to be glad or sorry. It's a funny sort of feeling. I can't bear the idea of no Findlaters at Stark Place . . . but it's exactly the sort of house we want."

"I'll see what they say and ring you up to-night. If they decide to sell you'll want it at once, won't you? You'll want to — to alter it a bit."

"Just a little," said Roger uncomfortably. "I mean — for a school —"

Mary replied to the tone more than to the words. "Don't worry, Roger. We would have to sell it sooner or later — and somehow I shan't mind so much if the dear old Place is a boys' school with lots of little nippers running about playing cricket and having fun. Yes, it's the right thing, Roger. It's time there was some young life about Stark Place — hope and happiness instead of sad memories."

Roger knew she was thinking of Ian when she spoke of sad memories, for Ian had been one of those bright-spirited beings whose death leaves a gaping void in the lives of their friends. Ian Findlater had had "everything": good looks, abounding vitality and a natural charm of manner which had endeared him to old and young. When Roger heard the words, "Age shall not weary them, nor the years condemn" he thought instinctively of Ian Findlater, and of his own beautiful Clare.

It was because these two — who had never met — were bracketed together in his mind that Roger spoke of Clare now, to Mary. He scarcely ever spoke of Clare — in fact he never spoke of her if he could help it — but this morning he found he wanted to.

"I wish Clare had seen Amberwell," he said. "She liked me to tell her about it."

"Clare and I were great friends."

"I know. She often talked about you, Mary."

"It must have been frightful for you," said Mary in a low voice. "I meant to write to you at the time, but when I tried I couldn't."

"It was — frightful. We were so happy together. We were everything to each other, so there was nothing left — nothing that mattered. People say you get over things in time, but I haven't found it."

"Perhaps someday —"

"I don't think so," said Roger.

Mary hesitated and then she said, "Your Clare and my Ian! I suppose it isn't the right way of thinking — but they were very special, weren't they? I sometimes feel there are other people who could have been more easily spared."

They walked on through the woods which were carpeted with a blue sea of wild hyacinths and stopped at the gate leading on to the moors. The gate marked the boundary between Amberwell and Stark Place. Summerhill Moors had happy memories for Roger; the Ayrtons and the Findlaters had played here when they were children; played at Red Indians and Cowboys, tracking each other amongst the moss-hags and hillocks and the deep fissures carved by innumerable little burns. Later when he was older Roger had shot over the moors with Sir Andrew Findlater; it was here Roger had shot his first grouse. To the right of where they were standing was an old quarry which they had often used for picnics. Amberwell House had been built of the stone quarried here, and St. Stephen's Church and the cottages upon Amberwell Estate.

Mary knew all this as well as Roger, of course. They leant together upon the gate and talked about it.

"I suppose I had better go home — or I shall be late for lunch," said Roger at last in reluctant tones.

"We'll both be late," said Mary.

They would both be late for lunch but still they lingered for it was such a beautiful morning; so peaceful and sunny and warm. There were two cuckoos in the wood, calling to each other, and there was a lark soaring and singing above the moor.

"What fun we had when we were children!" said Roger.

"Yes, it was fun," Mary agreed. "No worries, no responsibilities. I often think of all the things we did. We were happier than you were."

This was true. The three Findlater children had led a very carefree existence for their parents had been reasonably indulgent, and, whereas Roger and Tom never knew when they would be pounced upon and punished for some mysterious crime, Ian and Andy and Mary could get off with a good deal of mischief without serious trouble. They could even argue with their parents and justify their behaviour which had seemed to the Ayrtons most extraordinary.

"Do you remember —" began Mary and then she glanced at her watch and exclaimed in dismay. "Goodness, I really must fly!"

"We'll play at 'Do you remember?' some other time," said Roger smiling.

"Yes, let's! Good-bye, Roger. I'll ring you up to-night — about Stark Place."

Mary's thoughts, as she hurried home, were entirely different. She could hardly believe she had been so foolish as to feel annoyed with Roger. Roger was a dear. He had been awfully nice about Stark Place — so kind and understanding — and she liked his manners. Manners were important, she thought. He had walked with her to the boundary of his property and seen her on to her own ground. Nothing had been said about this small act of courtesy but Mary understood and appreciated it. Nowadays when off-hand manners were fashionable one appreciated small acts of courtesy all the more. Roger might be wealthy but he was not spoilt

— that was obvious. He was neither proud nor ashamed of his money. It had come to him without his volition and he had just taken it naturally and was spending it wisely, using it to improve his property and to help other people. Mary realised that the school was intended not only to benefit Stephen but to benefit other boys less fortunate and to give Arnold Maddon a worth-while job. It was not a "charity" but something even better. She understood Roger's motives very clearly and this was strange because he had not explained them to her.

There was an old Scots saying that came into Mary's head as she hurried through the neglected gardens of her home:

> It's no' what ye ha'e,
> It's what ye dae wi' what ye ha'e
> That matters.

CHAPTER
SIX

1

Roger stood upon the terrace at Stark Place and waved his hand. He said, "We must have a door here so that the boys can go straight into the changing-room after games. We can't have them barging in at the front door and making a mess of everything."

"Yes, Major Ayrton," agreed the architect, writing busily in his notebook.

Arnold said nothing. He was so tired and dazed that he had almost lost interest in the proceedings and his leg was aching intolerably. The three of them had been here all afternoon and had explored Stark Place from attic to cellar. At first Arnold had tried to curb his new employer's extravagance a little but Roger was determined that the school should be perfect. "We want things to be right from the beginning. It's cheapest in the long run." Roger had said — and the architect, whose name was Mr. Strow, had caught on to the idea and suggested all sorts of plans which entailed more expenditure, never any plan which entailed less. Some of Mr. Strow's suggestions were welcomed by Roger (though not by Arnold) but even Roger balked when Mr. Strow suggested a lift.

"A lift!" exclaimed Roger. "This is to be a boys' school not a home for old ladies."

"I just thought it would be useful — for luggage," said Mr. Strow hastily.

"We must have lots of baths and washing-basins and showers," Roger had said. "This big room can be a bathroom. I want tiles on the floor and half-way up the walls. It will take four baths easily."

"The floor must slope to a drain in the centre," put in Mr. Strow.

"I don't think that will be necessary —" began Arnold.

"It's absolutely necessary," said Mr. Strow. "Boys splash about like anything. I know what my own boys are like."

"We may as well do the thing properly while we're at it," said Roger.

"It's cheaper in the long run," agreed Mr. Strow.

"The suite at the end of the corridor will do for the matron," said Roger. "There's a bathroom already, and the sick-room can be next door."

"Most convenient," agreed Mr. Strow, licking his finger and turning over the leaves of his notebook. "*Most* convenient!"

Roger looked round. He said, "We must put a door here in the passage to close off the whole suite."

"A curtain would do —" began Arnold.

"A door would be better," said Roger. "The matron must have privacy. If there isn't a door people can barge in and disturb her at any hour."

"You're absolutely right, Major Ayrton," said Mr. Strow.

The headmaster was to have privacy too. His suite was to be on the ground-floor, looking out on to the rose-garden. It comprised two bedrooms, a sitting-room and an office — and of course a private bathroom.

"I shan't want all that accommodation," said Arnold.

"Nonsense," said Roger. "You might want a fellow to stay. Besides the rooms are here. We must shut off this suite with a door — make a note of it, Mr. Strow."

Mr. Strow made a note of it.

But that had all happened in the early part of the afternoon and by the time they had arrived at the changing-room, and the side door which was to be made so that the boys would not go barging in at the front door and making a mess of everything, Arnold was beyond speech and even Mr. Strow was reduced to saying, "Yes, of course, Major Ayrton," and making notes. Mr. Strow had two feet, which gave him an advantage over Arnold, but the advantage was diminished by the fact that he had corns. All Mr. Strow wanted was to sit down on the steps and take off his smart new brown shoes which he had donned for the occasion.

"Well, that's about all," said Roger with satisfaction. "I think we've got it pretty well taped out — unless either of you can suggest anything?"

Neither of them could.

"Perhaps we ought to have another look at the attic," said Roger doubtfully. "I mean the one where we're going to enlarge the window."

"Quite unnecessary, Major Ayrton," declared Mr. Strow with conviction.

2

There was nobody in the house when Arnold got home. He removed his foot, swallowed three aspirin tablets and lay down upon his bed. For a time he could think of nothing but his physical discomfort but presently the pain ebbed away and his brain began to work. He reached for the writing-tablet which he kept beside his bed and started making notes. Fortunately Arnold's memory was extremely good so he was able to think back and retrace the whole tour without much difficulty, and as he went from room to room and remembered all that had been said his admiration for his friend increased. Roger had been splendid. Roger had known exactly what he wanted and was determined to have it. Even the extravagances seemed sensible when viewed in retrospect. That door into the matron's suite, which had seemed unnecessary, was really quite a good idea. A matron needed privacy . . . so did a headmaster when one thought of it. But as Arnold's admiration for his friend increased so did his dislike for Mr. Strow.

It was a pity Arnold disliked Mr. Strow, for he would have a lot to do with him, but it could not be helped. The man was an absolute bounder.

Arnold had seen through Mr. Strow very early in the proceedings; he had watched Mr. Strow's face when he was talking to Roger and unluckily for its owner it was not a poker face. It was a fat face, fair and rosy-cheeked, and full of expression. Although he was not much older than Arnold Mr. Strow had the beginnings of a double chin, his mouth was full-lipped and shapeless and his eyes were too small. Worst of all, in Arnold's opinion, his ears were very small indeed and were glued closely to his head. The description sounds unpleasant, but the whole effect, at first sight, was not unpleasant. Mr. Strow gave the appearance of a cheerful, hearty sort of fellow and it was only when one observed him closely that one realised he was false.

Was false too strong a word? No, not really, thought Arnold. His expression when he was talking to Roger gave him away. Here's a mutt, Mr. Strow had said to himself. Here's a fellow with more money than sense. I'm on to a good thing if I play my cards well.

Mr. Strow had played his cards admirably so far as his employer was concerned (he had only gone wrong once, when he had suggested the lift) but he had not concerned himself with the third member of the party. "No need to bother about him," Mr. Strow had thought, glancing contemptuously at the shabbily dressed schoolmaster with the leather patches on his elbows and the well-worn flannel slacks . . . and as time went on, and the third member of the party became more and more silent and merely followed from room to room in a sort of trance, Mr. Strow's conviction was strengthened. "No need to bother about *him*," Mr. Strow had thought.

Mr. Strow had not realised — did not realise even now — that Major Ayrton was going back to Germany when his leave was over and that Mr. Maddon would be left in charge of everything — with *carte blanche*.

Dr. Maddon came in while Arnold was still busy with his notes. He stood at the foot of the bed and looked at his son. "Tired?" he asked anxiously.

"Dead beat," replied Arnold frankly. "Dead beat, but very happy. Sit down, Dad, I want to talk to you."

"I'll make a cup of tea first," said Dr. Maddon. "Don't move. I'll bring it in here."

Arnold had finished his notes and was lying, staring at the ceiling, when his father came in with the tray. He watched his father's preparations without speaking. He liked watching his father; the large strong hands which had done so much good in their time were still firm and capable. Presently all was in order, the table cleared and brought over to the bed, the tea-tray neatly arranged, the bread buttered and cut into thin slices.

"Now we're right," said Dr. Maddon cheerfully. "You'll feel better when you've had a cup of tea."

"I feel better just looking at you," Arnold replied.

Dr. Maddon cocked one bushy eyebrow. "That's my bedside manner." He poured out the tea and added, "So you're happy?"

"Happy as a king. I can scarcely believe my luck. It's the sort of job I've dreamed of — and I know I can do it."

"You'll do it well," nodded Dr. Maddon.

"After all these months of misery!"

"I know. You've had a bad time."

"So have you. I've been a perfect nuisance to you, Dad."

"Och, away!"

"Dad," said Arnold earnestly. "Do you consider that I'm all right now? I mean, apart from my foot, would you say I was reasonably healthy? Tell me honestly: supposing I made a success of the school and — and that sort of thing — would I be justified in asking a girl to marry me?"

Dr. Maddon showed no surprise. "I don't see why not," he replied in matter of fact tones.

There was no need to say more. These two had always understood each other and since Arnold's return from hospital they had grown even closer together. Often at nights when Arnold had lain sleepless and racked with pain he had heard a slight sound and seen the door opening to admit the tall bulky figure with the blue-striped pyjamas and the tousled grey hair. "Silly young fool, why did you not ring for me?" Dr. Maddon would mutter crossly . . . and then would come the sharp prick and the blissful drift into sleep. Latterly there had been no need for these nocturnal visits and they had been discontinued — or so Arnold had imagined — but one morning he had found a large white handkerchief lying on the floor by his bed, so perhaps they had not been discontinued entirely.

"Tell me about Stark Place," said Dr. Maddon after a short silence. "Is it all plain sailing? Are there no snags at all?"

"There's Mr. Strow, the architect. I don't like Mr. Strow."

"Any special reason?"

"Nobody makes tea as well as you," said Arnold, sipping the strong brew with enjoyment. "Yes, several reasons: small ears, stuck closely on to his head, and a squashy sort of mouth . . . but principally because he took Roger for a sucker."

"M'mm," said Dr. Maddon.

"But he didn't take me into account," added Arnold with a chuckle. "I'll see he doesn't pile up his expenses! I'll sort him!"

Dr. Maddon looked at his son approvingly and his heart was joyful. For months he had watched Arnold slipping downhill, searching for a job — any sort of job — frustrated at every turn, becoming hopeless and embittered by disappointment. Now, despite his only too obvious exhaustion, there was new life in the boy's eyes. Dr. Maddon was almost pleased to learn that the architect was a twister, for a battle would do Arnold all the good in the world.

"You'll earn your salary, eh?" said Dr. Maddon.

"You old wizard!" exclaimed Arnold. "How did you know that's what I've been thinking?"

"Just guessed."

"You guessed right. I've been worrying. It seemed all wrong to pocket the money and sit back until the place was ready. I told Roger I would get a temporary job but he wouldn't hear of it — said he wanted me to be on the spot to keep an eye on things. Well, here I am, and I intend to keep both eyes firmly fixed on Mr. Strow."

"H'mm," said Dr. Maddon.

This ejaculation was a sort of grunt accomplished with compressed lips. It could mean all manner of things depending upon the occasion. It could mean that the doctor was amused or incredulous, it could express accord or disagreement, satisfaction or dismay. His patients knew the doctor's grunt. When the doctor took your temperature and examined his thermometer you waited anxiously for the grunt "H'mm!" he would say, shaking down the mercury — and you knew at once without any manner of doubt whether you had gone up to a hundred-and-one or down to normal.

Of course Arnold was familiar with the famous grunt and knew better than anybody how to interpret its meaning. On this particular occasion it expressed amusement.

"What's so funny about it?" Arnold inquired.

"I'm just a wee bit sorry for Stow — or whatever his name is."

"He'll be sorry for himself before I've done with him!"

"I wouldn't wonder."

"Look here, Dad!" said Arnold. "Yes, I *will* have another cup. I'll tell you one thing that happened — just to show you. There's a big room — we're making it into a dormitory — it's at the end of the house and has a window looking east. It will take six beds easily. Strow said that with six boys in the room there wouldn't be enough air. He said there should be two windows, preferably facing different ways, so that there would be a current of air through the room. He proposed knocking a hole in the wall and making a window facing south."

"I'd have agreed with him," said Dr. Maddon promptly.

"Not if you'd seen the wall. It's four feet thick. Now listen, Dad; there's a smaller room next door with a window facing south, and it would be as easy as pie to take down the partition-wall between the two rooms. That would give us the two windows and the current of air, and it would make a splendid big dormitory which could accommodate nine boys."

"I call that clever," said Dr Maddon judicially.

"Yes it was," agreed Arnold with a deplorable lack of modesty. "It was very clever of me. In fact it was a stroke of genius."

"Was the man pleased with your stroke of genius?"

"He was not," declared Arnold. "He turned it down and went on blethering about his hole in the wall."

"H'mm!"

"Yes, I don't wonder you're disgusted," agreed Arnold. "But there's no need to worry. I shall get my own back all right. Roger said I could have *carte blanche* and I intend to take full advantage of it."

"You'd better finish up the bread and butter," said Dr. Maddon.

Arnold obeyed without thinking. "There was another thing," he said. "We're having a door made so that the boys can go straight into the changing-room after games. Strow decided where the door was to be and marked the wall with a piece of chalk. By that time I was too tired to bother — I was speechless — but now

I realise that Strow was wrong. There's a large window in the room and surely it would be easier and a lot cheaper to make the window into a door than to cut an entirely new opening through four feet of solid stone."

"What about light?" asked Dr. Maddon.

"Glass in the door is the answer. A glass panel — and you needn't say it would break when they banged it, because nowadays you can get glass that's practically unbreakable — and we could put a spring on the door."

Dr. Maddon had been going to say just that, so he said nothing.

"Look here, Dad," said Arnold, struck with another brilliant idea. "Look here, what about you coming over to Stark Place and having a prowl round?"

"I will," declared Dr. Maddon. He said it so promptly that Arnold knew he had made up his mind to come from the very beginning, whether he was asked or not.

3

Roger's account of the afternoon's work was slightly different from Arnold's.

"That fellow Strow is quite good value," said Roger. "He's got all sorts of ideas about the alterations."

"That's what he's paid for, isn't it?" said Nell without enthusiasm. It was impossible for Nell to be enthusiastic about Roger's project, for the school would rob her of Stephen. She was unhappy about it not so much for her own sake — though of course she would miss him unbearably — but because she doubted whether it was the right thing for the child. Was it really necessary, was it really the right thing for a sensitive little boy to be thrown into a whirlpool of rough noisy contemporaries and left to sink or swim? Nell thought of this while she listened with one ear to Roger's glowing description of tiled bathrooms, airy classrooms and thoroughly remodelled kitchen-premises.

Stephen was listening too, but more intently. "It's my school, isn't it?" he said. "And Uncle Arnold is going to be the headmaster."

"No," said Roger. "Look here, you must get this straight. It isn't your school any more than anybody else's, and you'll have to call Uncle Arnold 'Mr. Maddon.'"

"Why?" asked Stephen in surprise.

"Because the other boys will. Everybody is alike at school. It would never do for one boy to be different from the others."

Stephen nodded. He saw the point. "But it will be difficult," he said.

"You had better practise," Roger told him. "The sooner you get it into your head that you'll be just one little pebble on the beach the better it will be for you."

"Oh Roger —" began Nell in dismay.

"Honestly, Nell," declared Roger. "That's exactly the reason why I want him to go to school."

Stephen was quite undaunted, for he had a firm footing of love and affection, and although he looked delicate there was plenty of spirit in him. As a matter of fact he was looking forward to school. It seemed to Stephen that his father's plan was ideal, for he could go

68

to school — like other boys — and yet he would be near Amberwell.

Having settled this important matter Roger returned to the subject of the alterations. "Some of Strow's ideas are a bit far-fetched," continued Roger. "For instance he suggested a lift. Did you ever hear of such nonsense?"

"Oh Daddy, a lift would be fun!" cried Stephen. "We could play with it on wet days, couldn't we?"

"Well, there isn't going to be a lift," said Roger laughing.

"What did Arnold say?" asked Nell.

"Very little," replied Roger. As a matter of fact Roger was just a trifle disappointed in Arnold.

Unlike his two companions Roger was not in the least tired after the tour of Stark Place so when Stephen suggested that he should come out into the garden he rose at once.

"I'm going to have a running lesson," said Stephen. "We do it on the bowling-green. You'll come and see, won't you?"

Roger remembered that Nannie had mentioned running lessons but he had been too busy to think about it. "Oh yes — running," he said vaguely.

"Miss Glassford runs like the wind," declared Stephen proudly.

"And what about you?"

"I'm shaping well," replied Stephen, obviously quoting his instructress.

The bowling-green was some distance from the house. It was a very large square lawn surrounded by a yew hedge. As they approached, and stopped at the wrought-iron gate, Roger saw that the lawn had been marked out with whitening. There was a line all round, about ten feet from the hedge, and upon this improvised track Georgina was running. She was clad in a white shirt, open at the neck, and white tennis-shorts. The long legs, seen without trousers, were admirably shaped. They really were beautiful.

"She's doing her mile," said Stephen in a low voice. "We mustn't interrupt her."

Roger had no wish to interrupt her. It is always delightful to see an expert performer — whether it be running or dancing or tennis or any other activity — and although Roger knew very little about running he knew he was seeing something good. Georgina ran so easily, so lightly, that her feet seemed scarcely to touch the ground. The sight pleased Roger in a purely aesthetic way, for he was not interested in women. There had been one woman in his life — and one only. He would have been equally interested and enthralled if the runner had been Milanion — not Atalanta.

"She's nearly finished now, and then you'll see me," said Stephen.

"How do you know she's nearly finished?"

"Because she does the last lap faster of course."

Georgina completed her last lap at a terrific pace; then she looked round and saw them at the gate and came towards them. Roger was interested to notice that although she was breathing quickly she showed no other signs of distress.

"I say, you can run!" he exclaimed.

70

"I've always been keen," replied Georgina. "I did quite a lot of running when I was at Cambridge. We had a very good coach."

"It must be difficult to practise here, all by yourself."

"Yes, and I've got nobody to time me."

Roger wondered how long she took to run her mile. It would be interesting to know but he did not like to show his ignorance by asking.

"I've measured it out very carefully," she continued, pointing to the white lines. "Mr. Gray said he was sure you wouldn't mind."

"I don't mind a bit as long as you don't ask me to run," replied Roger.

This was intended as a joke but Georgina took it seriously. "You aren't the right build," she replied. "Neither is Emmie of course."

"But Stephen is shaping well?"

"Yes," said Georgina. "Yes, Stephen is splendid."

It crossed Roger's mind that she had no sense of humour, but perhaps Atalanta had had none either.

Stephen having removed his sweater and changed his shoes was now ready and anxious to show his paces. He began to prance like a little pony and to flap his arms. "This is to loosen my muscles," he explained. "It's very important to loosen your muscles before you start."

When Stephen had loosened his muscles sufficiently he got down on the mark in a very professional posture and the lesson began.

Roger was amused, but he managed to hide his amusement for pupil and instructress were both very serious indeed. He noticed that Stephen, who was "a sedulous little ape," ran exactly like Georgina; his head well up and his legs moving in long easy strides. Roger watched for some time; he was anxious to see that Stephen's strength was not being over-taxed, but Georgina was careful. It was obvious that she knew when to stop . . . and having satisfied himself that all was well Roger left them to get on with it.

CHAPTER
SEVEN

1

Saturday was a holiday and the Ayrton family decided to have a picnic on the shore. Nell made up a lunch basket and they all set out together. The party consisted of Roger and Nell, Stephen and Emmie and Georgina Glassford. Anne had been invited but had refused, saying she was too busy. They all walked through the walled-garden, chatted for a few minutes to Mr. Gray, who was pottering happily amongst his beans, and emerged through a wooden door on to a steep path which led to the shore.

"Gray is getting old," said Roger to Nell. "I see a lot of difference in him. Do you think he needs more help?"

"We might get another boy," replied Nell thoughtfully.

"What about a man? I mean who's going to take over when Gray has to give up?"

"Bob Grainger," said Nell promptly. "Oh I know he's young, but Mr. Gray has taught him everything and I'm sure he could do it. You remember he's the boy who saved Tom's life when the *Starfish* went down."

Roger remembered. "He wasn't much good at first, was he?" objected Roger.

"No," agreed Nell smiling. "He knew nothing about gardens. He pulled up the seedlings and left the weeds to flourish — poor Bob! I don't believe Mr. Gray would have kept him if it hadn't been for Tom. Tom talked Mr. Gray into giving him another chance — and then another. Tom can talk people into anything," added Nell.

"Yes, I know — but all the same —"

"Oh, once Bob got into the way of things it was all right and I really don't know what we would do without him now."

"Is he still living with the Grays?"

"Oh yes, he's just like a son to the Grays. He does all sorts of little jobs for them. Of course he adores Tom and Tom is very good to him. Tom is always sending him brightly-coloured post-cards from some outlandish place or other."

"Tom doesn't bother to write to me very often," said Roger.

"Perhaps you don't write very often to him," suggested Nell.

Georgina and the two children had run on and by this time they had reached the shore. It was a little bay, sheltered by rocks. There was a tiny cave in the cliff which had been known to the Ayrton children as The Smugglers' Cave, for no other reason than that all caves were believed by them to have belonged to smugglers. Stephen and Emmie knew it well, of course, but Georgina had not been here before so they had the pleasure of showing it to her and telling her all about it. Georgina thought it was splendid.

74

Everything was splendid according to Georgina: the view, the sea, the bathe and the little chicken patties which Mrs. Duff had made for their picnic-lunch. Nell found her enthusiasm amusing, for Georgina's predecessor, Miss Paterson, had been difficult to please . . . or at least (thought Nell trying to be strictly fair) one had never known whether Miss Paterson was pleased or not. She was reserved and inscrutable. This girl was better for the children, thought Nell, as she watched Georgina paddling with them and helping them to catch crabs in the little pools left by the receding tide.

"She asked me to call her Georgina," said Roger suddenly.

"Oh Roger!" exclaimed Nell.

"I don't see why not," declared Roger. "She's just a child, really. Look at her playing with Stephen and Emmie. I shan't find any difficulty in calling her Georgina, the name suits her quite well."

Nell said no more, but she was a little uneasy. It was odd, to say the least of it.

2

"I'm very cross with you," said Mr. Orme to his housekeeper.

"Oh dear, how dreadful! What have I done now?" exclaimed his housekeeper in feigned dismay.

"Why didn't you go to the picnic with the others?"

"Who would have cooked your sweetbreads, I should like to know."

"Nobody of course. I would have been perfectly happy with bread and cheese — and an apple."

Anne laughed. She knew this was perfectly true. Mr. Orme did not notice what he ate. He ate what was placed before him. In some ways this was good but in other ways a little disappointing for his housekeeper. It was disappointing when one had cooked a particularly appetising meal to watch it being eaten without undue appreciation; but on the other hand if a pudding were not what it should be — if it fell to pieces or was slightly burnt — there was no need to worry. Mr. Orme ate it quite happily.

They had finished their meal. Anne rose to fetch the coffee and as she passed his chair she bent over and kissed him lightly on the forehead. It was a butterfly caress and exactly expressed the relationship between them, which was almost that of father and daughter, but not quite. Fathers and daughters have always known each other and take their affection for granted as a natural thing, but these two had found each other and were grateful.

As Mr. Orme sat and waited for his coffee he thought about this. He was very grateful for Anne's love. He had enjoyed her companionship for more than a year and now he did not know how he could have lived without it . . . but there were responsibilities in his life which he had not had before and sometimes he found himself worrying about them. He was old — quite old enough to be Anne's grandfather — and for years he had suffered from an unusual heart-condition which necessitated the greatest care. Dr. Maddon had warned him that he might die at any moment but Mr. Orme had not minded; it had not worried him in the least; he had just accepted it and gone about his usual avocations taking reasonable care and no more. Now things had altered and Mr. Orme found himself less ready to die. It was because of Anne, because it would make her unhappy. How curious it was (he thought). How often in this life the unexpected happens!

When he had taken Anne and Emmie under his roof he had envisaged other troubles: Anne might find it dull; Mrs. Ayrton might be stubborn and refuse to forgive her; Emmie might be a little disturbing to his peace . . . but all these fears proved groundless and he found himself worrying about his own health! He found himself taking more care, doing a little less and resting more frequently. This new *régime* certainly suited his health, and he felt the better of it, but was it right in principle? Was it right to pamper oneself so that one could hang on to life a few years longer?

"You could do without me quite comfortably," said Anne, continuing the conversation as she brought in the coffee. "I don't know why you bother to have a cook when you could live on bread and cheese and apples."

"Bread and cheese and apples make good fare," replied Mr. Orme. "But there are other things besides food — and I couldn't do without you quite comfortably. You and Emmie have become necessary to my comfort. You've pampered me."

"That's nonsense," declared Anne, dropping her teasing manner and speaking seriously. "It's the other way round. You've pampered us. You've given us things we never had before — protection and love."

"My dear child!"

"It's true," she said with a little catch in her breath. "I never had that before. I never knew what it was to feel safe. I'm happier now than I've ever been in all my life."

"So am I," said Mr. Orme gravely.

"Well, that's all right, isn't it? We're both happy. There's nothing wrong in being happy."

"No, indeed!"

"Well then?"

"But I'm nearly eighty, you know. People don't live for ever. I've been wondering —"

"Don't let's think about the future," said Anne interrupting him.

"But we should," declared Mr. Orme. "I've been wondering if you could go back to Amberwell — someday."

"No, no, I couldn't!"

"If you ever felt you could go back —"

"No, never. I've told you why."

Mr. Orme sighed. "Oh well, you won't be penniless," he said. "I haven't great possessions but all I have will be yours and it will be enough for you and Emmie to live on."

"I wish you wouldn't talk — like that!" she exclaimed in dismay. "You don't feel — ill — or — anything, do you?"

"No, my dear. I feel perfectly well but I'm nearly eighty," replied Mr. Orme smiling a little. "I just

78

wanted you to know that there's no need for you to worry; that's all."

"I don't worry about money. I worry about you, when you're ill, and about Emmie when she gets a cold. Other things don't matter. I used to worry myself nearly crazy about money — about how I was to make ends meet and pay for Emmie's education — but not now." She hesitated and then added in a lower voice, "You've taught me to trust God and enjoy my daily bread, that's why I said don't let's think about the future."

Mr. Orme could say no more — and at any rate he had said what he had intended. He had wanted Anne to know that she and Emmie would be independent. They need not return to Amberwell. Perhaps Anne would marry again for she was still very young and in Mr. Orme's eyes she was beautiful. Mr. Orme had a shrewd idea that she was beautiful to other eyes as well.

"I haven't — thanked you," said Anne in a shaky voice. "I can't — really. You must promise not to talk like this again."

"I promise," he said solemnly. "We'll trust God and enjoy our daily bread together."

3

It was a habit of Dr. Maddon's to look in and see Mr. Orme quite frequently (he came partly in a professional capacity and partly because they were very old friends and enjoyed a chat) so neither Anne nor Mr. Orme was surprised when they saw Dr. Maddon coming up the path. Arnold was with him and this was not surprising either.

"It's a good thing I made lots of coffee," said Anne. "I'll just go and heat it up for them. I expect they've come to tell us all about Stark Place."

They had, of course. Arnold was making rather an amusing story of the tour of Stark Place when Anne came in with the coffee.

"Ha, coffee!" exclaimed Dr. Maddon. "I don't know why it is but I can't make good coffee. I can make very good tea but coffee seems to be beyond me."

"Have I missed anything?" asked Anne.

"Not really," replied Arnold smiling. "I was just being funny. We went all over the house from attic to cellar with the architect fellow and fixed up everything. Of course there will have to be a good many alterations — Roger has big ideas. It's to be a super school."

"Lucky boys," said Mr. Orme.

"Yes indeed," agreed Anne. "Emmie and I are annoyed; we think you ought to take girls as well."

Arnold laughed and said he would take Emmie like a shot if her mother wanted her to come.

It was delightful to hear Arnold laughing and to see him looking happy. Anne had been very sorry for Arnold during the last few months. She had heard about his hopes and his disappointments, and had listened with sympathy, for she knew from bitter experience what it was like to search for a job and to find that nobody wanted you.

Presently Anne and Arnold went out into the garden and left the two old friends together.

"The Old Uns enjoy their chat, don't they?" said Arnold. "And it's very good for them too."

"I hope Dr. Maddon will sound his heart," said Anne.

"He will. He knows you're worried."

"He knows!"

"Yes, I saw him looking at you. Has he had another heart attack?"

"No, he's been wonderfully well lately."

"But you *are* worried, aren't you?"

"He was talking about — about being eighty."

"It's hateful when people get old."

"Hateful — especially when you've got all your eggs in one basket."

"You've got Emmie. I've got nobody except Dad."

This conversation was elliptical and might have been obscure to a stranger but Anne and Arnold understood each other perfectly. They had spent a good deal of time together lately (while "the Old Uns" talked) and their friendship founded in childhood had ripened. To-day they wandered idly along the path, stood for a few minutes watching a thrush picking up crumbs upon Mr. Orme's home-made bird-table, and then sat down on the garden-seat.

"I'm glad you're so happy about the school," said Anne.

"It's wonderful! I feel like a different creature! I have to keep on pinching myself to make sure I'm not dreaming. At first I just couldn't believe it, I thought it would all fall through —"

"It won't fall through if Roger has anything to do with it," declared Roger's sister emphatically.

"Oh, I'm not worrying. I'm just — gloating. And that reminds me that I want to apologise to you. I never realised until now what an awful bore I've been — coming here and moaning."

"You haven't —"

"Yes I have — moaning and groaning! You've been awfully good to me. I've made up my mind that I'm not going to the other extreme and bore people by talking about the school. That would be almost as bad."

"But I'd like to hear about it."

"Yes, but not all the time. Let's talk about you for a change. Why didn't you tell me you were an author?"

"An author?" echoed Anne in surprise.

Arnold took a little book out of his pocket and showed it to her. It was a child's book with a brightly-coloured picture on the cover.

"Oh — that!" exclaimed Anne. "I just wrote that to amuse myself and Emmie."

"I think it's charming . . . Yes, really. It's original and amusing and the little pictures are delightful."

"Who told you about it?" Anne wanted to know.

"Nobody told me. I saw it on the bookstall at Westkirk Station and recognised the picture on the cover. It's the mermaid-fountain, of course. The other pictures are all of Amberwell Gardens, too. Here's the potting-shed and here's the bowling-green; here's the Smugglers' Cave!"

"Yes," admitted Anne. "Yes, it's Amberwell."

"And the story is all about you when you were children! There's even a bit about me. I'm Alan of course. I'm the boy who climbed the Monkey Puzzle and tore his shorts."

"Yes, of course you are," said Anne smiling.

"But why Alan? Why not Arnold?"

"I changed all the names," explained Anne. "I wrote it just for fun to please Emmie, because I couldn't afford to buy her picture books, and then when we decided to publish it to make some money I had to change the names."

"Did you make some money?"

"Yes, much more than I expected — and it came in very useful. I bought new clothes for myself and Emmie and I put the rest of it into the bank. It was wonderful to know we had something to fall back on for a rainy day."

Arnold knew a little about the "lost years" but he had not realised it had been as bad as that.

"The publishers tried to persuade me to write another," continued the author. "But of course I couldn't. You see *that* book is all true. I couldn't make up a story to save my life." She paused for a moment and then added thoughtfully, "It's funny how things happen. If it wasn't for that little book I wouldn't be here now."

"You wouldn't be here now!"

"No," said Anne.

Arnold waited for more information but none was forthcoming. At last he could bear it no longer. "Is it a secret?" he inquired.

"A secret? Oh no, I was just thinking — wondering where I would have been. You see Nell bought the book in Glasgow for Stephen and when she saw the picture she knew at once that it must have been written by me, so she took it to Mr. Orme and he got my address from the publishers and came to me — and found me — and brought me here. That was how it happened."

"How strange!" said Arnold thoughtfully. He closed the little book and put it into his inside pocket as if it had suddenly become more valuable to him than before.

"What made you think I had written it?" asked Anne with interest. "It might have been Nell or Connie —"

"Ah, but I'm Poirot. I use my little grey cells. It couldn't have been Nell or Connie or anybody but you." He paused and looked at her teasingly.

"I don't see why," declared Anne after a moment's thought.

"Because you were the only one who saw me climb the Monkey Puzzle — the others were bathing — and it was you who went and got me a pair of Tom's shorts because I couldn't go home in my own."

Anne laughed. "They were Roger's shorts. I took them out of his drawer. Nannie couldn't think where they had gone. She hunted for them everywhere — and I never said a word. We were deceitful children."

"Deceitful?"

"Yes, I'm afraid so — but it wasn't really our fault. We never knew when we were doing something very naughty and when we weren't. Grown-ups were our enemies — they were queer and unreasonable — so we deceived them. Emmie is quite different, she tells me everything — good things and bad things — she's as open as the day."

"Perhaps it's because you're not queer and unreasonable," suggested Arnold smiling.

After that they talked some more about the school, for although Arnold had made up his mind not to be a bore he found it difficult to keep off the subject. He told Anne that the school was not to be called Stark Place (Sir Andrew did not want them to use the name) and both he and Roger were glad of this because it seemed to them unsuitable. Mary Findlater had suggested Summerhills. It was an old name for a part of the Stark Place estate.

"Oh yes — Summerhill Moor!" exclaimed Anne. "And Summerhill Quarry where we used to have picnics."

"Do you think it's a good name for a school?"

"Yes," said Anne thoughtfully. "Yes, it's nice — Summerhills — it makes me think of little boys playing in the sunshine."

"That's exactly what you're meant to think of!" Arnold assured her. "When Daddy and Mummy are looking for a nice school for dear little Jackie, it will make them think the same. 'We must send him to Summerhills' they'll say. 'Let's write to the headmaster at once.'"

The headmaster of Summerhills put on an important air as he said these words, arranging his shabby old tie and pulling down the frayed cuffs of his jacket. Anne laughed — she was meant to laugh — but she did not laugh very heartily. She would have liked to mend the jacket and wash the tie and smarten up the headmaster a little . . . there was no woman to look after Arnold and his father, to mend their clothes and keep them up to the mark; two men, living alone, were very helpless.

"The headmaster will have to get a new suit," suggested Anne.

"Oh, he will," was the reply. "He's got that in mind. He's just waiting until he's collected his first month's salary."

It was now time to go. Arnold rose reluctantly and said that "the Old Uns" would have finished their chat . . . and be wondering . . .

This was found to be correct. In fact "the Old Uns" were just coming to look for "the Young Uns" and all four met on the path. The Maddons took their leave and Mr. Orme and Anne saw them off the premises.

"What did the doctor say about you?" asked Anne.

"He said, 'H'mm,'" replied Mr. Orme smiling. "It was a surprised and pleased sort of 'H'mm.' Apparently my heart is ticking along quite nicely and may go on for years. Does that satisfy you?"

"Yes," said Anne, squeezing his arm fondly.

CHAPTER
EIGHT

1

The Ayrtons were having tea on the terrace. It was exactly the tea-party Roger had imagined when he was in the plane. Nell behind the silver tea-pot; Stephen beside her eating scones and honey and Mrs. Ayrton in her chaise-longue with the little table conveniently near. Roger had been at home for nearly a fortnight but this was the first afternoon that they had had tea together like this. Some days had been a little too chilly for the meal to be taken out of doors and they had had it in the morning-room; other days Roger had been out. Roger had been very busy indeed settling up matters at Stark Place and talking things over with Arnold and rushing up to Glasgow to see Mr. Strow, so he had not been with his family as much as he would have liked. All the same Roger had enjoyed it and he was delighted with the progress he had made.

"To-morrow is Sunday," said Stephen suddenly. "You don't have to go over to Summerhills on Sundays, do you, Daddy?"

(They were all trying to call it Summerhills but Stephen was the only member of the family to whom it came easily.)

"Yes, I'm afraid so," replied Roger. "You see the builders are starting on Monday morning and there are one or two things I want to look at before they come."

Stephen sighed. He knew the school was important but it took up such a lot of time.

"We'll bathe in the afternoon," said Roger smiling at his little son. "Church in the morning, bathe in the afternoon and Summerhills after tea."

"Is it a promise, Daddy?"

"Yes, it's a promise."

While they were talking the post had arrived and Roger saw that there were several letters for him but did not bother to open them. The only important letters were letters from home — and he was here with his family round him. Mrs. Ayrton had a letter from Connie, full of news about the children, and Nell had received an air-mail letter which she was scanning with interest.

"It's from Dennis," said Nell, putting it down as she poured out Roger's second cup of tea. "He's on his way home. This is from Cairo."

"Dennis who?" asked Roger in surprise.

"Dennis Weatherby — I'd forgotten you don't know him. He was in the *Starfish* with Tom when they ran into that mine and he came here for a few days when Tom got out of hospital. You'd like Dennis," she added.

Roger remembered now. Tom had mentioned his friend, Dennis Weatherby, and had said that Dennis had "gone off the deep end about Nell"; but that was three years ago, and as Roger had heard no more he had dismissed it from his mind. Tom was constantly "going off the deep end" about some girl or other, and if his friend were like him (as was probable) there was no need to attach any importance to the matter. Now, however, it appeared that the fellow had been corresponding with Nell which looked as if there might be something in it.

"Commander Weatherby's mother lives near Harrogate," said Mrs. Ayrton.

Nell looked at her in surprise for as a rule Mrs. Ayrton found great difficulty in following the conversation — especially the rapid conversation of the younger generation — and was usually left far behind utterly and absolutely bewildered.

"I remember distinctly," declared Mrs. Ayrton. "His mother lives in a large house near Harrogate. He told me about it; he was a very well-mannered young man."

"He brought me a bear," put in Stephen. "It was a huge enormous Teddy bear — of course I was quite young then. Why don't you open your letters, Daddy? There's one with a foreign stamp. Can I have it for my collection?"

The letter with the foreign stamp was addressed to Roger in thin spidery foreign writing. He opened it and tore off the stamp for Stephen.

For a few moments there was silence.

"I say!" exclaimed Roger. "What on earth are we to do about this? Aunt Beatrice is ill — in Rome."

"Aunt Beatrice — in Rome!" echoed Nell.

"Yes, frightfully ill. This is from the woman who runs the Pensione where she's staying."

Neither Roger nor Nell had seen Aunt Beatrice for years — there had been a quarrel in the family — so they were not exactly heartbroken by the unexpected news, but they were naturally upset.

"Oh, poor Aunt Beatrice, how miserable for her!" exclaimed the sympathetic Nell. "It's bad enough being ill at home, but everything is so much more *difficult* when you're abroad."

"Yes, it's pretty grim," agreed Roger.

"Beatrice was always difficult," said Mrs. Ayrton vaguely. "She was so dreadfully interfering. I used to have her to stay quite often but it was always a strain because she didn't get on at all well with your father ... and then, when she encouraged Anne to get married without permission, your father was very angry indeed and wrote her a very strong letter."

"I know," agreed Nell. "But she's ill, so —"

"If Beatrice is ill she should send for the doctor. We can't have her at Amberwell," declared Mrs. Ayrton.

"She's in Rome," explained Nell patiently.

"In Rome? Oh no, dear, there must be some mistake. Beatrice lives in Edinburgh. Anne was staying with her when she met Mr. Selby."

"I know," repeated Nell. "I suppose she must have gone to Rome for a holiday — she often did. She used to tell us about the Pensione Valetta where she always stayed. It was run by a Frenchwoman called Madame Le Brun. There was a roof-garden —"

"This is from Madame Le Brun," said Roger, holding up the letter.

"It was all Beatrice's fault," continued Mrs. Ayrton. "Anne was a mere child and never would have thought of marrying anyone we didn't approve of. Your father was quite right when he decided to have nothing more to do with Beatrice."

"I wonder if I could get a sleeper to-night," said Roger with a little frown.

"Oh Roger, must you?" cried Nell.

"What else can we do? We can't just leave the old lady to her fate. Somebody must do something."

This was true of course. Nell saw that as clearly as Roger.

Stephen had been following the conversation with growing dismay. "Oh Daddy, have you got to go away? Is Aunt Beatrice very important? You said we were going to bathe to-morrow. You promised."

"Yes," said Roger doubtfully. "Well, perhaps it would do if I went on Monday. I could fly out, couldn't I?"

"I suppose you must," agreed Nell with a sigh.

"It may not take long," said Roger. "I can see Aunt Beatrice and fix things up" — but he spoke without conviction for he did not see how his mission was to be accomplished quickly.

2

The programme which Roger had suggested for Sunday was carried out. In the morning the whole party went to St. Stephen's. Georgina went too — which was unusual. She had put on a coat and skirt for the occasion and a very becoming blue hat. She walked beside Roger asking him questions about Summerhills and showing an intelligent interest in his plans . . . and Roger was pleased for his mind was full of his plans.

"I think it's a splendid idea," said Georgina. "It will be so good for Stephen to go to school. I shall be terribly sorry to leave Amberwell, but that can't be helped."

"Oh, it won't be ready till Easter," Roger told her. "There are so many alterations to be made and the staff to be engaged and all sorts of things to be arranged."

"Easter!" said Georgina. "Amberwell must be beautiful in spring."

Roger glanced at her. She looked very sad. He wondered whether she would like to stay on and teach Emmie, or perhaps she would like a post in the school; but he would have to ask Arnold before offering her a post at Summerhills. It was Arnold's prerogative to choose the staff.

"I'm so happy here," added Georgina with a sigh.

"I'm glad of that," said Roger rather uncomfortably. "And Easter is a long way off. I mean all sorts of things could happen before Easter."

"What sort of things?" asked Georgina. She turned her head and looked at him inquiringly with her large soft brown eyes.

"I was wondering whether —" began Roger . . . but he did not continue, for by this time they had reached the wicket-gate which led into the churchyard and Mrs. Lambert was approaching, so Roger was obliged to hasten forward and open the gate for her.

"Oh, thank you, Roger," said Mrs. Lambert with her most charming smile.

After that there was no opportunity for private talk, they all filed into church together and the Ayrton family took up its usual position in the Amberwell pew.

St. Stephen's was not large, but it was well-designed and solidly built. It had been erected by Henry Ayrton as a memorial to his father and there was a plaque upon the wall commemorating the fact. Beside this plaque was another larger one with the names and dates of all the Ayrtons beginning with the first William who had built Amberwell and continuing in unbroken line with Roger, Stephen, Henry, William Henry and William the Third.

Roger had seen this plaque hundreds and hundreds of times but he still liked looking at it and thinking about the family history which was implicit in these names and dates. Some day his own name would be added and, below that, Stephen Ayrton . . . after that who knew? Stephen should call his eldest son Henry; it was time there was another Henry in the family. To-day Roger was in an imaginative mood and he reflected that it would be very pleasant if the old Roger and Stephen and Henry and all those Williams could return from the shades for a brief visit and take up their positions in the Amberwell pew. How interesting it would be to trace the family resemblance in their features, to talk to them about Amberwell and hear their views! Each would be dressed in the fashion of his time with the formal precision due to the occasion. The modern Roger, in his well-cut lounge suit of grey worsted tweed, would find himself very much out of step with the fine broadcloth of his forebears. (They wouldn't think much of me, thought the modern Roger with an involuntary smile.)

Roger noticed that his son's eyes were fixed upon the plaque and he wondered what Stephen was thinking . . . but there was no time for any more reflections for the service had begun.

Unlike most churches nowadays St. Stephen's was always well-filled, which probably was due to the personality of the rector. Mr. Orme was good and wise; he inspired affection. It was his custom to preach for ten minutes exactly, to take one idea for his theme and one idea only — so all the members of his congregation went home with it clearly in mind — and Mr. Orme's sermons had the unusual merit of being interesting to adults yet not above the heads of his youngest listeners. Lately he had formed the habit of trying out his ideas upon Emmie — who was one of his youngest listeners — and of altering his notes accordingly. To Mr. Orme religion was simple, there was nothing complicated about it — nothing abstruse. Mr. Orme's religion made him happy and his chief object in life was to share his happiness with his neighbours.

This morning Mr. Orme had taken Strength as his theme: "The Lord is my Strength and my Shield; my heart trusted in Him and I am helped." If we trust our own strength (said Mr. Orme) it may sustain us up to a certain point and then give way and let us down just at the moment when we need it most, but if the Lord is our strength, and our hearts trust in Him, He gives us

His help in time of trouble. All the great men of history had the Lord as their strength: Drake, Nelson, Gordon — and a host of others. In modern times we need look no farther than Churchill who was sustained through terrible strains and stresses by the Lord's hand. But it is not only great occasions which call for strength beyond our own; ordinary people who go about their daily duties feel the need of God's strength to help them, and God's shield to protect them from harm. The chief cause of unhappiness in modern times is fear, said Mr. Orme; fear of illness, fear of the future, fear of death; but the heart that trusts in the Lord fears nothing.

The theme was by no means new — most of Mr. Orme's listeners had heard sermons before on the same subject — but the sermon was strangely impressive for it was so absolutely sincere. Most of Mr. Orme's listeners were aware that for years the speaker himself had lived in the Shadow of Death and had seen him going about undismayed and cheerful with a ready smile for everybody.

When the service was over there was the usual gathering in the churchyard, but the Amberwell party did not stay long. They greeted their friends and set off home without delay. Roger had regained his sanity by this time; he realised that he had nearly done an exceedingly foolish thing; he had very nearly asked Georgina if she would like a post on the staff at Summerhills after Easter, and he had no business to do this without the permission of the man he had chosen to be headmaster of the school. Arnold would not mind of course (Roger felt sure of this) but that did not make it right. Arnold must ask Georgina himself.

Having made this decision it was wiser to avoid any further *tête à tête* conversation with Georgina and Roger accomplished this by the simple method of seizing Stephen's hand and walking home with him.

"We're going to bathe in the afternoon, aren't we?" said Stephen happily.

Roger nodded. It was not a particularly warm day, there was a fresh westerly breeze and he was aware that the sea would be rough and somewhat chilly; but he had promised and promises were important especially to a child. Indeed if Roger had not promised his son to bathe this afternoon he would even now be on his way to Rome.

They bathed together and as it was even colder than Roger had expected they did not stay in long, but there was another bather that afternoon who had swum far out beyond the waves and was disporting himself in the water like a seal . . . and when at last he came ashore, borne upon the crest of a breaker, the courageous mortal proved to be Bob Grainger.

When Bob had dressed and had emerged from behind a rock, clad in slacks and a fisherman's jersey, Roger went over to speak to him. It seemed a good opportunity for a quiet chat. Although Nell had sung his praises Roger was not sure that Bob was quite the right chap to take over the management of Amberwell Gardens. You needed something more than knowledge of plants to be a successful head-gardener. You needed the ability to manage men and get the best out of them

— and this boy was so young! But Roger had not spoken to Bob for more than five minutes before he changed his mind; the boy was young, certainly (and looked even younger than his nineteen years with his hair all rumpled with the towelling he had given it) but there was a strange dignity about him which betokened strength of character. He was respectful — but he had the fearless independence of the true Fifer, and looked you in the eye.

When they had been chatting for a bit Bob produced a postcard from his pocket and showed it to Roger proudly. "It's from Mr. Tom," he said. "I just thought maybe you'd like to see it."

The postcard was from Trinidad and there was a good deal written upon it in Tom's small neat "doctor's writing," and after obtaining permission from its owner Roger read it.

Hallo Bob, Tom had written. This is a fine town. Lots to see and do. Lots of pretty girls. Nice hot sun and gorgeous bathing. You would open your eyes if you could see the flowers. They are marvellous. Just got your nice long letter. Most interesting. I shall be home for Christmas. Cheerioh. T.A.

Roger smiled as he handed it back. It was difficult to know what to say. He himself would not have written quite like that to a garden-boy, but Tom was different. Tom was "hail-fellow-well-met" with everybody . . . and of course there was a special sort of bond between

Tom and Bob Grainger. Bob had jumped into the sea and saved Tom's life when the *Starfish* was blown up by a mine.

"It tells you a lot," said Bob as he put the postcard back in his pocket.

Roger agreed that it did.

CHAPTER
NINE

1

Tea was a hasty meal for Roger, and no sooner had he swallowed it than he set off to Summerhills in the car. He parked it in the drive and ran upstairs to have another look round and to make sure about one or two measurements in the big dormitory. The Findlaters had sold a good deal of their furniture to Roger and the rest had been stored until they found a suitable house. Meantime they had all gone to Harrogate for a restful holiday; Stark Place — or Summerhills — was empty. Roger was pleased to be there by himself, without Arnold or Mr. Strow, for he could look round quietly and brood upon his plans, a copy of which he had brought with him.

Suddenly there was a noise. The hall-door was opening and somebody was coming into the hall. Roger went down to see who it was and met Mary Findlater on the stairs. He was surprised to see Mary, not only because he had thought she was in Harrogate but also because she had said that she did not want to come back to Stark Place. Roger had understood her feeling perfectly . . . but here she was.

"Hallo, I thought you had gone to Harrogate!" he exclaimed.

"Yes, I did," replied Mary. "I got the parents comfortably settled in the hotel and then I came back. I'm staying with the Lamberts at Merlewood." She hesitated and then added, "I thought I'd come over."

"Yes, of course. Why shouldn't you?" said Roger, trying to speak as if it were the most natural thing in the world.

"It seemed silly not to come."

"Yes, of course. At least I don't think it was a bit silly, but still —"

"It seemed silly," repeated Mary. "So I just made up my mind to come. Really and truly I'm awfully interested in what you're doing and I thought I might be some use — knowing the place so well." She looked round the big empty hall as she spoke. Roger noticed that her face was white and strained. He felt very sorry for her.

"Are you making any alterations here?" asked Mary.

"Hardly any," said Roger hastily. "We're just — er — we're just going to put in a radiator and — and that sort of thing."

"Where? Tell me about it, Roger."

Roger told her somewhat awkwardly; it seemed all wrong to be making alterations in Mary's home.

"Don't worry, Roger," said Mary. "You've got to alter the old place to make it into a school. As a matter of fact I've been thinking about it and I was going to suggest one or two things."

"Grand! Go ahead, Mary!"

"A hatch in the dining-room for one thing — but perhaps you've thought of that already."

Roger nodded. "Yes, but there isn't a suitable place."

"Oh, there is! I'll show you. If you put it at the far end of the room it will open on to the passage just outside the kitchen door."

This was an excellent suggestion and soon Roger and Mary were busily tapping the wall and measuring and deciding exactly where the hatch was to be put . . . And Mary took the piece of chalk from Roger's hand and marked the wall firmly. After this there was no awkwardness, and the two of them went all over the house together, tapping walls and measuring and making a lot of notes.

"It is good of you," declared Roger as they came out of the front door and lingered on the steps in the sunshine. "You've been a tremendous help and I appreciate it more than I can say. I hope . . ." He paused and looked at her.

"It's all right," she replied. "It was just the first few minutes. I'm glad I came. You see, Roger, I understand what you're doing; I mean it's a worth-while plan to start a school for boys whose parents couldn't afford to send them to a very expensive place . . . people like us," said Mary, looking up at Roger and smiling rather sadly. "People who used to have enough money, but haven't enough now. The new poor."

Roger nodded. "That was the idea."

"I just wanted you to know that I understand, and that I'm awfully glad you bought Stark Place."

"If you feel like that perhaps you'll come again?"

"Yes, of course, if you want me."

"I shan't be here," Roger told her. "I've got to fly to Rome to-morrow. Aunt Beatrice is ill — in Rome — and I've got to go and see what I can do for her. It's an awful nuisance," said Roger frankly, "but there it is. Arnold will carry on here. It would be a help to Arnold if you could look in occasionally."

Mary said she would.

After that they wandered round the gardens; Roger had plans for the gardens too, and Mary listened and made several suggestions.

The meadow lay beyond the gardens (it was to be levelled and made into playing-fields); at one end of the meadow was a big oak tree with a huge spread of branches.

"You'll have to take it down, won't you?" said Mary sadly.

Roger hesitated. "I've been wondering about it," he said. "I hate the idea of taking it down. Do you remember one afternoon when Ian climbed on to that big branch and dared me to come after him?"

Mary smiled at him. "Yes, and you stuck half-way and Nell and I ran and got the gardener's ladder for you."

"What a fool I felt!"

"Nobody could climb that tree except Ian. We called it Ian's tree. He used to dare all sorts of people to climb it — and they always stuck."

"I shan't take it down," said Roger. "We'll rearrange the playing-fields."

"Roger, you mustn't —"

102

"We'll manage," declared Roger. "It's a beautiful tree. I hate cutting down trees, don't you?"

Mary said nothing — she could not speak — and they walked on in silence for a while.

"How long are you staying with the Lamberts?" asked Roger at last. "I mean if you're staying for some time it really would be a tremendous help if you could come over here now and then and keep an eye on things. The fact is — between you and me — I'm just a bit worried. Arnold and Mr. Strow don't pull together very well. Arnold is the boss — I'm writing to Strow to-night and making that perfectly clear — but I wish Arnold had a bit more drive."

"Perhaps he will when he's on his own," suggested Mary.

"Yes, perhaps. I hoped Nell would help, but Nell is a bit half-hearted. She thinks the school is a good plan but she's not keen to get on with it quickly."

He glanced at Mary to see if she understood and saw that her eyes were twinkling with amusement.

"Yes," said Roger with an answering grin. "Yes, our Nell will be only too pleased if Stark Place — I mean Summerhills — takes a long, long time to get going."

2

Mary had intended to stay with the Lamberts for a few days only, but after her talk with Roger she decided to ask her hostess if she might stay on. She was practically certain that Mrs. Lambert would not mind. So when Mrs. Lambert appeared at Mary's bedside to say good night — as was her very pleasant custom — Mary broached the subject.

"It's lovely being here," said Mary. "And the parents seem perfectly happy without me, so if you could possibly have me a bit longer —"

"Stay as long as you possibly can," said Mrs. Lambert warmly. "We both love having you, Mary dear."

They both loved having her, not only because they had known her all her life and were very fond of her, but also because she was an easy guest, always cheerful and amusing and no bother in the house . . . which in these days, as everybody knows, meant that Mary made her bed neatly every morning, dusted her room and was always ready to help with the washing-up. It also meant that Mary could knock up a very appetising omelet on the cook's night off and that she left the kitchen spotlessly clean and in excellent order for the cook's return. In spite of these activities Mary found her visit to the Lambert's a pleasant rest-cure, for Merlewood was modern and labour-saving and, compared with Stark Place, it was small.

Mr. Lambert was a cheerful hearty man, big and burly. Mrs. Lambert (who was known as Poppet to her friends) was a tiny fairy-like creature with an amusing tongue. They were contemporaries of Mary's parents but seemed a good deal younger because they had had a much less wearing life. Even the war had not affected them much; for at the beginning of the war Gerald was already a useful member of his father's shipbuilding firm and therefore exempt from military service.

"That *is* kind of you," said Mary. "The fact is Roger has asked me to keep an eye on Stark Place — and I think I'd like to. I went over there this afternoon and Roger showed me the plans for the alterations. It was horrid at first but afterwards I didn't mind a bit."

"Roger is very attractive," said Poppet smiling.

"Roger won't be there," said Mary hastily. "He's going to Italy to-morrow."

"What is he going to Italy for?" asked Poppet, who was always interested in the affairs of her fellow creatures.

Mary told her.

"Beatrice," said Poppet thoughtfully. "I haven't seen Beatrice for years; she must be about eighty."

At this stage in the conversation it occurred to Mrs. Lambert to sit down, so she perched herself on the end of the bed and arranged herself comfortably. She was wearing a pale pink peignoir and a pale pink boudoir cap trimmed with narrow lace. Thus arrayed for bed Poppet looked even more dainty and fascinating than in her usual clothes.

"We must ask Roger to dinner when he comes back from Italy," said Poppet. "I saw him in church this morning. He reminds me of his father."

"Of his father!" exclaimed Mary in surprise. "But Mr. Ayrton was —"

"I mean long ago — before you were born," said Poppet with a smile. "When Will Ayrton was young he was very attractive indeed; he was tall and fair and he had a sort of glow and he was full of vigour. Poor Will lost his glow when he married Marion — and no wonder! I'll tell you a secret, Mary," said Poppet lowering her voice. "I very nearly married him myself."

Mary was so astonished at this revelation that she was speechless.

"It isn't nice of you to be so surprised," complained Poppet. "I dare say you won't believe it, but I was very pretty when I was a girl."

"It isn't that at all! You're pretty *now*. Very pretty indeed."

"That's better," said Poppet approvingly.

"It's just that it seems — so queer —"

"That's not so good," said Poppet shaking her head.

Mary laughed and said no more.

"I know what you mean of course," continued Poppet reflectively. "You can't imagine us young; but we were, you know. We were just like you when we were young. We had hearts and legs — though we didn't show them so conspicuously as you do. We had a lot more leisure of course because we didn't need to wash the dishes or make the beds, but I'm not sure that it was good for us. We had too much time to think about ourselves, to be introspective. I know I had," said Poppet with a sigh. "I was a silly little creature. I read novels by Ethel Dell and Florence Barclay instead of washing the dishes and it wasn't nearly so good for me."

Mary was fascinated by this recital; she hoped more was coming.

"Will and I were engaged," continued Poppet. "We kept it a secret; not because anybody would have objected — our parents would have been delighted —

but because I was a romantic with my head in the clouds. I wore Will's ring on a ribbon round my neck instead of on my finger and made elaborate plans so that we could meet without anybody knowing. It was thrilling — and utterly idiotic. Men are straight-forward creatures; they don't like conspiracies; they don't like holes and corners and pretendings. Will wanted to tell everybody and be properly engaged, but I wouldn't. Of course it led to trouble."

Poppet was silent for a few moments, gazing into the distance, and Mary began to think this was all she was to be told. She was very anxious to hear the end of the story.

"Of course it led to trouble," repeated Poppet. "There was another girl, you see. She flirted with Will and I didn't like it."

"No wonder! It was horrid!" exclaimed Mary.

"Not really horrid. She wouldn't have done it if she had known we were engaged."

"But he knew! He should have —"

"Men are so helpless," said Poppet. "And the nicer they are the more helpless they are — besides it was quite a mild sort of flirtation — but I was a fool in those days so I was angry with Will . . . and Will just laughed and said it was all my fault for not being properly engaged. Even then it wasn't too late; I could have had him back quite easily — but I had no sense at all. So we quarrelled and it all fell through and I was so furious that I married Johnnie. It's a silly story, isn't it?" said Poppet. "I don't know why I told you — except as a sort of Gypsy's Warning — but you don't read Ethel Dell, do you?"

"I never even heard of her," said Mary, who had been trying to follow and was getting positively breathless in the attempt.

"You'd laugh at her," said Poppet, looking at Mary critically. "Yes, I believe you'd laugh. We didn't laugh. We were thrilled to bits at her stories — all about strong silent men with sadistic tendencies — so perhaps we weren't very like you after all."

Mary wondered if she were expected to show sympathy — it was a little difficult — but Poppet had an uncanny knack of reading one's thoughts.

"You needn't be the least bit sorry for me," said Poppet. "I've been very happy with Johnnie for nearly forty years. He's not a hero of romance but he's a dear, nice, good, kind creature and we suit each other admirably."

Mary nodded. She was aware of this.

"I wonder what started me off," said Poppet with a thoughtful look. "I believe it was you saying Roger was so attractive."

"I didn't!" cried Mary indignantly.

"Didn't you?" asked Poppet in surprise.

"No, I never said such a thing."

"But you thought it, didn't you?"

"No, of course not."

"Well then, you must be blind," declared Poppet with a mischievous smile. "You must be absolutely stone blind. Roger is quite beautiful to look at and that slight air of sadness adds to his appeal. If I were a girl I should fall in love with Roger, head over heels."

Mary had blushed like a rose. She said, "Oh, but Roger doesn't take any notice of girls. He's still — sad — about Clare."

"Yes, but he's beginning to get over it and that's the most dangerous time. You know, Mary," said Poppet earnestly, "that girl with the long legs means to have Roger."

"Oh no!" cried Mary in dismay. "Oh no, not her!"

"I don't like her either," agreed Poppet.

"She's not nearly good enough for Roger."

"Not nearly — but she means to have him if she can. It would be a thousand pities if she got him. I'd much rather have you as a next-door-neighbour," added Poppet in confidential tones.

Mary had been pink before but now she was scarlet. "You're — awful!" she exclaimed.

"Yes," said Poppet nodding. "I know I'm awful — everybody says I am — but it's such fun to be awful, and sometimes it does people good to shake them up a bit." And with that Poppet kissed her guest fondly and tripped away to bed.

Mary thought about the story of Poppet's broken romance and wondered why it had been told to her; for Poppet was clever — not silly at all — and the story had been told with a purpose. Was it really a Gypsy's Warning (as Poppet had said) and, if so, to warn Mary of what? There was no moral in the tale — none whatever — for Poppet's foolish behaviour had not led to her downfall but to forty years of married bliss.

Poppet *is* awful, thought Mary, as she cuddled down into the comfortable bed provided for the Lamberts' guests. I could call her Poppet quite easily (thought Mary). I very nearly did it to-night — by mistake. It would be rather cheek for me to call her Poppet, but I believe she'd like it . . . and I wonder why it is that she can say anything — be as awful as awful — and you don't really mind . . .

CHAPTER
TEN

1

Stephen sat upon Roger's bed and watched him packing his suitcase. He had sat upon the same bed only a fortnight ago and watched his father unpack with very different feelings.

"Daddy, do you want to go and see Aunt Beatrice?" asked Stephen.

"No, of course not."

"I thought grown-up people could always do what they wanted."

Roger could not help smiling. "I thought the same when I was eight," he said. "I thought that when there was nobody to tell you what to do, you could do whatever you liked . . . but you can't. When you grow up you have responsibilities, especially when you're the head of the family."

"The head of the family?"

"Yes, that's what I am. It means I've got to look after all the other people in the family — see?" He glanced at his little son's face to be sure that he understood. You could never be sure with Stephen. Sometimes he seemed mature beyond his years and at other times quite babyish. It was being so much with grown-up people, Roger thought. It was being with Nell and chatting to her and trotting in and out of the kitchen, hob-nobbing with dear old Mrs. Duff. He had Emmie to play with but Emmie was "old-fashioned" too. She had been her mother's close friend and companion and still was. They had weathered hardships together . . .

"It's important being head of the family, isn't it?" said Stephen, thoughtfully. "Like being a King, really."

"Something like that," agreed Roger, wondering whether he should take a dinner-jacket and deciding he need not. "One of these days you'll be the head of the family," added Roger.

"Me!"

"Not until I'm dead, of course."

"But you'll live to be a hundred," replied Stephen cheerfully.

"Who said so?"

"Mr. Gray. Mr. Gray said, 'The major's that strong and active I wouldn't wonder but he'll live to be a hundred.'"

Roger chuckled. Stephen had "got" Mr. Gray exactly, even to the slightly husky voice.

"Oh well," said Roger. "In that case it will be a long time before you're King of Amberwell."

There was no reply for a few moments and Roger, glancing towards the bed, saw that his son was engaged in an arithmetical problem. He was muttering to himself and counting on his fingers. "Sixty-seven years," he said at last with obvious satisfaction.

This little talk remained in Roger's memory very clearly; perhaps because the mixture of matter-of-fact sense and childish innocence was "so like Stephen." It was comical and pathetic and this was "so like Stephen" too. Roger reflected that it was a pity children had to grow up; by this time next year Stephen would be a schoolboy and the childish innocence would have vanished . . . but one could not help it of course. One could only do one's best to see that the child grew into a boy and the boy into a man smoothly, and with the least possible suffering . . . and that there were as few "nasty things" as possible in his cupboard of memory to roll out unexpectedly and make him uncomfortable.

These thoughts and others like them passed through Roger's mind as the plane in which he was travelling was flying over the Mediterranean Sea. He had left Amberwell that morning and now he was approaching Rome. Looking down from the little window Roger saw the coast of the Italian Riviera, the long line of white towns and villas embowered in green, the small yachts with their white sails and the hazy mountains beyond. He knew the country, for he had been here during the war, but it looked different from the air; it looked unreal. Perhaps the air of unreality was partly due to Roger's own feelings; for this trip (unlike his flight from Hamburg to Renfrew) had come upon him suddenly and unawares. Two days ago Roger had had no more idea that he would be flying to Rome to see Aunt Beatrice than that he would be flying to the moon.

Even now Roger could hardly believe that he was flying to Rome to see Aunt Beatrice . . .

The plane swayed and bumped and the old man who was sitting opposite to Roger looked about him anxiously.

"We're crossing Sardinia," his companion told him — and began to explain about warm air rising from the island and creating a disturbance in the atmosphere. The explanation was not scientifically correct (and the island happened to be Corsica) but it had the desired effect and the old man was pacified.

This little incident changed the tenor of Roger's thoughts and he reflected with some amusement that it really was possible to be in two places at once. His room at Amberwell, untidy with packing (and his small son sitting upon the bed, counting on his fingers) was every bit as real to Roger as the interior of the plane. At the same moment he was there — and here!

The plane roared on and Roger began to think of Summerhills, for since he had begun work on the place it had never been far from his thoughts. He had gone at it tooth and nail. While he was on the job he had thought about the job and not about himself at all, but now that he was idle he had a rare moment of introspection. It's done me good, he thought in surprise.

It was Roger's mind that felt better. His health had never bothered him. Ever since Clare's death Roger had felt only half-alive. He had explained this feeling to Mary by saying that he had nothing left — nothing that mattered. It was as good an explanation as he could give. But now, quite suddenly, he realised that things had begun to give him pleasure: food tasted better, colours looked brighter and his spirit was lightened of its burden. Roger had never had a serious illness, but he had been wounded in the war and he had felt like this when recovering. Yes, it was like convalescence.

The thought worried him. He had been certain that he would walk in sackcloth all his life — invisible sackcloth of course — but here he was enjoying things again. Was this uplift of spirit an infidelity to the memory of Clare?

But it isn't a woman, thought Roger. It's a job, and a worthwhile job at that. So there's no need to worry.

What a pity he could not be at Summerhills to-day! The builders were starting work. Mr. Strow would be there and Arnold; perhaps Mary would go over. Mary had been most useful — that hatch was a very good idea — he had asked Mary how long she was going to stay with the Lamberts, but she had not replied. He wondered if she would still be there when he got home.

The air-hostess came down the passage. "Fasten your safety belts," she said. She smiled at all her charges but the smile she gave Roger was a little more real and friendly for she liked the look of him. There was something about him . . . it was not only his broad shoulders and his fair hair and his sea-blue eyes . . . "And I'm afraid you must put out your cigarette," she added in regretful tones.

"Oh, of course!" exclaimed Roger, stubbing it out hastily.

Having booked a room at the hotel Roger left his
suitcase in charge of the hall-porter and set out on foot
for the Pensione Valetta. Now that he had almost
arrived at his destination his heart began to fail him
and he wondered what he would find, for it was six
days since Madame Le Brun had written that letter
saying Miss Ayrton was ill, and quite a lot could
happen in six days. Aunt Beatrice might be dead — one
had to face it — or on the other hand she might be
better. If she were better he would be allowed to see
her.

The prospect of an interview with Aunt Beatrice was
not very pleasant, for Roger had no idea what her
feelings towards him might be. He felt somewhat guilty.
Of course she had been very stupid about Anne —
urging Anne to marry without her parents' consent —
but all that had happened long ago and should have
been forgiven and forgotten. Roger had done nothing,
he had just let matters drift; he was home so seldom
and there was always so much to do that he had never
got round to making up the feud. He remembered now
that Tom had visited Aunt Beatrice when his ship was
at Rosyth and had reported that the old lady was very
friendly and had given him an excellent lunch . . . but
even that was years and years ago, before Tom left the
Navy.

Oh well, thought Roger, as he pushed his way
through the crowded streets with an armful of flowers
which he had bought as a peace-offering. Oh well, if she

doesn't want to see me that's her look-out. I've done the right thing to come.

The Pensione Valetta was not easy to find for Roger could not speak Italian and the people he asked seemed unable to direct him. He knew it was near "The Spanish Steps," and he expected it to be a large flourishing establishment in the wide square, so when at last he was shown a narrow alley in a side street, with several extremely dirty children playing about the entrance, he could hardly believe he had come to the right place. The children stopped playing and gazed at him with large soft brown eyes — although dirty they were beautiful — and Roger was prompted to give them each a flower from Aunt Beatrice's bouquet. This gesture was a tremendous success and he was pursued by cries of pleasure and gratitude as he went on down the alley and emerged into a little courtyard. One small girl followed him and when he said "Pensione Valetta?" in an inquiring tone of voice she pointed to an archway and a flight of steps and held out her hand for another flower as payment. It was greedy of course, thought Roger as he gave it to her — children in his own country would not have asked — but when he saw one dimpling smile on her grubby little face he forgave her. Children in his own country would not have smiled so sweetly for the gift of a flower.

Roger went on, up the narrow unprepossessing stairs, and presently arrived upon a broad landing bathed in sunshine. It was a surprisingly pleasant place compared with its approach. The child, who had followed him up the stairs, pointed to a door with a brass plate inscribed "Pensione Valetta" and held out her hand for another flower.

This time Roger refused the request, shaking his head and saying, "No, you greedy little creature"; but he said it with a smile.

He rang the bell, which jangled loudly, and waited for some time; he was about to ring again when the door was opened by a short stout woman dressed in black satin with a mass of gold chains round her neck. She looked him up and down and burst into a flood of Italian.

"I'm sorry I don't speak Italian," Roger said. He added a trifle diffidently, "*Parlez vous Français?*"

"*Je suit Française, moi,*" replied the woman. "But I spik Ingleese or Gairmain — or wot you plees. Eet ees all one to me."

It was not all one to Roger so he chose to make his business known in his native tongue. (Afterwards he discovered that it was not all one to her either, for her command of the English language was extremely limited.)

"Oh good," said Roger. "Well the fact is I'm Miss Ayrton's nephew. I think you wrote to me — if you're Madame Le Brun."

She did not welcome him with the enthusiasm he had expected but she opened the door a little wider and allowed him to come in. He found himself in a very large hall paved with parquet and furnished with small tables and easy-chairs. At the far end of the hall there were double doors which opened on to a roof-garden. The hall itself was dim and cool but the garden was bright with masses of flowers, lighted by the afternoon sunshine.

"I hope my aunt is better," said Roger a trifle diffidently for his cool reception had daunted him.

"Mees Ayrton ees seek — but to-day a leetle better," replied Madame Le Brun. "You 'ave taken a long time. I am worried a lot."

Roger began to explain that he had thought it better to come than to write and that as he lived in Scotland the letter had taken several days to reach him, but he soon realised that Madame Le Brun did not understand a word. She still continued to look at him crossly with her black beady eyes.

"For Miss Ayrton," said Roger, handing her the flowers in the hope that they would pacify her.

"But wot to do?" she said, frowning. "I do not tell 'er I write. See? I write because ze docteur say write — and she look vairy seek and I sink it good that peoples of 'er own are 'ere."

"Yes, of course," said Roger.

"Now she ees better you go away," added Madame Le Brun, waving towards the door.

"Go away!" exclaimed Roger. "Do you mean without seeing her?"

"Ze docteur say quiet ees best."

Roger hesitated. He did not particularly want to see Aunt Beatrice, but after coming all this way it seemed ridiculous to be turned away at her door. Besides he did not like this woman at all; he did not trust her, and he was very much annoyed with her. She had written to him because she was afraid Aunt Beatrice was dying, and he had come at her behest — now all she wanted was to get rid of him. She was completely selfish, thought Roger, looking at her in distaste.

Perhaps she sensed his feelings. "Look you," she said in a more conciliatory tone. "Mees Ayrton ees vairy deeficult, *n'est ce pas*? I ask me will she be glad you come or will she be vairy angree. Angree is bad for 'er — see?"

Roger realised that there was some truth in this. He had no idea whether Aunt Beatrice would be glad to see him or very angry indeed.

"Yes," he said doubtfully. "I haven't seen her for years. She might be — upset." He had been about to say angry, but substituted the other word.

"So you must go away," said Madame Le Brun, nodding.

"But how is she?" asked Roger. "What's the matter with her?"

"She ees seek," replied Madame Le Brun. "When I write she ees vairy seek but now she is a leetle better."

This information was vague, to say the least of it, but Roger could discover no more; he could not make up his mind whether Madame Le Brun was being vague deliberately or whether the difficulty was due to their inability to communicate with each other — they could not speak the same language! It crossed Roger's mind that if only he had learnt a modern language at school (if he had spent all the hours devoted to the study of Latin in learning to speak French or Italian fluently) he would not have felt so helpless. He made up his mind then and there that the boys of Summerhills should be

120

taught modern languages which would be of use to them in a modern world.

At last Roger gave up the struggle to get any satisfaction out of Madame Le Brun.

"I must see the doctor and speak to him," said Roger with a sigh.

Madame Le Brun smiled grimly. "You can see 'im but you not spik to 'im," she replied.

"Not speak to him?"

"'E not spik Inglese."

"Not any English at all?"

"Vairy little. Not good like me. *C'est amusant, n'est ce pas?*" she added with a titter.

Roger was not amused. It seemed to him a very poor joke. "Oh," he said. "Well, I'd like to see him all the same."

"Eet will be no good."

"Perhaps not, but I mean to see him. Where does he live?"

Madame Le Brun did not understand — or pretended not to understand — this perfectly simple question and Roger was obliged to repeat it several times before she answered.

At last she said reluctantly, "You see 'im 'ere eef you want to see 'im. 'E come at ten hours of the morning — but eet will be no good."

CHAPTER
ELEVEN

1

When Roger got back to the hotel he was informed by the hall-porter that a visitor had called and asked for him and on being told that Major Ayrton was out had left a message to say he would come back after dinner.

"Who was he? What was his name?" asked Roger.

"I think he was your brother," replied the hall-porter.

This seemed impossible, for Nell had said that Tom was in Bermuda. "Are you sure?" inquired Roger.

"He looked like you," was the answer.

"If he looked like me he wasn't my brother," declared Roger.

This curious statement was perfectly true. Tom was lightly built, with dark hair and brown eyes. The two brothers were quite unlike each other.

"But he looked like you," repeated the hall-porter.

It was obvious that the man did not understand and Roger saw no object in explaining matters further; he was just turning away when a very beautiful young woman rushed up to the desk and addressed the hall-porter in an unknown tongue (which certainly was not French or German or Italian) and the hall-porter replied to her fluently. Hall-porters were wonderful, thought Roger. How useful to have had one on the Tower of Babel!

By this time Roger was very hungry so he went in to dinner, but as he ate the excellent meal he continued to puzzle over the identity of his visitor. Roger had no friends in Rome. Nobody knew he was here except his own family. Two days ago he had not known he would be here himself. Who on earth could it be?

The mystery was solved when Roger went into the lounge to have his coffee; there was a man sitting by himself in the corner reading the *Daily Mail*. He looked up as Roger came in and, putting down the paper, rose and came across the room. The man was a large fair Briton, not unlike himself, but a complete stranger.

"Are you Major Ayrton?" he asked.

"Yes."

"Oh good! I'm Dennis Weatherby. You don't know me of course, but I'm a friend of Tom's."

"I've heard a lot about you," said Roger, smiling as they shook hands.

"I called before," said Dennis Weatherby. "The hall-porter didn't get my name — it's a difficult name for foreigners — but he said he would tell you."

"He did. He said you were my brother — said you looked like me — wouldn't believe me when I told him that if you looked like me you couldn't be my brother. It was too difficult."

Dennis smiled. "Certainly you aren't like Tom. We're more like each other — both large and fair!"

The hall-porter's mistake tided them over the slight awkwardness of their meeting. It was mildly amusing.

Roger's coffee was brought and the two large fair young men sat down together at the corner table. They talked about Tom, which was a natural subject for conversation, and Roger discovered that Tom's friend shared his own views.

"Yes, of course Tom should settle down and practise medicine seriously," agreed Dennis. "But I don't think he will, you know. He likes wandering about the world and seeing new places and he loves the sea. Tom ought to have gone into the Navy."

"I know. He always wanted to," agreed Roger.

All this time Roger had been wondering how Dennis Weatherby had known he was in Rome. At last he asked the question.

"I'm on my way home," explained Dennis. "I've been out East for three years so I've got a good long spell of leave. I'm staying here with some cousins who have a villa up in the hills. You see my mother's sister married an Italian — so the cousins are half English. I used to spend my holidays with them sometimes when I was a boy, but I haven't seen them for quite a long time so I thought it was a good opportunity to go and see them on my way home. Of course I'm only staying here for a few days."

Roger nodded and waited for more. Dennis had explained his presence in Rome but he had not answered the question.

"Nell told me you were here," added Dennis after a short pause.

"Nell told you!"

"Yes. You see I — er — I rang her up last night."

124

"You rang her up!"

"Yes," said Dennis. "I just thought — it was a sudden idea — and we got a very good connection. I mean it was worth it." He hesitated again and then added, "When you've been abroad for years it's rather nice to — to talk to people."

This was true of course, Roger had experienced it himself, but all the same it looked as if Tom were right. It was "nice to talk to people" when you had been abroad for years, but only if you happened to like them in rather a special sort of way.

"Nell told me about your aunt," continued Dennis. "She suggested I should look you up and see if I could be of any help. You see I know the lingo, more or less."

"How frightfully good of you!"

"Not a bit. I wanted to meet you. Is there anything I can do?"

"Yes," said Roger. "At least — I hardly like to ask you. The fact is I'm in a bit of a hole — but I don't see why you should bother."

"No bother at all," declared Dennis fervently.

It was true, thought Roger. No fellow in his senses would volunteer so eagerly to help another fellow out of a mysterious hole unless he were extremely interested in the other fellow's sister.

"If it's money I can help you quite easily," Dennis continued. "I can borrow it from my cousins and you can pay me back when you get home. Nell thought you might be short of money. If you've got to pay the doctor or put your aunt into a hospital —"

"I haven't got round to that yet," said Roger ruefully. "I haven't done anything at all. I don't even know what's the matter with her and I can't find out . . ." and he proceeded to tell Dennis the whole story.

"Why don't you trust the Frenchwoman?" Dennis inquired.

"I don't know. It's just a feeling. Probably I'm quite wrong and she's the soul of honour, but I didn't like her." Roger smiled and added, "She was short and stout and her black dress fitted her so tightly that she looked like an old-fashioned pin-cushion stuffed with sawdust. She had lots of gold chains round her neck and her eyes were like beads."

They laughed together over the description.

"I'll come with you to-morrow," said Dennis. "I can talk to the doctor and find out the state of affairs. Then we'll know what to do — whether Miss Ayrton should be moved to a hospital."

This offer was such a relief to Roger's mind that his objections and protestations were somewhat half-hearted.

"Of course I'll come," said Dennis. "It isn't a bother at all. I'm longing to see the pin-cushion. We'll make a little hole in her and see if the sawdust pours out."

"It will," declared Roger with conviction.

Having settled to meet and go to the Pensione Valetta on the following morning the two young men began to talk of other things. Dennis did most of the talking, and Roger as he listened became more than ever convinced that his new friend was talking with a purpose. It was unusual, to say the least of it, for a casual acquaintance to tell one so much about his affairs. By the time Dennis left Roger knew all about his background.

Dennis Weatherby's father died when he was a child. His mother continued to live at Weatherby Manor. Although it was much too large for comfort she had hopes that some day things would change for the better and her son would be able to take up his residence in his old home. Lately it had become increasingly difficult to carry on. The house was some miles from Harrogate and so isolated that Mrs. Weatherby could not get any domestic help and as it was quite impossible to live in the place alone she had been obliged to shut it up and take rooms in a hotel. Now however she had managed to find a small house in Harrogate with a pleasant garden and Dennis was going to help her move into it and get settled there.

So far Weatherby Manor had not been sold, it was standing empty; they had had one or two offers for it but the offers were so ridiculous that they could not be considered. Nobody wanted an enormous house, miles from anywhere.

Dennis spoke of his mother with deep affection, he was obviously devoted to her. He told Roger that she was only twenty years older than himself and young for her age. For years she had lived like a hermit in Weatherby Manor, seeing few people and working far too hard, but she was interested in people and he hoped the move into Harrogate would be a success. Already she had made friends with some people in the hotel and was going about and enjoying herself. Dennis did not exactly state his income — that would have been a little too obvious — but he gave Roger to understand that his mother had enough to live on and would have more if they could sell the Manor, and that although he himself had very little beyond his pay he was well on his way to promotion in the Service. There was no mention of Nell, but Dennis was well up-to-date in news of the Ayrton family; he knew about Summerhills and Roger's plans for the school, and he could not have known all this unless Nell had written and told him . . . so they were corresponding regularly!

If Roger and Dennis had met elsewhere it would have taken them much longer to become acquainted; but meeting here, in a foreign country, produced an intimacy between them in record time. He's a good fellow, thought Roger as he went upstairs to bed. If he's the Right One for Nell I shan't be sorry . . . though what will happen to Amberwell if Nell decides to marry him Heaven alone knows.

Dennis was Tom's friend, which was strange, for he was not the least like Tom. Tom was a dear fellow; he was amusing and attractive, he could wile the birds off the trees, but you could not call him sound. Dennis Weatherby was sound — if Roger knew anything about men.

Perhaps Roger's estimate of his new friend was slightly coloured by his relief at finding a fellow countryman in strange surroundings, and a fellow countryman who was eager to help him out of a hole, but Roger was used to people who showed eagerness to be of service to him and could see through them at once. The offer of help could have been made in a very

128

different way; it could have been difficult to accept without a feeling of obligation, but it had been made so naturally and spontaneously that there was no awkwardness at all. The offer of money to tide him over any temporary difficulties had been sensible and business-like. Roger had not thanked Dennis — there was no need — but he had appreciated it greatly; the more so because it was so unusual. Roger was frequently asked for the loan of money but he could not remember ever having been offered such a thing before.

This was a small matter, of course (he smiled when he thought of it), but it had its effect . . . and it was quite possible that he would have to take advantage of the offer, for the sum allowed to travellers by the British Government would not go very far if Aunt Beatrice had to be moved to a hospital.

2

Dennis appeared at the hotel punctually the next morning and, as Roger knew his way to the Pensione Valetta, he was able to lead his friend direct to the somewhat unsavoury entrance in the side street. There were no children here this morning — perhaps they were at school — but there was litter lying about in the form of tins and pieces of torn paper and orange skins. The place looked worse than Roger remembered and he was not surprised when Dennis commented upon it unfavourably.

"I know. It's horrible," agreed Roger. "But it's all right once you get inside."

Madame Le Brun opened the door to them; she was arrayed as before, tightly and creaselessly in black satin with the gold chains round her podgy neck. It was impossible to imagine her in any other garment or to believe that she removed it when she went to bed. Roger glanced at Dennis and noticed that he was endeavouring to hide a smile. The doctor had arrived before them and was waiting in the hall; he too was short and stout, but he looked more human. He looked as if he were made of flesh and blood — not sawdust.

When everybody had been introduced and had acknowledged the introductions politely they began to talk at once. Dennis had said that he knew the lingo, more or less, and now Roger realised that this statement had been extremely modest. Perhaps he did not talk quite so fast, and certainly he was less lavish of gesture than the other two, but he seemed to be holding his own. They talked for some minutes without stopping for breath and, to the anxious listener, it appeared that they were arguing fiercely and were all very angry indeed, but apparently the anxious listener was wrong.

"It doesn't sound too bad," said Dennis at last, turning to Roger and speaking in a rapid indistinct mumble which nobody but Roger could understand. "Doc says she's had a slight hæmorrhage on the brain — a sort of stroke, I suppose. At least that's what he thought at first, but now he's not so sure. It's all pretty technical and I wouldn't get it in English far less in Italian. He was anxious about her at first and told the pin-cushion to communicate with her relations, but

130

after a couple of days she was very much better and the improvement has continued. Her arm was paralysed — I think that's what he means — but that's better. He's surprised at the improvement and I have a feeling he's trying to save his face by making it all as mysterious as he can. Silly little ass, isn't he?"

Roger glanced at the silly little ass and saw that he was listening to the interpretation of his remarks with his head on one side and a beaming smile upon his chubby countenance. Madame Le Brun was listening too, she wore a frown and was trying her best to follow the conversation.

"Why you not speaking Ingleese?" she demanded suddenly.

"We prefer Urdu," replied Dennis slowly and clearly. "You have no objection, I hope."

"Eet is vairy foony, I sink," she declared suspiciously.

Roger thought it was "foony" too. He could not help chuckling.

Having made this explanation Dennis turned back to Roger and continued to converse in "Urdu." "She's still in bed," he muttered. "Hasn't been up at all, but if she goes on like this he's thinking of letting her up to-morrow."

"Does she want to see me?"

"They haven't told her you're here. Pin-cushion doesn't want you to see her. Doc says you can see her if you don't excite her. My impression is Doc doesn't want to take the responsibility of sending you away."

"Well, I don't know," mumbled Roger. "You'd better tell him I've no idea whether it'll excite her or not.

There was a fearful row in the family and I haven't seen the old lady for years. Might go off the deep end if I walked in."

"Better not mention the row. I'll just say it might excite her." He turned back to the others and explained.

The argument was resumed and now that Roger held the key he was able to follow it quite easily — not from the words of course but from the gestures. Madame Le Brun pointed to the door by which the two young men had entered, words poured from her mouth, she waved her arms dramatically and rolled her eyes like a prima donna in an Italian opera. The doctor shook his head violently and pointed to a door at the other end of the hall, which no doubt led to his patient's bedroom. Dennis had withdrawn from the contest and stood by, watching and listening.

The argument became more and more heated, the voices louder. Roger was convinced that very soon the contestants would come to blows. He seized his interpreter by the arm.

"Look here," he exclaimed. "I'd better not see her. I don't want to see her if it's going to make all this fuss. I only came because the woman wrote to me and I thought it was the right thing to do."

"You'd better see her. Doc says he'll take the responsibility. It's for him to say. Pin-cushion has nothing to do with it."

Roger was not so sure. "Let's go, for goodness' sake," he whispered. "Let's filter out and leave them to it."

"No. You'd better see her."

132

"Why?"

"I think there's some funny business going on."

"Funny business?"

"It's fishy," explained Dennis. "I mean why doesn't the pin-cushion want you to see her? That's what I'd like to know."

Before Roger could think of a reply the argument terminated. Madame Le Brun raised her palms upwards in a gesture of despair and, giving one last shriek of rage and disapproval, she swung round and clattered off down the hall leaving the little doctor victor of the field.

"Come," said the little doctor smiling agreeably. "I vill tak you — to see — ze ant."

"Go on," said Dennis encouragingly. "I'll wait."

Roger had no option but to follow the doctor's lead.

3

It was a small room and rather dark. Aunt Beatrice was lying propped up in bed. Roger's first impression was that she had not changed a bit since the last time he had seen her — and that was over ten years ago. Her hair was no whiter; it was still the same ugly iron-grey, and her strongly-marked, bony features were the type that seldom change much with the passing years. He would have known Aunt Beatrice anywhere.

"Hallo, Aunt Beatrice!" he said. "I'm sorry to hear you've been ill. I happened to be in Rome so I looked in to see you. I'm Roger," he added.

"Of course you're Roger," said Aunt Beatrice crossly. "I may be old — and ill — but I'm not gaga yet. Pull up the blind so that I can see you properly."

He did as he was told and sat down on the chair beside the bed. "I'm glad you're better," he told her.

"A lot of fuss about nothing — but that's just like these foreigners. They didn't send for you, did they?"

"No, of course not," he replied . . . but Roger wasn't a good liar at the best of times and with those sharp brown eyes fixed upon his face he made a poor job of it.

"Oh, they did, did they? They thought I was going to die. I don't intend to die in a foreign country."

"No, of course not."

"You're older," said Aunt Beatrice. "Older and better-looking. In fact you're very like William."

"William?"

"Your father of course. He was extremely handsome when he was young."

It was difficult to know how to reply to this so Roger remained silent.

"How is your mother — I mean your step-mother?"

"She's — fairly well. She gets rather muddled sometimes."

"Muddled!" exclaimed Aunt Beatrice scornfully. "She has no right to get muddled at her age. Marion is younger than I am and I'm not muddled, am I?"

"No, you're not," replied Roger smiling.

"I hear Anne has turned up," continued Aunt Beatrice. "Anne treated me abominably. She hasn't written to me for years. All your family have treated me in the most extraordinary way — all except Tom. He comes to visit me sometimes when he happens to be near Edinburgh."

"Yes, I know," said Roger uncomfortably. He would have liked to stand up for his family — in his opinion it was Aunt Beatrice who had behaved badly — but it would be the height of folly to start an argument with her.

"I shall leave all my money to Tom," declared Aunt Beatrice.

Roger said nothing. He thought it an excellent plan but it was not for him to say so.

"There was no need for you to come," she continued, "but perhaps it is just as well. I don't feel up to travelling home alone."

"Travelling home!"

"Yes, we had better go by aeroplane. I have never been in one but I am told they're extremely comfortable."

"But we can't —"

"Why not? I shall pay the fares. You needn't worry about that."

Roger was not worrying about that. "I'm sure the doctor wouldn't hear of it," he declared. "You're not fit to travel."

"Not to-morrow, perhaps, but I shall be perfectly able for it the next day."

"But Aunt Beatrice —"

"Don't argue," said Aunt Beatrice irritably. "I can't stay here. Madame Le Brun has been exceedingly rude to me."

"We could move you into a hospital."

"A hospital! No, thank you!"

"You would be more comfortable —"

"I don't intend to go to a hospital and I can't stay here. As I said Madame Le Brun has been rude — unbearably rude. I have been coming here for years but I shall never come back, that's very certain. Her behaviour has been most extraordinary. Surely after all these years I had a right to complain about the food! It was for her own good that I told her the food was uneatable and the place was going downhill! There was no need to be rude about it." Aunt Beatrice paused and looked at Roger defiantly.

"No," said Roger in doubtful tones. "No, perhaps not. I suppose you had a row."

"You can call it that if you like," she retorted.

It must have been the grandfather of all rows, thought Roger, but he said nothing.

"Perhaps I said rather more than I intended," admitted Aunt Beatrice. "I certainly was somewhat annoyed, but she was so impertinent that I came straight into my bedroom and started to pack. Then suddenly I felt a little queer and my arm went numb."

"Yes, I see. It's very unfortunate."

"Most unfortunate — and most uncomfortable. I have been lying here for nearly a week, waited upon by Her. I have asked her repeatedly to allow the girl to bring me my food but she takes no notice. She brings the trays herself and bangs them down on the table and stumps out of the room without a word. It's like being in prison. I won't stay here a moment longer than is

136

absolutely necessary." She was working herself up (as Nannie would have said) and Roger was very much alarmed, for he had been warned not to excite her.

"It's all right," he said hastily. "I'll take you home the moment you're fit to travel — I promise faithfully I will — but you mustn't get excited or you won't be fit to travel for ages. The doctor said so."

"I'm not in the least excited and I shall be fit to travel the day after to-morrow," said Aunt Beatrice firmly.

Roger did not know what to do. The matter was beyond him . . . but anyhow it was time to go so he rose and said good-bye.

"Good-bye, Roger," said Aunt Beatrice, smiling quite pleasantly. "It was nice of you to come. You'll come and see me to-morrow, won't you?"

"Yes, of course I will."

"And don't forget to reserve seats in the aeroplane. I prefer to sit with my back to the engine," added Aunt Beatrice.

4

Dennis was waiting in the hall as he had promised. "I say, you've been ages!" he exclaimed.

"I know. It was frightful. Let's get out of this quickly."

"Don't you want to speak to the pin-cushion?"

"There's nothing I want less."

They let themselves out of the front door as quietly as possible and ran down the stairs . . . and, as they went, Roger gave a brief and somewhat incoherent account of his interview with his aunt.

"Of course the obvious thing to do is to move her into a hospital," said Roger when he had finished the recital.

"But she won't go?"

"No."

"You can't move her by force."

Roger was aware of this. "What the dickens am I to do!" he exclaimed in despair.

"You had better book the seats," Dennis told him. "If she can't travel they'll have to be cancelled, but from all accounts I should think your aunt must be a very determined old lady."

"Obstinate as a mule. In fact a mule is tractable compared with Aunt Beatrice."

"Well, there you are!" said Dennis.

The conversation lapsed for a few minutes while the two young men crossed the street. Crossing the street in Rome during the rush hour is not an easy matter and requires agility and concentration. When they had reached the opposite pavement, having dodged several large cars — apparently driven by homicidal maniacs — and a dozen or so motor scooters, Dennis resumed their talk.

"I wish I could help you," he said. "I mean I'd come with you in the plane if I could, but I shall have to fly home to-night. There's a man coming to-morrow to look at Weatherby Manor, and it sounds fairly hopeful. He's the representative of a syndicate that intends to start a country club. My mother wants me to see him."

138

"Of course," agreed Roger. "You can't miss the chance. You must certainly see him. You've been a tremendous help. Goodness knows what I should have done without you."

"It was nothing. I enjoyed it."

"You must come and stay with us for a bit," suggested Roger. "I mean when you've finished all the business with your house and got your mother settled. Just ring up and say when you can come."

"Yes, I should like to," replied Dennis without hesitation. "It may take some time to arrange everything but after that —"

A man bore down upon them carrying an enormous crate and Roger, in trying to avoid him, was pushed off the pavement. Fortunately Dennis was able to seize his arm and drag him to safety from the path of a motor lorry filled with wine barrels.

"I say, look out!" cried Dennis. "You've got to be careful of the traffic."

"I noticed that," returned Roger with mild sarcasm.

"I mean you've got to look out for yourself in Rome. Nobody else bothers about you . . . and for goodness' sake remember that it all goes like mad in the wrong direction."

Roger did not reply to this typically British statement, though as a matter of fact he agreed with it profoundly. "It all goes like mad in the wrong direction" seemed to him a perfectly fair description of the Roman traffic. The noise was appalling and the crowds, pushing and jostling along the pavement, made further conversation impossible so it was not until they had reached the hotel and had seated themselves in the lounge and ordered *apéritifs* that anything more was said.

"What if she dies on the plane?" said Roger.

"She won't," replied Dennis confidently. "Old ladies with obstinate natures are pretty tough — and she's made up her mind to go. If you ask me she's much more likely to die if she's thwarted."

"You really think I should take her?"

"What else can you do? You can't move her to a hospital by brute force and if you leave her where she is she'll probably have another row with the pin-cushion and die of rage . . . I say, am I being rude?"

"Frightfully rude," replied Roger smiling. "But you're absolutely right. I believe the aeroplane is the best chance of survival. I'll have to try and get her a seat with her back to the engine."

CHAPTER
TWELVE

1

The next day was wet and miserable and Roger's mood matched the weather. He had visited Aunt Beatrice in the morning and in the afternoon he went to the Vatican and spent some hours looking at the treasures of the Popes. In other circumstances he would have enjoyed it but the thought of the journey lay heavily on his mind. That night he slept badly, pursued by nightmares, and he arose the next morning with a headache, which was an unusual ailment for Roger and annoyed him the more on that account.

Everything seemed to go wrong that morning; he lost his collar-stud, his shoes were not cleaned and the key of his suitcase broke when he tried to lock it; the coffee at breakfast was luke-warm and there was difficulty in getting a taxi. Even when he had got the taxi and had put his suitcase into it and was on his way to the Pensione Valetta to fetch Aunt Beatrice his troubles were not over for he was still doubtful whether or not she would be fit to travel. She had said she would be well enough — but supposing she was not? Roger had burnt his boats, he had given up his room and paid his bill and what with one thing and another he had not much money left — so if Aunt Beatrice could not go to-day it would be a bit awkward. Fortunately Dennis with commendable foresight had given Roger a card with his cousin's name and telephone number. "They're half English of course," Dennis had said. "Their mother was my mother's sister, so don't hesitate to ring them up if you want any help — I've told them all about you." If it had not been for that card, which was safely lodged in his pocket-book, Roger would have been even more worried and apprehensive.

Leaving the taxi at the entrance to the alley Roger ran up the stairs and for the fourth time he rang the jangling bell. He hoped fervently it would be the last and that he would never see the place again.

Madame Le Brun opened the door before the bell ceased to jangle. "Eet ees madness!" she cried. "Mees Ayrton ees seek — she ees not well to travel — ze docteur say eet ees madness!"

"He said no such thing," declared Miss Ayrton, appearing in the doorway, fully clad, with a small suitcase in her hand.

"Did he say you could go?" asked Roger.

"No!" shrieked Madame Le Brun. "No, no, no!"

"Did he come this morning?" asked Roger, trying to get to the bottom of the matter.

"Yes," replied Aunt Beatrice. "And he said I was better."

"'E was 'ere, yes. 'E see Mees Ayrton in bed."

"Did he say you were unfit to travel, Aunt Beatrice?"

"No," said Aunt Beatrice firmly.

"'E nevaire sought to say!" screamed Madame Le Brun. "Why should 'e sink to say? 'E see Mees Ayrton

142

in bed. Zare ees talk that she will get up. Zere ees not any talk that she will go out. Zere ees not any talk that she mount in a plane and fly to England. Eef you ask 'im 'e would say: *No, eet ees madness.*"

"Possibly," admitted Aunt Beatrice. "The man is a fool and —"

"Eet is you is ze fool — and you also," added Madame Le Brun, turning to Roger.

Roger had a feeling this was true. "Perhaps we'd better wait a day or two longer —" he began.

Aunt Beatrice did not listen; she handed Roger the suitcase and her umbrella and led the way downstairs. Madame Le Brun rushed on to the landing and, leaning over the banister, screamed at her in Italian, and Aunt Beatrice halted and replied in the same language. Roger was struck anew by the conviction that Italian was a wonderful language if you happened to be in a rage . . . but rage was the worst thing for Aunt Beatrice and he wanted her to conserve her strength for the journey.

"Go on, Aunt Beatrice," he said. "We'll need all our time; the plane won't wait for us."

Thus abjured Aunt Beatrice went on down the stairs and Roger followed with the umbrella and suitcase. He was somewhat reassured by his aunt's upright carriage and determined manner. They were pursued by shrieks but not by Madame Le Brun in person.

"Such nonsense," muttered Aunt Beatrice crossly as she got into the taxi. "All this fuss about nothing . . ."

She continued to grumble all the way to the airfield, and then quite suddenly her ill-humour vanished. Quite suddenly she became an old lady, bewildered by the noise and the crowd, and grateful for a strong arm to lean on.

"It's all right," said Roger encouragingly. "We haven't far to walk. Once we get out of the crowd it will be easier."

Once he had got her out of the crowd and into the plane and had settled her comfortably in the seat "with her back to the engine" it was a great deal easier: Aunt Beatrice was interested in all she saw. She was interested in the plane and in her fellow passengers — so naïvely interested that if Roger had not been anxious about her he would have been amused. He was anxious about her because, now that he saw her sitting opposite to him in the plane, he realised that she looked very ill indeed. Her face was the colour of old parchment and there were dark shadows round her eyes. If Roger could have seen her properly before starting the crazy journey he would not have started at all . . . but it was too late to think of that, for already the plane had taxied to the end of the airfield and the four engines were roaring, impatient to be off.

Although he had flown so often Roger still suffered moments of terror in air-travel (there was the horrible moment on leaving the ground — when one wondered whether the plane would rise — and the equally terrifying moment of landing). He fully expected Aunt Beatrice to suffer in the same way, but it was not so. Aunt Beatrice, looking out of the window and seeing the ground recede, remarked, "Dear me, we are in the air already!"

"We are airborne," said Roger trying to smile.

"Airborne," repeated Aunt Beatrice, savouring the word. "It is a very pleasant sensation. When I get home I shall write to Elsie Cannan and tell her about it. She has never been airborne."

It was encouraging to discover that although she looked like death his charge had plenty of spirit. There was nothing yellow about Aunt Beatrice except her face.

When they had chatted for a little Roger persuaded her to rest, so she lay back and closed her eyes and soon was fast asleep. Roger himself had intended to stay awake and watch her carefully, but having had a very bad night sleep overcame him and the next thing he knew was the arrival of the luncheon trays.

His companion seemed a lot better for her nap. "What a very appetising little meal!" she exclaimed, taking up her spoon and starting upon her soup forthwith. "This really is a pleasant way of travelling, so clean and comfortable and so fast. That attractive young woman told me we shall be in London in half an hour. Quite incredible! Next year when I take my holiday I shall certainly fly —"

"But not to Rome," said Roger hastily.

"No, not to Rome," agreed Aunt Beatrice. "I have a feeling I should like to visit Copenhagen. It is a very beautiful city I am told."

Roger could not help smiling. He wondered whether he should begin to study Danish — just in case —

"You have been very kind to me," continued Aunt Beatrice. "Oh yes, you have indeed. There are not many young men who would have given up part of their holiday to come and rescue a disagreeable old aunt."

"You're not disagreeable," declared Roger — nor was she at the moment.

Unfortunately for herself Aunt Beatrice was one of those people who have little or no control of their tempers. When things went well nobody could be nicer, when things went ill few people could be nastier.

They were obliged to change planes at London Airport; the plane which carried them to Turnhouse was smaller and Roger was unable to get his companion the seat she wanted.

Aunt Beatrice was furious. "Ask those two men to change with us," she said.

"But we can't — honestly — they were here first."

"Ask them," said Aunt Beatrice in commanding tones.

There was nothing Roger disliked more than making a fuss, but he saw that he would have no peace until he carried out her orders, so he went over to the two men and explained matters, adding that his aunt had been ill. One of the men seemed willing to give up his seat but the other was a truculent individual and refused to budge.

"We'll stay where we are," he declared, glaring at Roger defiantly. "We chose these seats and we don't intend to give them up to anyone."

This settled the matter but it did not settle Aunt Beatrice. "I don't know what the world is coming to, nowadays," she declared in a loud voice which was only partly drowned by the roar of the engines. "When I was

146

young it was very different. Any gentleman would have been only too pleased to give up his seat to a lady."

"We can't do anything —" began Roger.

"Call that girl at once."

Roger was unwilling to call the air-hostess so Aunt Beatrice beckoned to her in a peremptory manner and explained what she wanted.

"But it doesn't matter which way you sit," said the air-hostess, smiling soothingly. "It isn't like a train, you know. These are very good seats, I'm sure you'll be quite comfortable here."

"I am not comfortable."

"Would you like me to tilt your seat back a little?"

"No," said Aunt Beatrice crossly.

"I'm going to bring you some tea in a few minutes. That will be nice, won't it?"

"I don't want tea. I want a seat with my back to the engine."

The girl glanced at Roger. "I'm afraid I can't do anything," she said regretfully.

"I know," said Roger. "It doesn't matter at all."

"It matters a great deal!" exclaimed Aunt Beatrice. "You're treating me as if I were six years old. It always gives me a headache if I sit facing the engine."

"My aunt has been ill," explained Roger. It was the only excuse he could find for her behaviour.

After that Aunt Beatrice grumbled continuously; she grumbled about the motion of the plane, the tea was too weak and the cake was stale. She complained of a headache but refused some aspirin tablets produced by the air hostess. Altogether she was thoroughly unpleasant and unreasonable. Roger realised that she was tired out, and probably felt ill, so he tried to make allowances for her, but he was so ashamed of all the fuss that he was thankful when at last they arrived at their destination. He was thankful to hand over the grumpy old lady to the care of her faithful maid, who had been with her for years in spite of her bad temper.

Roger's mission was accomplished; his one thought now was to go home to Amberwell as quickly as he could and as it was too late to get a train he hired a car for the journey.

She's alive, anyway, thought Roger as he lay back in the car and closed his eyes. She's come through the journey alive. If she dies now I can't help it — but she'll probably survive to go to Copenhagen next year — nothing could kill Aunt Beatrice. If she wants somebody to rescue her from Copenhagen she can get Tom — only Tom wouldn't be such a fool!

CHAPTER
THIRTEEN

1

Four days of Roger's precious leave had been wasted upon Aunt Beatrice (wasted was Roger's word for it and incidentally it seemed to him more like a fortnight than four days); so he had only three clear days at Amberwell before returning to his regiment. It was difficult to apportion his time between all the things he wanted to do. Mr. Gray was anxious to speak to him about the gardens; Nell wanted him to go over the accounts; it was essential to see what progress the builders were making at Summerhills and of course he must spend as much time as possible with Stephen.

The first thing he did on reaching home was to ring up Arnold, and Arnold suggested that everybody should meet at Summerhills the following afternoon. It would save time, said Arnold. If everybody were there — including Mr. Lumsden the builder — Roger could hear everybody's ideas.

"What d'you mean by everybody?" Roger inquired.

"Well, Dad would like to come and — and one or two other people. You don't mind, do you?"

Roger was somewhat doubtful. He explained that he wanted a quiet talk with Mr. Lumsden and that might be difficult to achieve if the house were full of people.

"Don't worry; I'll manage everything," said Arnold.

"We'll want Mary, of course," said Roger. "We must have Mary to explain her idea about the hatch in the dining-room."

"Mary can't come."

"Can't come?"

"No, she's gone to Edinburgh to stay with her cousins."

"What a pity —" began Roger.

"Oh, it doesn't matter," said Arnold cheerfully. "I've passed on her idea about the hatch to Lumsden and he's started work on it already."

"When is Mary coming back?"

"Next week, I expect — but we don't need her. We've got her ideas to work on."

Roger was silent.

"We want new ideas," continued Arnold. "Anne said she'd like to come and bring Emmie. She hasn't seen the place yet."

"Look here, Arnold. We don't want a crowd."

"I'll look after the crowd. There's no need for you to bother. We'll meet there early, you and I, before the others arrive. Will that do?"

"I suppose so," said Roger.

When Nell heard that Anne was to be at Summerhills she said she would come too, and bring Stephen.

"Oh well," said Roger with a sigh. "I suppose if there's got to be a crowd it may as well be a mob."

"Don't you want us to come?" asked Nell.

"Of course I want you to come," replied Roger impatiently. "You know perfectly well I've been trying to get you to take an interest in Summerhills for weeks."

It was so unlike Roger to be cross that Nell was quite alarmed, but on reflection she decided that the trip to Rome had upset him — and no wonder! Poor Roger had had a dreadful time with Aunt Beatrice.

Roger and Arnold met at Summerhills early, before the crowd arrived. They discussed the door into the changing-room (which was Arnold's pet idea) and Roger promised to speak to Mr. Lumsden about it.

"Now look here," said Roger. "What about a matron? Have you anybody in mind?"

"No, have you?"

"What about Georgina Glassford?"

"Georgina Glassford!" echoed Arnold in dismay. "Good lord, I wouldn't have her as a gift! That girl is an absolute menace. Look here, old fellow, you don't really mean it, do you?"

"I thought perhaps —"

"But she isn't the type!" cried Arnold. "We want a nice, comfy, motherly sort of woman —"

"All right, have it your own way," said Roger. He had been a little cross before, but now he was definitely out of temper — the more so because he knew in his inmost heart that Arnold was right. Georgina was not really the type they wanted as matron for Summerhills. "A nice, comfy, motherly woman" was the sort of woman for the post.

"Of course it's for you to say," continued Arnold in reluctant tones. "It's your school — and if you want Miss Glassford — but she'd cause a lot of trouble with the staff. I mean she's far too good-looking — and those trousers! And have you seen her running with her long legs?"

Roger had, of course. "All right, don't lose your hair," said Roger. "It was just a suggestion, that's all."

They discussed several other matters after that. Roger described his adventures in Rome and put forward his theory that modern boys should learn to speak modern languages.

"Not just school French," said Roger earnestly. "Not just *voici la plume de ma tante*. I learnt to say that when I was at school but it was a fat lot of use to me when I tried to talk to that blinking Frenchwoman! Let's get a Frenchman as one of the masters and make a Special Thing of modern languages."

Fortunately Arnold was able to agree whole-heartedly. In fact he went even farther than Roger and had plans for taking some of his future pupils abroad and "showing them the world."

They were still talking when the crowd arrived. It was a much bigger crowd than Roger had expected for Arnold had asked everybody who was remotely interested in Summerhills (except Mary, of course). He had even managed to round up some people from outlying districts who had young sons and might consider sending them to the school. Arnold had said he would look after the crowd and he carried out his promise. He gathered all the visitors together and took them for a personally conducted tour of the building.

2

Anne was one of the crowd which followed Arnold round the new school. She was pleased that Arnold had asked her and pleased to come. The little outing was enjoyable for she was so busy with her household duties at the Rectory that she did not go about very much. This outing, though not exactly a social occasion, gave Anne the opportunity of meeting friends whom she had not seen for years — and in addition she found it amusing. She could not help smiling as she watched the group of people following Arnold from room to room and listening to his discourse, for it reminded her of a group of tourists being shown over some historic castle . . . but instead of gaping dungeons and ruined battlements their guide was displaying airing-cupboards and comfortable dormitories and modern bathrooms in course of construction. It occurred to Anne that, whereas historic castles were relics of the past, Summerhills was looking towards the future.

The house was well-known to Anne (she had visited it as a child when the Findlaters were in residence) so she was interested in the alterations. In the bathrooms the alterations had just begun, which meant that the joiners had torn up the flooring and left the pipes exposed, but their guide explained what was going to be done, and described what the bathrooms would look like when finished, in a manner which left little to the imagination.

To-day Arnold was playing the part of headmaster — and was doing it well. He looked the part to perfection for he had bought his new suit, and his collar and tie and highly-polished shoes were all above reproach. He was much too busy to speak to his friends individually but he had asked the visitors to tell him about any brilliant ideas which might occur to them *en route*. A few sensible suggestions were made — and quite a number of foolish ones — all of which were carefully noted in the headmaster's book.

The tour finished in the hall, where it had begun, and the visitors melted away. They all went except Anne, who had lost Emmie.

"It's all right," said Arnold. "She'll be here soon. She and Stephen went off together to explore on their own. Let's sit down," he added, looking round for something to sit on.

Anne was aware that Arnold hated standing so she followed him into the dining-room where they found two chairs and sat down together.

"It went off all right, didn't it?" said Arnold. "Roger was annoyed with me for asking all those people — but we must try to advertise the school and get boys. As a matter of fact I've got the names of three boys this afternoon — they're coming at Easter — so it was worth it."

"It has been a nice party," Anne said.

"A funny sort of party! No food and nothing to drink!" returned the host somewhat ruefully. "But

154

never mind, we'll have a proper party later on — a slap-up affair. Look here, Anne, you didn't make any suggestions."

"I hadn't any to make."

Arnold took out his book. "I want your advice about colour schemes. What do you think would be nice for the matron's rooms — and the headmaster's rooms? Roger says I can choose what I like, but I'm no good at interior decoration. I haven't a clue."

"You should ask Nell. She knows far more about that sort of thing than I do."

"I'd rather have your advice. I mean that's why I wanted you to come this afternoon," explained Arnold. "Do you think it would look well to have cream paint — or would white be better? My sitting-room is rather dark so it must be a light sort of paint. And what about paper? Do you like plain paper or a pattern?"

"I don't know," replied Anne.

"You don't know?" echoed Arnold in surprise.

Anne smiled. "Honestly — you're asking the wrong person. I don't bother much about things like that. I've never decorated a room in my life. Ask Nell or Mary — or Mrs. Lambert. I believe Mrs. Lambert would be best. Merlewood is beautiful, isn't it? Yes, I think you should ask Mrs. Lambert."

The idea did not seem to please Arnold. "But people have different tastes," he said doubtfully . . . and then, as Anne said nothing, he added, "Oh well, there's no hurry. We shall have to get all the building finished before we start papering and painting the rooms."

While they were talking a man had approached. He was a curious-looking individual in a blue suit and tan shoes. Anne had noticed him going round the house with the rest of the party and had wondered who he was.

"You are the headmaster, I'm told," said the man, smiling in an ingratiating manner. "My name is Mr. Walker."

"Yes," said Arnold, not very cordially. "Do you want to speak to me?"

"About the furniture," said Mr. Walker. "You've got some very nice stuff here. It's far too good for a boys' school."

"The owner of this place has just bought it."

"We know that — but, if you'll excuse me saying so, it was a mistake. Now I have a little proposition to make: I'm a dealer in furniture — see? I'll take some of this furniture off your hands at a good price and you can buy some hardwearing stuff instead."

"Sell the good stuff and buy trash!"

"I didn't say that, did I?" said Mr. Walker reproachfully. "There's no need to buy trash. You can buy solid stuff that won't matter. The boys will knock this stuff to bits in a few months."

"They will not," replied Arnold. "I'll take good care they don't."

"Now Mr. Maddon, just listen a minute —"

"You're wasting your time, Mr. Walker. As a matter of fact it has nothing to do with me. If you want to do a deal you should ask Major Ayrton. But I can tell you it won't be any good. He and I have already discussed

156

the matter. There's no need for me to tell you any more — but I will," said Arnold frankly. "Our idea is to make this school different from other schools. We've got a beautiful house and we intend to have good furniture in it. We think that boys should be taught to respect good furniture and to take an interest in their surroundings . . ."

Anne could not help smiling for this was Arnold's hobby-horse and once he was mounted upon it he would not dismount in a hurry. Of course Mr. Walker had asked for it, so he could not complain, but she felt a little sorry for him. She and Arnold were sitting upon the only two chairs available so Mr. Walker was obliged to stand and listen to the headmaster's views about the education of the young.

"If you bring up a boy in an institution with a lot of deal furniture round him you can't blame him for kicking it, can you?" said Arnold. "That's what's the matter with the modern young. They haven't been taught how to behave in a well-furnished house. My boys are going to be taught to appreciate the finer things of life: good furniture and fine pictures and a beautiful old house with traditions of gracious living; they're going to be taught to appreciate the park and the lovely trees."

"But Mr. Maddon —" began Mr. Walker.

"I'm going to teach them manners," declared Arnold. "I'm not going to let them behave like boors and savages. We've got all sorts of plans. For instance, Major Ayrton is very anxious for them to learn to speak French fluently — and perhaps Italian as well. Modern languages are going to be a specially . . . and we have plans to take small parties of boys to the Continent so that they'll see other countries besides their own. It will widen their minds and broaden their outlook upon life —"

"It was the furniture, Mr. Maddon," said Mr. Walker unhappily.

"Oh yes, I know; but it's all part of the same thing. It's all part of the training. Now I'll tell you another thing I mean to do —"

"It sounds excellent," said Mr. Walker. "I'm sure it will be a great success, but I'm afraid I can't wait. It's a pity about the furniture —" he sidled towards the door.

"Look here," said Arnold. "Come back a minute. Who told you about the furniture?"

"Who told me?"

"Yes. It wasn't by any chance Mr. Strow, was it?"

"Mr. Strow?"

"Mr. Strow told you to ask me about it, didn't he?"

"Well — he just — happened to mention it," said Mr. Walker uncomfortably. "I saw him the other day and he — just — mentioned it."

"I thought so," said Arnold. "You can tell Mr. Strow to mind his own business — see?"

Mr. Walker had reached the door. He opened it and went away in haste.

"Poor man!" exclaimed Anne laughing. "You were a bit hard on him, Arnold."

"Perhaps I was — a little," admitted Arnold. "But I don't like it much. I don't like Strow having sent that chap to speak to me about selling the furniture. There's something fishy about it, Anne."

Anne stopped laughing and looked thoughtful. "How did you know Mr. Strow was at the bottom of it?"

"He's at the bottom of most things — besides I've had a feeling all along that Strow was interested in the furniture. I'd like to know why."

"Money," said Anne. "People like that are always out for money, aren't they?"

"You mean Strow and Walker got together and decided to do a deal with me?"

Anne nodded. "Yes, behind Roger's back. I'm sure of it. They'd have given you a rake-off."

"Gosh, how horrible!" Arnold exclaimed. "It's rather — frightening."

"There's no need to be frightened," said Anne sensibly. "You wouldn't dream of doing anything shady so you're perfectly safe. But I think you ought to tell Roger the whole thing."

"I shall," agreed Arnold. "If only we could bring it home to Strow we might get rid of the brute."

Soon after this the two children appeared. They had no idea it was so late and Stephen was surprised to discover that his relations had gone home without him.

"I'd better run," he said. "Good-bye, Uncle — I mean Mr. Maddon."

"Why this sudden formality?" inquired Arnold, who had enjoyed the status of adopted uncle since Stephen was two years old.

"Daddy said so," replied Stephen. "Daddy said I must practise, that's all. Good-bye, Mr. Maddon."

"Good-bye, Ayrton," returned his future headmaster with a smile.

Stephen looked a little surprised and then he laughed. "It *does* sound funny," he declared, and with that he waved cheerfully and ran off down the drive.

Anne and Emmie were the last to go. They left Arnold to lock up the house and walked home together.

"We had a lovely time," said Emmie. "We went all over the house — we even went into the cellars. There are huge cellars underneath the house. All crawly with spiders and things. Some day we're going to take a torch and explore them properly. We might find a secret passage like the boy in *The Moated Grange*. Wouldn't that be fun? If we found a secret passage Stephen could escape from the school whenever he wanted."

"Will he want to escape?" asked Anne with a good deal of interest.

"I don't think so — not really," replied Emmie frankly. "But it would be nice to know that he could. Stephen is pleased about the school. He thinks it will be a good thing." She sighed and added, "What a pity I'm not a boy!"

"I'm glad you're not a boy."

"I'm glad too — really and truly," said Emmie, putting her hand through her mother's arm. "We wouldn't be such friends if I was a boy, would we? I wouldn't be able to help you so much — but what's going to happen to me when Stephen goes to Summerhills?"

This matter had disturbed Anne a good deal, but fortunately she had discovered a small girls' school in

160

Westkirk, which was run by two ladies, and she had decided to send Emmie to it daily. It would do for a time at any rate. Later on when Emmie was older she would have to go to a boarding-school. Anne explained these plans to her daughter.

"I don't mind going to Miss Johnstone's," said Emmie. "But a boarding-school would be horrible. You never went to a boarding-school, so why need I?"

"I never learnt anything," said Anne with a sigh. This was a slight exaggeration, of course, but it was true that Anne's education had been inadequate. She and Connie and Nell had shared a governess and although Miss Clarke had done her best for her pupils she had not been a good teacher.

"We can't afford a boarding-school," declared Emmie in her old-fashioned way. "You know that, Mummie, so why think about it?"

"Uncle Roger has offered to pay. He says that later on when you're old enough he'll pay for you to go to St. Leonards, and it would be very silly to refuse. A good education is most important; it will give you a start in life and make you independent —"

Emmie had been listening with growing dismay. "But I couldn't!" she cried. "I couldn't possibly go away and leave you! It would be frightful. You couldn't manage without me. Who would make the toast and help you to wash the dishes? And Mr. Orme needs me to help him with his sermons! Oh Mummie, it's a horrible idea!"

Anne did not like the idea either. She dreaded the thought of parting with her little daughter — they had never been parted for a day since Emmie was born. "I

161

know it's horrible," she agreed. "But we'll have to bear it. We'll just have to. I'm not going to have you grow up ignorant — like me." She gave her daughter's arm a little squeeze and added, "But we needn't think about it now. It will be years before you're old enough — years and years."

"Perhaps something will turn up," suggested Emmie a little more cheerfully. "Perhaps something will happen so that I won't need to go."

Anne agreed. She did not want Emmie to worry about it.

"Things *do* turn up, don't they?" said Emmie. "Look at the way we got money from the book when we needed new clothes so badly! Look at the way Mr. Orme turned up when we had to leave Harestone and didn't know where to go!"

Anne could not help smiling. It was rather comical to discover that her daughter shared her own Micawber-like attitude to the troubles of the future. Life had certainly been hard at times but something had always turned up.

"It's like Elijah and the ravens," added Emmie thoughtfully. "They turned up in the nick of time, didn't they? I shall tell Mr. Orme and perhaps he'll make a sermon about it."

3

Anne and Emmie had agreed not to worry about school, but there was another problem on Anne's mind — quite a different sort of problem — and this could

162

not be shelved so easily nor could she discuss it with her daughter. She had thought about it for weeks without getting any nearer a solution and finally she decided to confide in Mr. Orme. Mr. Orme was not quite the person Anne would have chosen, he was too innocent and other-worldly, but there was nobody else at hand . . . and even if he could not solve her problem she knew he would listen sympathetically and respect her confidence.

"I wonder if you could advise me," said Anne.

She and Mr. Orme were sitting by the fire, reading. It was evening, the day's work was done and Emmie was safely in bed. Mr. Orme was reading an old book which he had read before at least a dozen times; it was *The Travels of St. Paul*. Anne was reading *Persuasion*. Her book was not new to her either but it was one of her favourites and she never grew tired of it.

At the sudden request Mr. Orme immediately laid aside *St. Paul* and took off his spectacles. He looked at Anne — how lovely she was! To-night she seemed even prettier than usual; there was a slight flush upon her cheeks and her eyes were very bright . . . yet somehow she looked a little upset.

"I'm so silly," added Anne with a sigh.

"I don't think so," objected Mr. Orme.

"Oh, but I am! Compared with Miss Austen's heroines I'm an idiot."

"Louisa was extremely foolish — if I remember rightly. Wasn't she the young woman who insisted on jumping off the steps at Lyme Regis and fractured her skull and caused her friends so much anxiety?"

"Yes," admitted Anne. "But I don't mean that sort of foolishness. I mean they knew how to manage their affairs."

"Their love affairs?"

Anne nodded.

Mr. Orme was no fool, nor was he blind. "I suppose it's Arnold," he said. "Well, he's a very nice young fellow — very nice indeed. I like Arnold immensely."

"So do I," agreed Anne. "He's a dear, nice creature and I'm very fond of him but I don't want to marry him."

"Are you sure?"

"Absolutely certain."

"Well — you'll have to tell him so," said Mr. Orme.

"I can't until he's asked me, can I?" she returned, smiling a little uncertainly. "You see it's a bit complicated. That's why I want your advice. How does a young woman explain to a young man that she doesn't want to marry him — before he's proposed to her?"

Mr. Orme had been asked his advice upon all manner of strange problems, but this was a new one.

"You see," continued Anne. "You see it would be so much better if I could make him understand now, at once, that I like having him as a friend but that I don't want . . . anything else. It seems unfair to let him go on thinking about me."

"But Anne —"

"I've tried to — to put him off. I've even tried being a little bit unkind to him, but it doesn't work. It just

164

makes him unhappy, that's all — and I don't want to make him unhappy."

"No, of course not. No, you mustn't be unkind to him."

Anne hesitated for a moment. "I wonder if you could —"

"No, no!" cried Mr. Orme. "No, that would never do. I couldn't possibly."

"But it seems a pity to wait and do nothing."

"Perhaps you won't have to wait very long. Perhaps he will say something soon."

"That's just what he won't do," declared Anne with conviction. "It may be years before he says anything. He won't say a word until he's firmly settled in his new job and is sure it's going to be a success. Then he'll ask me to marry him."

Mr. Orme did not doubt her for a moment. It crossed his mind that if he had been in Arnold's position — and Arnold's age — he would have done exactly that: waited until he was certain he could support a wife in comfort and then asked Anne to marry him.

"I know it sounds rather a ridiculous sort of problem," admitted Anne. "But it's important to me because I like Arnold so much. I feel I'm being unfair to him — and I hate unfairness."

Mr. Orme knew this already. Anne's passion for just dealing had sometimes amused him a little, but it did not amuse him on this occasion. He said, "If you like Arnold so much perhaps you might like him even more — in time."

"No," said Anne in a low voice.

"Why not wait and see?"

"No, Martin spoilt all that."

"But my dear, you're so young! You'll forget about the unhappy time with Martin."

She shook her head. It was a childish gesture; Mr. Orme remembered it of old. It took him back to a morning long ago when he had watched her dancing on the bowling-green and had spoken to her for the first time.

"You're so young," he repeated. "Your life is before you."

"No, darling, you don't understand," said Anne gravely. "It's all spoilt for me. I can never marry anybody. Martin frightened me so dreadfully."

"Frightened you?"

"Oh, he didn't — hit me. He was just unkind. I don't know why I was so frightened — really."

"Try to tell me," suggested Mr. Orme. He spoke quietly and persuasively for he knew that it would be good for her to bring her fears to light. She had told him a little about her marriage before — he knew she had been unhappy — but by nature she was reserved and tongue-tied so she had not told him much. To-night for some reason Anne's tongue was loosened — but he must go carefully. "Try to tell me why you were frightened," he repeated.

Anne hesitated. There were some things she could not tell anybody — least of all Mr. Orme. She could not tell him the worst things, the things that made another marriage utterly impossible, but she might tell

166

him some of the smaller unkindnesses which she had had to endure and perhaps he would understand. Anne was very anxious for him to understand.

"You told me how much you disliked being dependent upon him," said Mr. Orme, trying to help her.

"Yes," agreed Anne. "Money doesn't seem important when you have enough, but when you're absolutely dependent upon somebody for every penny — and you have to explain how you've spent every penny — it becomes very important indeed. That was bad, but there were other things too. Martin was a schoolmaster and he was very, very clever — I told you that before, didn't I? He thought I was stupid and badly educated, and of course I am. Sometimes he used to ask me things and laugh when I didn't know the answers, and say my mentality was equal to a child of seven years old. But honestly I wasn't quite as stupid as he thought. I mean Martin *made* me stupid. One day — it was Trafalgar Day — he asked me if I knew who won the Battle of Trafalgar. I couldn't think for a moment. I felt sort of paralysed. Then he said, 'Didn't you learn any history at all? It was Drake, wasn't it?' I said, 'Oh yes, of course!' Then he laughed and laughed. Of course I knew it was Nelson — really. It was just that I was frightened."

Mr. Orme said nothing. He could not trust himself to speak.

"I was frightened of him all the time," continued Anne in her low clear voice. "I was so frightened of Martin that I told him lies. They were stupid little lies.

For instance when he asked me what I had been doing all day I told him I had been washing or ironing or that I had taken Emmie for a walk — he couldn't find fault with me for that. I never dared to tell him if I had been to see the old woman next door and helped her to clean her house. She had rheumatism in her knees and I used to scrub her kitchen floor twice a week, but if Martin had known he would have been terribly angry.

"It all seems quite ridiculous when I think about it now," added Anne, looking round the comfortable little room with its atmosphere of peace. "It seems impossible that I could have been such a fool."

Anne had told her story simply and in a matter of fact sort of way which made it very moving. If she had been "sorry for herself" and demanded his sympathy Mr. Orme would have given it to her in full measure, but he would not have felt so upset. Although Mr. Orme was a good and saintly man he knew quite a lot about life, and was not quite the innocent Anne imagined, so he could fill the gaps in Anne's story of her marriage without much difficulty. He was so distressed; he was so furiously angry with the unspeakable Martin Selby that he found himself shaking all over and it took him several moments and a tremendous effort of will-power before he could control himself.

"Other men — are not like that," he said at last.

"Oh, I know," agreed Anne. "Arnold would never be horrid to me, but all the same I couldn't marry him — nor anybody else. It's all spoilt and — and dirty. You must believe me."

168

He did believe her.

"So now you see," said Anne. "Now you understand, don't you?"

"Yes," said Mr. Orme sadly.

"Tell me what I'm to do about Arnold."

There was quite a long silence.

At last Anne said, "Of course I could tell him that I shall never marry again, but he wouldn't believe me, would he? I mean he wouldn't believe me unless I told him all about Martin — and I couldn't do that."

"No, you couldn't do that," agreed Mr. Orme. "And even if you could tell him what you've told me it wouldn't have the desired effect. In fact quite the opposite."

"Are you sure?" asked Anne, wrinkling her brows.

"Yes," said Mr. Orme firmly.

"Well, what am I to do?"

Mr. Orme sighed. "I'll think about it," he said.

CHAPTER
FOURTEEN

1

Roger was always reluctant to leave Amberwell, but this time he was even more reluctant than usual . . . so very reluctant that he began to toy with the idea of sending in his papers, of retiring and settling down comfortably and attending to his duties as laird. He had thought of it before once or twice but he was doubtful if there would be enough to do to keep him busy and to employ his boundless energy. It was difficult to decide, for on the one hand he hated leaving home but on the other he was keenly interested in his profession and all it entailed.

Once he was back with his regiment Roger felt happier. He was popular with his brother officers and received a warm welcome. They all wanted to know what he had been doing and were interested to hear about the school. Those with young sons — or nephews — were very interested indeed.

Letters from home arrived frequently. Arnold wrote twice a week reporting good progress, asking advice and showing admirable keenness. Mr. Strow's letters were disgruntled; he hoped Major Ayrton would not be disappointed when he saw the big dormitory. Major Ayrton would remember that *his* plan for the apartment had been to make a new window facing south. Mr. Maddon had altered quite a number of the original plans — including the plan for the door into the changing-room — and Mr. Strow had been surprised to find that the builders had begun to construct a hatch at the far end of the dining-room. Would Major Ayrton write at once and say whether he approved.

Nell wrote as usual — she always wrote to Roger when he was away — but her letters were concerned with Amberwell and she scarcely mentioned Summerhills except to say that things seemed to be going on quite well. Mary's letters interested Roger most of all for not only were they full of detailed information about the work but they were also very amusing; Mary was an onlooker at the battle between the architect and the headmaster and saw most of the game.

"You asked me to support Arnold," wrote Mary. "But Arnold does not need any support. He is standing up to Mr. Strow on his own. If they disagree — which happens frequently — Arnold merely refers to the fact that he has been given *carte blanche* and if this does not settle the matter he suggests that Mr. Strow should write to you. It is amusing to watch Mr. Strow's face (which shows his feelings very plainly). He would like to tell Arnold to go to blazes and walk out with his head in the air — but then he remembers his fees and decides not to. Personally I think it would be a good thing if Mr. Strow took the huff; we could manage very well without him. He is not very good at his job. Did you ever notice his ears? They are stuck closely on to his head in a very odd way. I noticed it yesterday when he and Arnold were arguing about my hatch. (Of course he can't help his ears but I read somewhere or other that criminals have curious ears.) 'Miss Findlater's hatch' is a very sore subject to Mr. Strow — he feels almost as bitter about it as he does about the door into the changing-rooms. I like Mr. Lumsden immensely — and he really is going ahead with the work. At first he was somewhat bewildered at receiving two sets of instructions, but now he realises who is the boss so he listens politely to Mr. Strow and does what Arnold tells him. Has Arnold told you about Mr. Lumsden's son? He was wounded at the crossing of the Rhine and has an artificial hand. Of course this makes a tremendous bond between Arnold and Mr. Lumsden. One morning when I blew into Summerhills to see how things were going I found the two of them sitting together upon a packing-case in the bathroom — Arnold demonstrating to Mr. Lumsden how his foot worked! Arnold thinks young Lumsden might make a suitable janitor but I expect he will be telling you about this. If you could manage to get a few days' leave and come over I should like to speak to you about an Idea of mine. It would be rather difficult to explain my Idea in a letter. Of course I could tell Arnold about it, but I would rather see you first."

The next letter from Arnold was full of young Lumsden. Arnold had seen him and liked him; he was just the sort of fellow they wanted, strong and sturdy and cheerful. Did Roger think it mattered about his missing hand? It was his left hand — fortunately — and it was surprising what a lot he could do with the artificial gadget he had got in its place. Could Roger possibly get a few days' leave and come over and see the fellow himself?

It was now the beginning of August and the work at Summerhills had progressed so rapidly that Roger was longing to have a look at the place — and young Lumsden as well — and of course he wanted to hear about Mary's Idea, so he approached his Colonel and explained matters and was granted leave at once. The Colonel was particularly interested in Summerhills for the simple reason that he had two young nephews.

Having made all his arrangements Roger wrote to Nell and Arnold saying he was coming on Saturday, and to Mary saying he would meet her at Summerhills on Sunday afternoon. Sunday was an excellent day to meet Mary for they would have the whole place to themselves with no workmen to bother them and Mary could explain her Idea at leisure.

2

Mary was delighted when she received Roger's letter. She had hoped he would come. Unfortunately Sunday was cold and cloudy — not in the least like August — but Mary was undaunted by the weather. She walked over the moors to Summerhills and arrived there shortly after three o'clock. Roger's car was parked in the drive and Roger was waiting on the steps for her.

Mary had not seen Roger since her talk with Poppet and she discovered that she was looking at him with more discerning eyes. He *was* attractive. Poppet was quite right about that — but quite wrong about other things of course. All the same Mary's heart beat a little bit faster than usual as she went up the steps to meet him.

"Well, here I am," said Mary with a smile.

"It's awfully good of you to come," said Roger. "Your letters have been grand — so helpful and amusing!"

"It has been very amusing," Mary told him. "I haven't said much, you know. I've just looked on and —"

"What about the Big Idea? I'm all agog to hear what it is." He glanced at his watch and added, "I can't stay more than ten minutes."

"Ten minutes!" echoed Mary in dismay. "But Roger, it will take much longer. I want to show you —"

"Couldn't you explain it quickly?"

Mary hesitated. She could not understand it at all — and she was bitterly disappointed — Roger had said in his letter that they would have the whole place to themselves and there would be plenty of time for her to explain her idea at leisure.

"I'm sorry," said Roger uncomfortably. "But I'm afraid I'll have to go. It's Georgina, you see. She caught me just as I was coming out and asked me to come up to the bowling-green and time some runs for her. She wants me to be there at half-past three."

"But this is important! Honestly, Roger!"

"Couldn't you tell me about it quickly?"

"No, I couldn't possibly. It will take much longer than ten minutes to explain my plan."

"She made rather a Thing of it. You see there's nobody at Amberwell who can use a stop-watch . . . so it's difficult for her." He paused and then added, "Perhaps I could nip back and do it for her. It won't take long. You could wait here, couldn't you?"

Mary said nothing. She was very angry. She was angry with Georgina but oddly enough even more angry with Roger. If Roger thought she would wait for him while he "nipped back" to Amberwell — and Georgina — he could think again.

"It won't take long," repeated Roger. "I'm sorry about it, but I couldn't say no, could I?"

"You asked me to meet you here —" began Mary indignantly . . . and then she stopped . . . and glancing at Roger's face she laughed. (The nicer they are the more helpless they are, Poppet had said.)

"What's the joke, Mary?" asked Roger in bewilderment.

"Just — something I've remembered."

"Something you've remembered?"

"*The Gypsy's Warning.*"

Roger gazed at her.

"It's all right," declared Mary, trying to control herself. "I haven't gone mad. It was just — something

175

— I remembered. I'll sit here and wait for you while you nip back to Amberwell and time Georgina's mile."

"You don't mind?"

"Not a bit," declared Mary. She sat down upon a convenient packing-case and assumed a patient attitude. Perhaps the pose was slightly overdone but if so Roger did not notice.

"It seems awfully rude —" began Roger in doubtful tones.

"It's quite all right."

"You see I couldn't refuse. She made a Special Thing of it."

"You couldn't refuse," agreed Mary with conviction.

Roger hesitated. "But all the same — I mean I don't see why — oh dash it all, why should I bother about the woman? I want to hear about your idea."

"I'll tell you about it when you come back," replied Mary, sweetly reasonable.

Roger glanced at his watch and made for the door . . . and then he stopped. "I'm not going," he declared. "Why should I go? I can't think what possessed me to say I'd go."

"You couldn't refuse," Mary reminded him.

"I ought to have refused," replied Roger.

This was so true that Mary could not refute it. She was silent.

"I know what I'll do," said Roger. "I'll ring her up and tell her that I can't come."

The telephone was in the next room and as Roger had left the doors open Mary could not help overhearing Roger's side of the conversation. She could have moved, of course, but she did not feel inclined to move, so she stayed where she was. It was some time before Georgina could be found and brought to the phone — perhaps she was on her way to the bowling-green for it was nearly half-past three.

"Hallo, this is Roger," said Roger. "Yes, I know it's nearly half-past three but I can't come. That's what I rang up to tell you. No, I can't possibly come. Mary is here — Miss Findlater — and we've got something important to discuss."

There was a short pause.

"Yes, I know," agreed Roger. "But this is *more* important. Honestly, Georgina! We can do your mile to-morrow. I'm sorry about it but I can't manage it this afternoon. Miss Findlater is here and . . ."

There was another pause — longer this time — and Roger's voice was slightly cross when he spoke again.

"It isn't that at all," he declared. "As a matter of fact she offered to wait for me while I nipped back and timed your runs for you; so you see . . ."

This time the pause was short.

"I've told you why," said Roger very crossly indeed. "I've told you I'll do it to-morrow. Why won't to-morrow do?"

The pause was almost imperceptible.

"All right *don't* ask me again," said Roger angrily.

When Roger returned his face was flushed and his eyes were sparking. "She cut off," he said shortly.

"Perhaps you should have gone," Mary suggested.

"Why?" asked Roger. "Why should I have gone? Why on earth should I go and time her blinking mile when I don't want to?"

It was no good. Mary had to laugh . . . and after a few moments Roger began to chuckle. Roger's ill-temper never lasted long.

"Silly, isn't it?" he said. "The fact is it's so difficult to say no. I mean when a girl asks you . . ." He hesitated and then added, "She said she wouldn't ask me again."

Mary had gathered as much.

"But she will," said Roger with a sigh.

Mary was not so sure.

3

The telephone conversation had upset Roger quite a lot but presently he recovered and was able to give his attention to Mary's Big Idea. She led the way to the small suite of rooms which had been set aside for the use of the headmaster.

"You may think it's no good at all," said Mary. "That's why I wanted to discuss it with you before saying anything to Arnold — but I think this room is much too small for the headmaster's sitting-room."

"Arnold said it was big enough."

"I know — but look at it, Roger! This is the only room Arnold will have to receive the parents and give them tea. It's much too small — and dull. At least I think so."

Roger stood and looked round. "You're right," he said. "Of course it's much too small — and dull. Why on earth didn't we think of it before? It's absolutely essential for Arnold to have a nice, bright, cheerful room to receive the parents and give them tea."

"That's what I thought."

"We shall have to find another room."

"But there isn't another suitable room on the groundfloor."

"We shall have to give up one of the class-rooms. There's nothing else for it."

"Would a bow-window be very expensive?"

"A bow-window?"

"We could throw out a bow-window. That was my idea. It would make the room bigger and brighter, wouldn't it?"

"You've got it!" cried Roger. "A bow-window is the answer."

"Would it cost the earth?"

"I don't see why it should — and anyhow, what's the alternative? There isn't another suitable room on the groundfloor. A bow-window would transform this room."

"That's what I thought . . . and you see there's plenty of space outside."

They leaned out of the small window together and surveyed the ground beneath. Mary had spent the morning marking it out with sticks and string so that Roger could see her plan.

"There's plenty of space," agreed Roger. "In fact we could have a much bigger window than that. We might as well do the thing properly while we're at it."

179

Mary smiled. She wondered how often Roger had said these words in the last few months.

"It really is clever of you," continued Roger. "It's a brilliant idea. I should never have thought of it. Let's go outside and measure."

They went outside and measured the ground carefully and discovered that there was plenty of space for a large bow-window.

"But it will cost a lot, won't it," said Mary doubtfully.

"I'll ask Lumsden," said Roger. "I'll see him about it to-morrow. We won't say a word to Arnold until it's all fixed."

By this time the afternoon had deteriorated; it was damp and cold and cheerless and a thin drizzle had begun to fall.

"I'll run you back to Merlewood," said Roger. "You can't walk back in this. Perhaps Mrs. Lambert will give me a cup of tea."

"Yes, I'm sure she will," replied Mary but without much enthusiasm.

Of course Poppet would be only too pleased to see Roger and sustain him with tea and cakes, but Mary had not told Poppet she was going to meet Roger this afternoon . . . and would Poppet be awful?

Mary was a little worried about it, and it was with some trepidation that she ushered Roger into the drawing-room where her host and hostess were having tea beside a comfortable, warm fire, but she soon realised that her fears were without foundation. Poppet welcomed the visitor with cries of delight, scolded him

180

severely for not coming to see her before and was altogether charming. Soon they were all sitting round the fire and Roger was telling them about Mary's idea.

"How stupid men are!" said Poppet, shaking her head sadly. "Any woman would have thought of that at once. It's frightfully important to make a good first impression upon the parents."

"I'm afraid it will cost a lot —" began Mary.

"It's a good idea," declared Mr. Lambert. "I don't suppose the cost would be excessive. You could have it built of brick —"

"Brick!" cried Roger. "Goodness, no! It will have to be stone like the rest of the house. If it was built of brick it would look like a false nose stuck on to somebody's face."

Mr. Lambert laughed. He said, "Well, you can ask your builder, but building in stone is an expensive amusement nowadays."

"It would be worth it," declared Roger. "It would make a small poky room into a good room — a really fine room. Mary's bow-window is a splendid idea."

Mary smiled. She said, "First Mary's hatch, and now Mary's bow-window. I know I'm fat, but really —"

"You aren't fat!" cried Poppet indignantly. "You used to be plump but you're ever so much thinner lately."

"Must be in love," said Mr. Lambert teasingly. "Young women always lose weight when they're in love."

"What nonsense, Johnnie!"

"Not nonsense at all," declared Mr. Lambert, laughing in his cheery way. "Look at her — she's blushing!"

Mary knew she was blushing, but blushing is beyond one's control. She wished he would be quiet. It was just his fun of course — Mr. Lambert enjoyed teasing — but how she wished he would be quiet!

"I've got it!" continued Mr. Lambert. "I've guessed the secret. It's Arnold! That's why she's always trotting round to Summerhills. That's why she takes such an interest in a bow-window for the headmaster's room. Now we know. It's Arnold."

"Perhaps it's that man with the funny ears," suggested Poppet. "Mary meets him nearly every day — at Summerhills — and he's so attractive, isn't he? Just the sort of man to appeal to Mary."

Mary laughed quite cheerfully (clever Poppet had rescued her). "You're both wrong," said Mary. "It's Mr. Lumsden — if you must know. Mr. Lumsden is a perfect darling; I'm crazy about him. We share our elevenses and have long talks about toilet equipment — but it's quite, quite hopeless because he adores his wife."

They were all laughing now. Even Roger who had been looking rather startled joined in the merriment.

"We must have a party," said Poppet. "Johnnie, we must have a party."

"Just as you say, m'dear," replied Johnnie. "I'm going up to Glasgow to-morrow, so if you want cards printed —"

"Not that sort of party at all! I mean the sort of party when you just ask people you like. We'll have all the Ayrtons of course and dear Dr. Maddon and Arnold."

"Gerald and Connie?"

"They won't be able to come," said Poppet regretfully. "They've gone to North Berwick with the children; but we can have Mr. Orme and the Claytons and — and —"

"Cocktails, I suppose," said Mr. Lambert. "You'd better let me mix them. That's all I ask. Last time, when you and Gerald —"

"Oh, but they were lovely!" cried Poppet indignantly.

"They tasted all right, but —"

"They were lovely," Poppet repeated. "Everybody said so — and if you're thinking of little Mrs. Bannister (which I know you are) it was just because she didn't understand about cocktails — and anyhow Gerald was terribly kind and got her sobered up beautifully before he took her home, so nobody knew anything about it and there was no harm done. Even Mrs. Bannister thought it was the mushrooms she had eaten for lunch."

Gales of laughter greeted this simple tale, and Poppet (who had told this tale on purpose to amuse her audience) sat there looking as innocent as a kitten and as pretty as a flower-fairy.

"If you want me to come to your party it will have to be soon," said Roger when he had recovered sufficiently to speak.

"Of course I want you, darling Roger," said Poppet, opening her eyes very wide. "The party is specially for you. We'll have it to-morrow — no, Tuesday — and you must bring Nell and Marion and the pretty governess."

"You had better ask Nell about — about Miss Glassford," said Roger doubtfully. "Nell always arranges things like that." He hesitated and then added, "But I don't think there's any need to ask her — really."

This was a little unkind of Roger because Georgina would have enjoyed the party tremendously.

CHAPTER
FIFTEEN

1

Mary had been under the impression that the cocktail party was intended for Roger and his relations and one or two others — just the Lamberts' special friends — so on the Tuesday morning when she went to help Mr. Lambert to look out the glasses she was surprised to find him filling a large tray.

"We shan't need all those!" exclaimed Mary.

"Forty-four, forty-five, forty-six," muttered Mr. Lambert, counting busily. "Four dozen ought to be enough. Eh, Mary?"

"Too many," said Mary.

"Not a bit of it. You don't know Poppet as well as I do. Her parties are like snowballs, they get bigger and bigger every minute. Poppet is going to the town this morning and she'll ask everybody she sees ... and she'll remember other people and ring them up, and they'll ask her if they can bring their sisters and their cousins and their aunts ... and Poppet will say yes. If the party was next week we'd need six dozen glasses at least, but as it's to-day she won't have time to go into the highways and byways like that fellow in the Bible."

Mary smiled. She had always liked Mr. Lambert but since she had been staying at Merlewood she liked him even better. As Poppet had said he was a dear, nice, good, kind creature. Even when he teased her Mary liked him. He had teased her quite a lot about Mr. Lumsden, but that did not worry Mary at all.

"Couldn't Poppet tell us how many?" asked Mary as she began to wash and polish the glasses.

"She won't remember," replied Mr. Lambert with conviction. "Oh, I say, are you going to wash them? That's fine. If there's one thing I hate more than another it's washing wine-glasses. I usually twist the stems off them. I think I'll go and mix the booze if you can cope with these."

Poppet was not idle of course; she was arranging the flowers. The cook was making tiny biscuits and decorating them with anchovies and caviare. It was obvious that she had had experience of the Lamberts' parties for Mary had heard Poppet say, "There will be about a dozen people, Janet," and Janet was making enough little savoury biscuits to feed three times that number of guests.

The last few days had been cold and bleak, so cold that the drawing-room fire had been lighted at tea-time, but Tuesday was fine and warm and sunny. The Lamberts were pleased but not surprised at this sudden improvement in the weather for it appeared that the sun always shone on Poppet's parties. This was all the more fortunate because the drawing-room had double doors which opened on to the veranda and the guests could stroll in and out as they pleased . . . and they could walk round the garden and admire Poppet's roses, which were the best in the county and always

186

bloomed at the right moment. Poppet loved her roses; she looked after them herself. The gardener was not allowed to touch them.

Mary felt quite excited as she dressed for the party. She had a cherry-coloured frock of soft cashmere which seemed just right for the occasion.

"Not bad at all — really," said Mary to herself, and as she looked in the mirror and made a few adjustments to her dark brown curls the thought crossed her mind that perhaps — other people — might think she looked quite nice.

Poppet was ready and waiting in the drawing-room when Mary went downstairs. "Mary, you're perfectly sweet!" she exclaimed. "That frock is just your colour. May I pin these two roses on your front?" and as Poppet was an artist in dress the two lovely pink roses pinned to Mary's "front" completed the picture.

"Yes," said Poppet, surveying her guest critically. "Yes, you'll do. In fact I never saw you look better. Let's each have a cocktail before they arrive because we shan't have time afterwards. I never seem to get anything to eat or drink at my own parties. Where's Johnnie?"

Johnnie appeared at that very moment and made a bee-line for the table where the food and drink was arranged.

"One each before they come," said Johnnie firmly. "If you've got to go wandering round with a jug you never get any yourself. I think I'll have two while I'm about it."

"Yes, darling, do," said Poppet. "And have some of Janet's biscuits. The caviare ones are terribly good."

Westkirk was not a fashionable place, so the guests (who had been invited to come at six-thirty) arrived at the time appointed or quite soon after. The Lamberts' car had been all round the town collecting people who had not cars of their own; these included Mr. Orme and Anne, the two Maddons and little Mrs. Bannister. ("I didn't know Poppet had asked her," said Mr. Lambert to Mary. "We had better give her lemonade. She won't notice and it'll be safer.") Roger brought Mrs. Ayrton and Nell; he also brought Georgina, for Nell in the goodness of her heart had rung up the Lamberts and asked if she might come. The Claytons came and brought old Miss Cannan (who was Aunt Beatrice's special friend) and the remainder of the company consisted of people Poppet had met in the town that morning and people she had suddenly thought of and invited by telephone.

There were about forty guests; they filled the drawing-room and filtered on to the veranda and as they all knew each other well, meeting almost daily in the town or on the golf-course or at some of the many social functions which took place in Westkirk (such as the Women's Rural Institute, the Girl Guides Local Association and Church Bazaars), they were naturally enchanted to meet each other again in Poppet's drawing-room. They had so much to say to each other and so many things of common interest to discuss that the noise of talk and laughter became louder and louder every moment.

188

Georgina Glassford was the only stranger — she knew nobody — but Poppet remembered this and introduced her to everybody within reach. Luckily there were several personable young men who were all agog to make Georgina's acquaintance and soon she was the centre of a little group and was chatting to them happily. Although Poppet did not like Georgina (and most certainly did not want her as a next-door-neighbour) she was bound to admit that the girl was good-looking and well turned out and obviously attractive to the opposite sex, if not to her own. She was an asset to the party, which was a mark in her favour.

Poppet had not yet solved the mystery of Roger and Georgina. There was a mystery, she was sure; they had been as thick as thieves that Sunday when she had met the Amberwell party going to church and Roger had opened the gate for her. But Roger had not wanted the girl to be asked to the party, and he was not one of the group which had gathered round her to-night. Mary might know the reason, but Poppet did not intend to ask her, for Mary must not be teased about Roger any more.

There was not much that escaped Poppet's eye for she was a born hostess and deeply interested in the affairs of her friends. She noticed that Arnold Maddon and Anne Selby had drifted out into the garden to admire the roses; she noticed that Nell had been pinned down into a corner by old Miss Cannan; she noticed that Mary — dear little creature — was helping Johnnie to wait upon the guests; she noticed that Marion Ayrton had sat down upon the sofa and was looking slightly dazed . . . but it isn't the cocktails, thought Poppet, it's just the noise and heat. I must get somebody to take her on to the veranda. Dr. Maddon will do.

It was not easy to find Dr. Maddon amongst the crowd and in her search for him Poppet came across Roger standing near the door. Roger was not talking to anybody but was gazing over the heads of his fellow guests, which he could do quite easily.

"Darling Roger, you've got nobody to talk to!" exclaimed Poppet in dismay. "Shall I find somebody —?"

"No — please," replied Roger hastily. "I just like looking round."

"How nice to be so tall! I can't see where anybody is; it's a great disadvantage for a hostess."

Roger looked down at her and smiled. Her head reached the second button of his waistcoat. "I could lift you up," he suggested.

"That would be lovely," she agreed. "But perhaps a little too — too obvious. Tell me what's going on. Can you see Mary anywhere?"

Roger said he could.

"I do wish you'd get hold of her for me," said Poppet fretfully. "She's handing round biscuits — and there's no need. The young men ought to be handing the trays. Mary has been running about all day helping me. She's done quite enough. Do get hold of her, Roger, and tell her she's to stop handing trays and enjoy the party. Tell her I said so."

"Poppet's order," said Roger nodding. He hesitated and then exclaimed, "Oh, I'm sorry!"

190

"But I like it," said Poppet, laughing merrily. "Everybody calls me Poppet — if they don't do it to my face they do it behind my back — so just call me Poppet if you can do it easily."

Roger said he could do it very easily, and in fact he had been trying not to do it for some time, and with that he pushed off through the crowd on his errand. For a few moments Poppet watched him; she could see his fair head above the heads of her other guests. She would dearly have liked to stand upon a chair and see what happened when he reached his objective but unfortunately that was out of the question. Heaving a sigh of regret at her dwarfishness Poppet continued her search for Dr. Maddon. She was hampered considerably by the friendliness of her guests who all wanted to talk to her and tell her how much they were enjoying her hospitality . . . but presently she found Dr. Maddon, purely by luck and not by good guidance, and seizing him by the arm told him to rescue Marion Ayrton and take her into the garden.

"Drink this," said Johnnie's voice in her ear. "Go on, drink it up. You need it."

Johnnie really was sweet, thought Poppet as she smiled at him and obeyed.

"The show is going well," said Johnnie. "You can tell by the noise. Frightful din, isn't it?"

"Frightful," agreed the hostess with complacency.

"Have another wee drop before I go?"

"Well, just half. Oh Johnnie, what about Mrs. Bannister?"

"It's all right. Don't worry. I've got her on lemonade . . . but the governess is getting a bit high. Shall I put her on lemonade or would she notice?"

"Yes," said Poppet. "I mean put her on lemonade. It doesn't matter if she notices."

They parted and went their ways and the din increased.

2

It was peaceful and cool in the rose-garden. The din could be heard in the distance like the sound of the sea. Not even Amberwell roses were as beautiful as Poppet's.

"Look Arnold, they really are lovely," said Anne.

"Yes," agreed Arnold, but he said it vaguely as if his thoughts were elsewhere.

Anne was suddenly frightened. Why had she come here with Arnold? Why had she allowed Arnold to inveigle her into the rose-garden? He had suggested that they should come here and look at Poppet's roses — but he was not looking at them. He was going to "say something," she was sure. Of course in one way it would be better if he "said something," because she could tell him it was "no use" and make things absolutely clear; but in another way it would be dreadful. Anne did not think she could bear it. Her heart beat like a sledgehammer. She wished she had the courage to escape. It would be easy to escape from Arnold. He could not run after her. She could make some excuse and run up the steps, back to the crowded room and to safety. But Anne could think of no excuse, her brain was paralysed — she was rooted to the ground.

"Anne," said Arnold, "I brought you here to tell you something. The Old 'Uns have been discussing our affairs. I just wanted to tell you that it's all right. I understand."

Anne was dumb with terror.

"It's all right," repeated Arnold earnestly. "Your Old Boy told my Old Boy and he explained it to me — so you needn't worry any more. We're friends."

Anne was still dumb and Arnold hesitated, for it was difficult to know how to go on. His Old Boy had told him quite a lot about Anne — some of it in medical language — and had concluded the lecture by saying, "So if you really want her you may have to wait for years — but to my way of thinking she's worth waiting for."

"I could strangle him," Arnold had muttered.

"H'mm, I dare say you could, but murderous feelings never did anybody any good and if you take my advice you'll put all that out of your head."

"I'll try," said Arnold. "It won't be easy — but I'll try. And I don't mind waiting if you think there's any hope."

"I never said there was hope, did I? You'll be wise to get that out of your head as well. Mind you, Arnold," declared Arnold's Old Boy, wagging a finger at him. "Mind you, if you so much as breathe a word of love or marriage to that young woman you're done — finished for good and all. That young woman needs a friend, not a sweetheart. Maybe some day she'll need a husband — maybe not."

At first Arnold had decided to say nothing about it to Anne, but just to be a friend to her. It seemed the easiest way. But then he had changed his mind. Once or twice when they had been talking he had seen the look of a woodland fawn appear in Anne's clear eyes; it was a frightened, startled look — almost a look of horror. If Arnold had needed any confirmation of his Old Boy's assertions Anne's startled eyes would have given it to him.

This being so it seemed better to clear up the matter and state his position clearly.

"We're friends," repeated Arnold, smiling at Anne in a friendly sort of way.

"You mean it — really?" asked Anne incredulously.

"I mean it," replied Arnold with conviction. "We're friends and we'll always be friends. That's all I want — ever." (God forgive me for the lie, thought Arnold.)

"Oh Arnold, I'm glad! I was afraid —"

"Well, you needn't be afraid any more."

She sighed with relief and pleasure.

"That's what you want, isn't it?" asked Arnold.

"Yes — it's marvellous. Nothing could be better. You see I like you so very, very much."

The grey eyes were raised to his with such a look of affection and trustfulness that Arnold was repaid. "That's — all right then," he said with a catch in his breath. "We know where we are, don't we?"

"Yes, we know where we are," agreed Anne smiling. "It really is simply perfect. And now I can be as nice as I like without — without you thinking —"

"Yes, of course," agreed Arnold. He hesitated and then added, "Well, now that it's settled perhaps we'd better go back," because he felt he had had as much as he could bear for the moment.

3

Nell was talking to old Miss Cannan — or rather old Miss Cannan was talking to Nell.

"Beatrice is quite herself again," said Miss Cannan.

Nell said she was very glad to hear it.

"Oh *quite* herself," nodded Miss Cannan. "She has *quite* regained her — her determination. I have been staying with her in Edinburgh for a few days and we went to some of the Festival Concerts. It was most enjoyable."

Nell said she was glad.

"That was a very curious little attack Beatrice had in Rome, wasn't it?"

"Yes," agreed Nell. "I wonder —"

"It must have been most unpleasant for her to be laid up in the Pensione, and Madame Le Brun seems to have behaved in an extraordinary way."

"Yes," said Nell. "Poor Aunt Beatrice was —"

"But she thoroughly enjoyed her journey home in the aeroplane. In fact she enjoyed it so much that she intends to fly to Copenhagen next year for her holiday and she is very anxious for me to go with her."

"It would be nice," suggested Nell.

"I have never been — airborne," said Miss Cannan in doubtful tones. "Beatrice assures me it is a delightful sensation but I am not a good sailor and I might feel unwell."

"There are things you can take," Nell told her. "Roger says Avomine is good."

Miss Cannan rummaged in her bag. "I must write it down in my little book," she said. "I don't really intend to go (Bournemouth would be much more restful), but Beatrice is so very — persuasive —"

"Yes," said Nell. "She is, isn't she?"

4

Meanwhile Roger had found Mary and delivered his message. He removed the tray of biscuits from her grasp and, handing it to one of Poppet's personable young men who happened to be standing near, told him to get on with it.

"Yes, sir," said the P.Y.M. smartly. (He was doing his National Service and knew a superior officer — even in plain clothes — when he met one.) "Yes sir, I'll circulate the biscuits. I'd have offered before, only —"

"There are some chairs on the veranda," said Roger, taking Mary's elbow the better to steer her through the crowd.

"But I think I ought to —" began Mary.

"Poppet's orders," said Roger firmly.

They settled themselves comfortably upon two chairs at the end of the veranda. Roger offered his companion a cigarette and lighted one for himself. "This is nice," he said. "It's frightfully hot and noisy inside, isn't it?"

"Yes, but it's fun. It's fun seeing everybody in their best clothes. Don't you think so?"

"Some people," said Roger, looking at Mary. "Some people look — awfully nice — in their best clothes."

"What about the bow-window?" asked Mary.

"Oh yes — the bow-window. I saw Lumsden about it this morning and he says it's a grand idea. Of course we'll have to get Strow to draw up some plans but Lumsden will keep him up to the mark."

"Must you have Mr. Strow?"

"I'm afraid so, unless I sack him completely. He's been rather useless, hasn't he?"

"Absolutely useless."

"Arnold came along while Lumsden and I were measuring it out," continued Roger. "At first he said it was an unnecessary expense — his usual reaction — but when I pointed out that unless the room could be enlarged we should have to bag one of his classrooms to entertain the parents he gave in at once, and became quite keen about it."

"Good," nodded Mary.

"You'll let me know how he gets on, won't you? I mean you'll keep on writing to me and telling me things?"

"Yes, of course."

"I like your letters. They're full of you. When I read them I can hear you talking."

"Can you, Roger?" She hesitated and then added, "So are yours — full of you, I mean."

For a moment Roger was silent and then he sighed. "I wish I needn't go back to Germany," he said. "Sometimes I've thought of chucking it and settling down at Amberwell. What do you think, Mary?"

"I think you're too young," she replied with a thoughtful smile. "Too young — and too energetic. There wouldn't be enough for you to do. It's bad for people not to have enough to do."

They went on talking about it. Roger explained how he was pulled both ways — by Amberwell, and by the fascination of his career — and Mary listened with interest. They went on talking until the din, which had been raging in the distance, suddenly decreased and they realised that the party was over.

CHAPTER
SIXTEEN

1

It was September before Dennis Weatherby was able to take advantage of the invitation given him in Rome. Weatherby Manor was sold to the syndicate and was being turned into a Country Club and Mrs. Weatherby moved into her new house in Harrogate. Dennis was pleased with the little house, it was comfortable and modern; the garden, though somewhat neglected, had possibilities.

The relationship between Dennis and his mother was a delightful one; they understood each other and enjoyed the same jokes and, best of all, they liked the same people.

If there had not been so much to do, so much bother with lawyers and removers, Dennis would have gone to Amberwell before, but he made up his mind to get the necessary business over first so that he would be free and could enjoy his visit to Amberwell with a clear conscience. Several times he had been on the point of telling his mother about Nell Ayrton but on each occasion something had prevented him . . . and anyhow there was nothing much to tell. There was nothing, except that he had fallen in love with Nell before he went to Burma and that they had carried on a regular, but strictly platonic, correspondence for three years. His dearest wish was to marry Nell, but until he had seen her and put his fate to the test it was no use talking about it. Of course his mother knew that Tom Ayrton was one of his greatest friends and he had told her about meeting Roger in Rome and all about "Aunt Beatrice." He had made a very amusing story of the affair and they had laughed over it together.

"Oh Den, what is she *like*?" asked Mrs. Weatherby.

"But that's just it! I never *saw* the old lady! I heard plenty about her from Roger and the doctor and the black satin pin-cushion — and they all told me something different. The only thing they had in common was terror; they were all scared to death of Aunt Beatrice."

After this it was easy enough to explain that Roger had asked him to visit Amberwell, and it was quite unnecessary to mention that by this time Roger's leave was over and he had returned to his regiment in Germany.

"You must go," said Mrs. Weatherby. "You deserve a holiday after all your hard work. Why not ring up your friend to-night and arrange it?"

Dennis rang up his friend — it was Nell not Roger of course — and the visit was arranged.

2

Amberwell had been so much in his thoughts that when Dennis saw it again it seemed well-known and friendly. The old grey house, so strongly built and beautifully

200

proportioned, was not large and grand and proud like Weatherby Manor — it was a comfortable building which had been erected by an Ayrton and had sheltered the Ayrton family for nearly a hundred and fifty years. Amberwell was a family house — no more and no less — thought Dennis as he drove up to the door. There was kindness about it, an air of benevolence which embraced not only its own family but the stranger within its gates.

He had been longing to see Nell, but now that he was so near his desire Dennis felt anxious; Nell was shy and there might be some awkwardness at first. He must be careful to assume the right manner and neither frighten her with too much friendliness nor chill her with too little . . . but he soon found that these fears were groundless and he had been reckoning without his hosts. Amberwell welcomed its visitors with benevolence and the people who lived in Amberwell did the same. Perhaps if Nell had met Dennis elsewhere she might have been shy and awkward but here she was on her own ground and her instinct of hospitality was supreme. It was not only Nell who welcomed him warmly; Mrs. Ayrton remembered him quite well and inquired after his mother, and Stephen received him with joyful exuberance as if he had been a long-lost uncle.

"D'you remember Him?" cried Stephen, flourishing an extremely dilapidated Teddy bear. "You brought him to me last time you came, when I was a little boy. I wonder what you —"

"Be quiet, Stephen!" exclaimed Nell.

"It's all right," declared Stephen unsubdued. "I wasn't going to say that; I was just going to say I wonder what — what you would like to do to-morrow. We might have a picnic at the Smugglers' Cave or — or something."

Fortunately Dennis had brought a gift for Stephen so he opened his suitcase and produced a large, oddly-shaped, flabby sort of parcel and handed it to him then and there.

"You shouldn't," said Nell, smiling. "He's a greedy little monster, but it isn't his fault really. It's because Roger and Tom always bring him parcels when they come home. I've told him he shouldn't expect it."

"I don't expect it," declared Stephen, not quite truthfully. "But it's nice when it comes. I wonder what it can be. It feels like a bath-mat."

But it was not a bath-mat; it was a rubber goose which was intended to float in a swimming-pool, and when inflated was large enough for a small boy to ride on. Naturally Stephen wished to blow it up at once and, refusing all offers of help, proceeded to do it himself and became very flushed and breathless in the process.

Thanks to Stephen there was no awkwardness at all and Dennis stepped straight into the middle of the Amberwell household as if he had known its members all his life. He had arrived just before tea-time, which is the best time for a guest to arrive, and as they sat on the terrace in the mellow glow of the summer sunshine he began to feel happy and relaxed. He was here at last

. . . and there was Nell sitting behind the silver tea-pot pouring out his tea. For the moment he wanted no more, it was all exactly as he remembered it: the peace and quietness, the mellow sunshine, the shadows of the trees upon the lawn. Best of all Nell was the same sweet, gentle creature who had lived in his heart for three years.

Now that Dennis was here it seemed impossible that he had been so far away and had seen so much. The glaring eastern sun, the bustling cities, the brown men and women in their gaily-coloured garments might have been a dream he had dreamed in one night.

At first they had talked about Stephen and his goose (it was a large ungainly bird ashore, but no doubt it would assume a more graceful appearance in the water), and then Dennis was asked for an account of his mother's new house and described it in detail.

"It sounds lovely," said Nell.

"It isn't lovely," replied Dennis. "But it's very comfortable and easily run and I'm sure my mother will be happy there. The garden is just the right size to give her plenty of scope without being a burden. When I came away she was planning to reorganise it completely. She likes that," added Dennis with a smile. "She likes doing things with her own hands and seeing the results of her labours. That's why I had to get her out of the Manor; she was killing herself trying to keep the place in order."

There was a little silence after that, a peaceful companionable silence.

"You're like Roger," said Nell at last. "Tom is your friend, I know, but you're much more like Roger . . . and I don't mean only to look at, I mean in yourself."

"How?" asked Dennis with interest.

"You're peaceful for one thing," replied Nell thoughtfully. "When Tom comes home he stirs us all up, but Roger seems to adapt himself to our slow-moving lives. Another thing is you don't change. Tom has a dozen different personalities, but Roger is always the same."

Dennis was satisfied with this, and so he should have been, for it was something to build on. He had known from the beginning he would have to go slowly with Nell; he would have to make friends with her before he could make love to her — that was how he put it to himself — and as there had not been time to make friends with Nell before he went to Burma he had left without saying a word and had contented himself with writing her long friendly letters. He wondered now, as he looked at her and met the friendly glance of her cornflower-blue eyes, how long it would be before he could move on to the second part of his programme with safety.

Several days passed and Dennis established himself as one of the household; they had a picnic on the shore and the goose was taken to bathe and proved itself an excellent swimmer. He walked on the moor, visited the Rectory and was taken to see over Summerhills. In addition to these social pleasures Dennis made himself useful, he oiled the garage-doors and mended a faulty catch on the bathroom window.

Mrs. Duff wanted a shelf put up in the kitchen and had been waiting for weeks for the joiner to come from Westkirk, so when Dennis offered to put it up for her she accepted the offer with delight. All the necessary tools and impedimenta were assembled; Dennis got on to the job with workmanlike precision while Mrs. Duff looked on and admired his skill. Nannie, who was ironing on the kitchen table, joined in the chat.

Dennis had been surprised to find that Mrs. Duff and Nannie remembered him — in three years they might easily have forgotten his existence — and he was surprised to find them so interesting and so well-informed. It was a new experience to talk to people like Mrs. Duff and Nannie and he found great difficulty in "placing" them. For instance it was a little startling to be asked by Mrs. Duff whether he had been to Rangoon while he was in Burma and to be told quite casually that her nephew was the manager of a large and flourishing shipping firm in that city.

"Mr. William Duff?" exclaimed Dennis, pausing in his work.

"That's him," agreed Mrs. Duff calmly. "Willie has done quite well for himself — I will say that. He's got a nice house and a lot of black servants. I've not seen Willie for years, but we write at Christmas and he tells me what he's doing. He was wanting me to go out and visit him last winter but I'm too old for junketing about the world in aeroplanes."

Dennis had met Mr. Duff and remembered him as an important person with a fine figure and a noble head and a slight Scots accent . . . and now that he looked at

Mrs. Duff he could see a very faint but unmistakable family resemblance.

"You were a fool not to have gone," said Nannie, thumping away with her iron. "I told you so at the time."

"It was too far. Amberwell's good enough for me. I was born at Amberwell and I'll die at Amberwell," said Mrs. Duff firmly.

"You were born here?" asked Dennis with interest.

"I was indeed. Father was old Mr. Ayrton's coachman."

"There's no place like Amberwell to be born in," declared Nannie in a sarcastic tone of voice.

"To my way of thinking there's not," retorted Mrs. Duff. "I'd a deal rather be born in Amberwell than in — some other places I could name."

There was an uncomfortable pause punctuated by the thumps of Nannie's iron. Dennis had a feeling that they were approaching unknown shoals and although it would have been interesting to know the nature of the shoals he decided it was time to change course and steer for calm water.

"Was your nephew born here?" he inquired.

"Born and reared at Amberwell," said Mrs. Duff proudly. "My brother had a big family. He was glad enough to get rid of Willie and we were glad enough to have him, so he stayed with us and got his schooling at Westkirk. Willie was a nice wee boy with a taking manner and very keen on his books."

"It's a small world," declared Nannie.

Dennis had been thinking the same. It was almost incredible that Mr. William Duff whom he had met in Rangoon should have been born and brought up at Amberwell.

"It's a big enough world to my mind," declared Mrs. Duff. "And what's more there's far too many folks in it. Give me Amberwell where there's room to turn —"

"And room to think," put in Dennis.

Mrs. Duff nodded. "There's a deal of truth in that."

For a few moments there was silence and then Mrs. Duff continued, "Maybe you're wondering why I'm Mrs. Duff and Willie's my nephew. I married my cousin, you see. He was a steward in the *Lusitania* and went down with the ship. That was in May, 1915, you'll remember."

"Kate, you never told me that!" Nannie exclaimed in surprise.

"Maybe not," replied Mrs. Duff calmly. "It's not a thing I care to speak about, but I just thought I'd like Commander Weatherby to know."

Dennis was touched. He said, "Thank you, Mrs. Duff. I'm sorry. It must have been dreadful for you." But he said no more, for Mrs. Duff had made it clear, not only by her words but by her manner, that she preferred not to speak about the tragedy.

When the shelf was finished Dennis stood back and surveyed his work with satisfaction. "It's solid, anyhow," he said.

"It's a fine solid job," agreed Mrs. Duff. "Sailors are neat with their hands — I always say. Mr. Tom would have done it for me if he'd been here, but he'd have done it no better."

This, from Mrs. Duff, was the highest possible praise, for "Mr. Tom" was her favourite. She would have died for "Mr. Tom" joyfully.

"Tom!" exclaimed Nannie, laying down her iron. "Tom would have begun it and left it half finished . . . and you know that as well as I do, Kate Duff. If you go into the back kitchen this minute you'll see the vegetable-rack Tom started last time he was here . . . and if you're not careful you'll fall over it."

"He was busy —" began Tom's champion.

"He was busy," agreed Nannie with scorn.

Dennis felt it was time to go, so he gathered up his tools and left them arguing.

3

Dennis had been dreaming about Nell — which was not unusual — and when he was awakened by a slight noise and on opening his eyes saw her standing beside his bed he imagined he was still dreaming. Nell was clad in a blue silk dressing-gown, her fair curls were slightly disordered and there was a flush upon her lovely face. It was a marvellous dream and Dennis had no desire to wake from it, so he did not try to speak but merely gazed at the apparition in silence.

"Oh Dennis, I don't know what to do! Can you help me?"

This too was part of the dream. Dennis had imagined it often. "Can you help me, Dennis?" No other words could have sounded more sweetly in his ears.

"Dennis! Please! I'm awfully sorry to waken you so early but I don't know what to do —"

"It's real!" cried Dennis, sitting up suddenly in full possession of his senses — for his training had accustomed him to sudden awakenings.

"Yes, it's real. Did you think you were dreaming? Oh Dennis, it's Mrs. Duff. She's fallen downstairs and I'm afraid she's hurt herself badly. I've telephoned for the doctor but he's out. I left a message —"

Dennis had already leapt out of bed and seized his dressing-gown. "I'll come," he said. "Where is she? Don't move her whatever you do."

"I thought you could help us to carry her upstairs."

"Better not."

"She always gets up early," said Nell in a shaky voice as they went downstairs together. "Fortunately I was awake and I heard — I don't know what I heard — but I thought I'd better go and see — and I found her —"

"It's a good thing you went to see."

"I very nearly didn't," said Nell with a sob. "I very nearly — turned over — and went to sleep. Oh Dennis, it was dreadful to see her lying there! Oh Dennis!"

"Don't worry too much —" began Dennis and then he stopped, for this was something to worry about. His heart sank when he saw the crumpled little figure lying at the bottom of the stairs.

"Oh Duffy darling!" cried Nell, kneeling down and seizing a limp hand. "Oh Duffy, speak to me! Oh Duffy, you're not dead! I can't bear it!"

"She isn't dead," said Dennis. "Nell, listen! You must pull yourself together. Go and get two blankets. Waken Nannie. Tell her to fill hot-water bottles. We've got to keep her warm."

"Couldn't you — carry her up to bed?"

"Not till the doctor comes. Honestly, Nell, it's much better not to move her. Hurry up and do as I say."

When Nell had gone to do his bidding Dennis knelt down and tried to discover the extent of the damage — like most sailors he had some knowledge of First Aid. Mrs. Duff was unconscious and breathing heavily but her pulse was fairly good; there was a gash on her forehead and one arm was twisted beneath her. Quite definitely the arm was broken and possibly the collar-bone as well. Dennis straightened her out very carefully and slipped a cushion under her head.

She did not look so bad when he had got that done; he began to feel more hopeful and the sick feeling in his stomach disappeared. Dennis had been all through the war; his ship had been blown up by a mine and he had seen men killed before his eyes, but somehow this accident affected him more strongly and in a different way. You expected casualties in action, and there was a queer sort of excitement which buoyed you up and kept you at concert pitch. There was no fear of losing your head — so Dennis had found. But the sight of dear old Mrs. Duff lying in a disordered heap at the bottom of the stairs had upset him so horribly that it had taken him all his time to keep his wits about him.

Nannie appeared in a few minutes; she was fully dressed but her hair was in curlers and her face was white and pinched. Dennis did not allow her time to "flap," he sent her off to fill hot-water bottles. Nell and the blankets arrived soon after and between them they tucked up their patient securely. There was nothing more to be done until the doctor came.

CHAPTER
SEVENTEEN

1

"Dearest Mother," wrote Dennis — and then he paused. Usually he could write to his mother as easily as he could talk, his pen flying over the paper at a tremendous speed; but this letter was difficult, this letter was very important, there could be no rushing along like an express train.

Dennis was alone in the morning-room sitting by the fire with a block of writing-paper on his knee. It was nearly midnight and everybody else had gone to bed. Dennis would have liked to go to bed himself but this letter must be written and since Mrs. Duff's accident there had been no time to get down to a letter which required concentration. Mrs. Duff's accident had disrupted the Amberwell household, not only because her work remained undone but also because everybody — and especially Nell — was so worried and anxious.

Dennis sighed and continued his letter:

Sorry not to have written before but I have been very busy. As you know I intended to come home on Friday but I am afraid I shall have to put it off. I hope you will not be too disappointed that I shall not be there to go with you to the Newtons'

212

dinner-party. You must make my excuses and explain that I am "unavoidably detained." The fact is there is serious trouble here. Old Mrs. Duff, the cook-housekeeper, fell downstairs and was very badly injured. At first we could not get the doctor, he had been out all night at a confinement, but after a bit he came and sent straight off for an ambulance to take her to hospital in Ayr. Nell and I followed in the car and waited to hear the results of the X-ray.

Dennis paused again and looked at the last sentence he had written . . . just a few words to describe hours of anxiety. He thought of the long drive with Nell sitting beside him, white-faced and miserable, and of the interminable wait in the hospital lounge. He had tried to make Nell talk, for her frozen silence seemed unnatural, and after a little he had succeeded.

"She's so good," Nell had said. "She's so kind and understanding. I wish I had appreciated her more . . . at least I don't mean appreciated because I did appreciate her, but I could have — have shown her more of what I felt."

"I'm sure she knows."

"She doesn't know how much I love her. Oh dear, why didn't I — show her — ?"

"You'll be able to show her later — when she's better."

"Oh Dennis, then you think there's hope? She looked so — so dreadful."

"Of course there's hope."

"She's old, you know — nearly seventy. Roger was saying the last time he was here that she and Nannie were getting very old. We were planning to build them a little cottage near the Grays. They would be happy in a little cottage together and I would have them near. I could see they were all right and —"

"But not together, surely! I mean they quarrel, don't they?"

"Oh yes, they quarrel, but they love each other dearly. They enjoy quarrelling you know."

"Where was Nannie born?" asked Dennis, not so much because he wanted to know but just to keep Nell talking.

"It's funny you should ask that. We used to ask her when we were children but she would never tell us . . . and then somehow or other we discovered the secret. Nannie was born in Khartoum. Her father was a sergeant in the K.O.S.B.'s. Of course there was nothing disgraceful about it — quite the reverse — and I don't know why she tried to keep it dark. Perhaps it was just that she didn't like the idea of not having been born in Scotland and we used to wonder about it. We wondered why Nannie wasn't black. We thought that if you had been born in Africa you would naturally be black. We were very ignorant about things like that — Anne and I — and it never occurred to us to ask. We just talked about it and wondered. Silly, wasn't it?"

"Not silly, really."

"I think it was silly — and of course it was silly of Nannie to make a mystery of it. I wonder why she did."

"She's ashamed of it, that's why."

214

"Oh Dennis! But that's absurd. How do you know?" Dennis told her.

"So Duffy knows Nannie's secret!" said Nell with a wan smile.

"Yes, but she was too much of a lady to reveal it."

"She is a lady," said Nell with a little catch in her breath. "She thinks of other people all the time — and that makes her manners — perfect. Nobody has more beautiful manners — than Duffy."

"Nannie is different —" began Dennis, trying to steer the conversation into a safer channel.

"Quite different," agreed Nell. "Nannie is a dear kind creature and we all owe her a tremendous lot — more than we can ever repay — but she has to be humoured, you know. You can't talk to Nannie and tell her things. She's not wise like Duffy. Oh Dennis, they're taking an awfully long time!"

"Not really. It seems a long time to us because we're waiting."

"How long?"

Dennis looked at his watch. "Twenty minutes, that's all."

"It seems much longer," said Nell with a sigh.

Dennis felt the same. He said, "Did you know Willie Duff?"

"Willie Duff? Yes, of course. He's Duffy's nephew. He used to live with the old Duffs in the stable cottage. I don't remember him as a boy, because he was much older than all of us, but I used to hear Father talking about him. He was a clever boy. Father got him a very good post in Burma and he used to come and see us sometimes when he came home."

"Have you seen him lately?"

"No, not for ages — but he always sends Mother a card at Christmas."

"I met him in Burma," said Dennis . . . and he began to tell her all about the important Mr. William Duff.

For a few minutes Nell listened to the story and then she interrupted it. "Dennis, you won't have to go away on Friday, will you?" she asked.

"Not if you want me to stay."

"Yes — please — if you can. I know I'm being horribly selfish — it can't be much fun for you — but you're such a — comfort."

"Of course I'll stay."

"If your mother wants you —"

"She won't mind a bit. I'll write to her and explain."

There was a short silence. Dennis had come to the end of his resources.

"I shall have to get a cook," said Nell at last. "Just a temporary one, of course — just until — until Duffy's better. It's rather an awful thought, because I don't like new people, but — but I must. You see if I don't get somebody Nannie will try to do all Duffy's work as well as her own — and she's old, too."

"We'll telephone to a registry."

"Yes."

"Listen, Nell, there's somebody coming!" exclaimed Dennis.

They listened. Footsteps approached the door and paused.

216

"Oh dear!" said Nell with a sob. "Oh goodness, they're being a long time, aren't they?"

"It's a good sign, really."

"You mean they wouldn't bother so much if — if it was — hopeless?"

Dennis had meant something like that but he would not have put it so crudely. He said hastily, "It takes ages to X-ray a person thoroughly. That's what I meant."

"Do you think they can have forgotten to tell us? I mean they're so busy in a big hospital; they might have — forgotten."

"I'll go and see," said Dennis, rising as he spoke. "Perhaps I could find someone —"

He was lucky enough to find the young doctor who had been helping to do the X-ray and the report was not as bad as he had expected. He knew already that the collar-bone was fractured, and the left arm, but apart from this the X-ray had shown no other damage.

"She's badly bruised," declared the young doctor. "And the cut on her head may be troublesome but on the whole she's got off lightly. She might easily have fractured a femur and that's no fun when you're her age. She's suffering from shock of course, so you'd better not disturb her, but you can look in to-morrow."

"You mean there's no need to worry?" asked Dennis anxiously.

"Oh well — I wouldn't say that, exactly. I mean she's old, isn't she?"

Dennis fetched Nell and, having explained Mrs. Duff's condition in a moderately reassuring manner, he drove her home.

That was what happened at the hospital — but it was unnecessary for Dennis to tell his mother all the details of the long miserable wait. He looked over what he had written and continued his letter:

Fortunately the X-ray showed that there were no very serious breakages, but Mrs. Duff is an old woman and even if all goes well she will have to be in hospital for some time. We were allowed to see her this morning for a few minutes and she looked frail and ill. Nell was very upset about her. Mrs. Duff has been at Amberwell for so many years that she is just like one of the family — in fact she is more like a mother to Nell than anything else. I expect you will be thinking, *Yes, but what has all this got to do with Den? Why doesn't he come home?* The answer is I can't leave Nell while she is in trouble. For years you have been teasing me because I didn't take any interest in girls and sometimes when I was home on leave you trotted out attractive young females for my inspection. You told me half-jokingly that you would like a nice daughter-in-law. Now, at last, I am hoping to get one for you. Yes, it is Nell of course. Nell Ayrton is lovely. She is beautiful to look at — fair hair and cornflower-blue eyes — and she is beautiful inside as well. I don't believe she has ever had an unkind thought in her head or done anything ungracious. Her voice is low and sweet like music. I expect you will smile when you read this and will realise that I have "got it badly." Perhaps I have got it so very badly because I never had it before. Girls have never interested me — as you know. I think I must have been waiting for Nell.

Dennis stopped for a moment and read it over. Was this the right line to take? It was so frightfully important to take the right line so that the two people he loved best in the world would love one another. He was not really afraid, for they were both lovable, but all the same Dennis realised that his mother was bound to feel just a little bit sad. He and his mother had been everything to each other, they had been perfectly happy in each other's company and had never wanted anybody else. That was changed now. He still loved his mother dearly but it would not — could not — be quite the same.

He took another sheet of paper and continued:

You will love Nell — I know that for certain — and Nell will love you. Her own mother has never been a real proper mother (not as you and I know the relationship), but you will make up for that . . . but here I am, writing as if everything were settled and nothing is settled at all. I have not yet dared to speak to Nell and tell her I love her.

> "He either fears his fate too much
> "Or his deserts are small
> "That puts it not unto the touch
> "To win or lose it all."

Which of these two cases applies to me. I wonder. Perhaps both. The Great Marquis was a gambler by nature and I am no gambler. I want to see my way clear before I step forward. I fear my fate, and I know I am not nearly good enough for Nell. Perhaps I should explain that my love for Nell is not a sudden thing. I did not tell you about it before but the truth is I have loved her for three years. You remember when the old *Starfish* was sunk and Tom Ayrton was so ill and I came to Amberwell to see him? It was then that I saw Nell first and fell head over heels in love with her. Of course it was no good saying anything *then*, because I had to go out to Burma — and Nell is not the sort of girl to be rushed. It would only have frightened her if I had said anything. She was a little scared when I asked her to write to me but after some persuasion she said she would and we have written to each other regularly ever since. At first her letters were a little stilted — for my lovely darling is shy — but after a while they became warm and friendly. They were the sort of letters a girl writes to a brother who is serving abroad and is feeling rather lonely. As a matter of fact I happen to know that Nell writes to her brothers in exactly the same way because Tom used to show me some of her letters. So far so good — but now I am beginning to wonder whether I have been a fool to teach Nell to look on me as a brother. She does just that. I rank with Roger and Tom. She scolds me if I forget to change my shoes — just as she would scold Roger or Tom — she takes my socks out of my drawer and mends them; she teases me in a gentle sort of way and we have jokes together. In the evenings after Mrs. Ayrton has gone to bed we sit together like Darby and Joan until the clock strikes ten. Then Nell smiles at me and says, "Good night, Dennis. Sleep well. You'll see everything's locked up, won't you?" and off she goes to bed. I am surprised she doesn't kiss me. She always kisses Roger and Tom good night. What am I to do, Mother? How am I to teach Nell that I am not a third brother?

Your loving son,

DEN

P.S. — On reading this over I think I may have given you the impression that Nell is a helpless sort of female and therefore quite unfit to be the wife of a naval officer, but on the contrary she is very capable indeed. She runs Amberwell for Roger; she manages the house, keeps all the accounts and arranges the work in the garden and she has brought up Roger's little son since he was a few weeks old. But she is not an officious sort of person as so many capable women are (remember how we used to laugh at the Captain's wife who managed everything and everybody — including the Captain — with such a firm hand?). Nell is not like that, thank goodness. She is not "managing" by nature. In fact if there happens to be someone at hand to lean on, Nell is delighted to lean. At the

221

moment she is leaning on Dennis. Dennis, helping with the accounts; Dennis is supervising the plumbers who are putting new pipes in one of the bathrooms; Dennis is going to the station to-morrow to meet the temporary cook; Dennis locks up the house at night (but I have told you this already). Of course Dennis likes it. In fact he would be perfectly happy if only he could be sure that some day he would be more than a brother to Nell.

Oh Mother, I must have Nell! There never has been anyone else; there never will be. Tell me how I am to get her.

DEN

It was very late indeed when Dennis finished his letter; he collected the sheets, tucked them neatly into a large envelope and went upstairs to bed.

3

Mrs. Corner was arriving the following afternoon and Dennis went to meet her — it was one of the little jobs he was glad to do for Nell. He had not yet posted the letter to his mother and while he waited for the train he took it out and re-read it carefully, trying to imagine what his mother would think when she received it. He decided it was not bad. Some parts of it were a bit muddled — he had told her twice about locking up the house — but if he re-wrote the letter it would not sound spontaneous, and if at this important moment she received a letter which sounded careful she might be hurt. Besides he had no time to re-write the whole thing.

Dennis shut up the letter and posted it in the station pillarbox.

Shortly after that the train came in and Mrs. Corner emerged from it.

Dennis did not know Mrs. Corner of course, but she was the only female passenger to alight at Westkirk so there was no doubt about her identity. She had several suitcases with her and a large assortment of baskets and handbags and various packages tied up in brown paper and string.

"I'll need a barra' for that lot," said the porter in disgust and went away to fetch one.

Now that Dennis had time to look at Mrs. Corner properly he saw that she was a bulky shapeless woman with a squashy sort of hat. The face beneath the hat was squashy too, except the nose, which was thin and pointed.

"I hope you had a good journey," said Dennis politely, shaking hands.

Mrs. Corner smiled in a patient manner and replied that it might have been worse. "You'll be Mr. Hayrton?" she suggested.

"Oh no, I'm just a friend," said Dennis hastily. "Weatherby is my name. I'm staying at Amberwell and Miss Ayrton asked me to meet you. She would have come herself, but she's very busy. I mean of course you heard about poor Mrs. Duff falling down the stairs — and — and all that."

He burbled on nervously as he led the way to the car and helped the porter to load the luggage. Dennis was not often nervous, he got on well with all sorts of people, but Mrs. Corner made him feel uncomfortable. Perhaps it was just because she was different from what he had expected. They had been told by the registry that Mrs. Corner was a very nice woman, very superior, and an excellent cook . . . and somehow Dennis did not think she looked "nice" or "superior." He hoped he was wrong. It would make all the difference to Nell — the difference between comfort and misery.

"It's a very small town," said Mrs. Corner disparagingly as they drove through Westkirk. "I've been accustomed to living in a proper town with good shops and cinemas. It's more cheery. Birmingham is my 'ome, Mr. Weatherley. We 'ad a very nice little flat in Birmingham when me 'usband was alive — very comfortable we were. I dunno what me 'usband would say if 'e knew I'd come down to this." She sighed heavily.

"I'm sure you'll be very comfortable at Amberwell," Dennis told her.

"I 'ope so," returned Mrs. Corner in doubtful tones. "I wouldn't never 'ave come all this way if the registry 'adn't persuaded me. I 'aven't been to Scotland before."

"A new experience for you," suggested Dennis.

"I've 'ad lots of experience," declared Mrs. Corner. "I've been in very good places. I was 'ousekeeper to Lady Seven for eighteen munce."

"This is Amberwell," said Dennis as they swept in through the gates. "It really is a lovely place. The gardens are beautiful."

Mrs. Corner was silent but her large bulky form exuded disapproval. She preferred Birmingham.

The household at Amberwell had been prepared to like Mrs. Corner, to help her as much as possible and to get her into the way of things — for of course she would find it difficult at first — but in twenty-four hours she had won the dislike of everybody in the place. She had won it by disapproving of everything. In the eyes of Mrs. Corner nothing was right, nothing was as it should be. This atmosphere of disapproval permeated the whole house, it was as pervasive as the smell of onions. The moment you entered the front door you could smell it.

It began when Nell showed Mrs. Corner the kitchen.

"I'm accustomed to small kitchings," said Mrs. Corner. "Small kitchings is cosier than big kitchings — and more convenient."

Nell had been prepared to make quite a lot of alterations for her new cook, for of course she might like things different, but it was not possible to reduce the size of the "kitching."

"It's really quite warm," Nell assured her. "The stove keeps it beautifully warm."

"I wouldn't never 'ave come if I'd known it was one of them sulky stoves," said Mrs. Corner, looking down her nose at the stove, which was the pride of Duffy's heart.

225

This was the first time Nell had heard her use the phrase but it was by no means the last. Mrs. Corner wouldn't never have come if she had known that she would have to make porridge every morning or that the baker only called twice a week or that she was expected to prepare the vegetables with her own hands. She wouldn't never have dreamed of coming if she had known her bedroom would be upstairs. Nell, looking at her, wished she had known.

Nannie was the worst sufferer, for Nannie had her meals with Mrs. Corner and was obliged to listen to her complaints. Occasionally the complaints about the inconveniences of Amberwell were varied by stories about the "good places" in which Mrs. Corner had held sway. She had worked for "reel ladies" who had provided Mrs. Corner with "kitching maids" to do all the vegetables and wash the dishes for her. "Reel ladies" did not order in the stores from the grocer, they left it to their cooks. "Reel ladies" did not expect you to get up at half-past seven.

"Maybe they brought you your tea in bed," suggested Nannie.

Mrs. Corner hesitated — and then changed the subject.

All this was hard for Nannie to bear but she soon discovered it was wiser to say nothing — so she held her tongue.

The only other subject which Mrs. Corner liked to discuss was her married life in Birmingham . . . and of course her husband.

"Corner was an 'e man," said Mrs. Corner proudly.

226

Nannie did not understand, but she did not ask for an explanation; she just wondered what the letter E stood for. Perhaps Mr. Corner had been an electric light fitter or an engine-driver ... or could he have been the keeper of the elephant-house at the zoo? It did not seem likely but Nannie could not think of any other occupation beginning with an E.

"'E was a butcher," added Mrs. Corner. "So 'e knew what was what in the way of meat. You couldn't put 'im off with a bit of scrag-end for 'is dinner."

"But I thought you said he was an E. man," said Nannie before she could prevent herself.

"And so 'e was," replied Mrs. Corner. "Corner was an 'e man right enough. If things wasn't to 'is liking 'e let you know about it. There was one day the chops was overdone and 'e shook me till the teeth rattled in me 'ead ... and drink! You'd 'ardly believe the amount of beer Corner could put through 'is face — *and* be none the worse of!"

Nannie gazed at her in silence.

In a strange perverted way Nannie enjoyed Mrs. Corner. She found it was possible to enjoy Mrs. Corner if you looked upon her as a music-hall turn and refused to allow her vagaries to annoy you. (She's just a poor sumph, thought Nannie, looking at the squashy face and the long thin nose with pitying scorn. This reflection helped Nannie a lot for you would be a sumph yourself if you allowed a poor sumph to annoy you.) And of course it was only temporary for Mrs. Duff was getting on quite well now. Soon she would come home. What a lot there would be to tell her!

Nell suggested to Nannie that Mrs. Corner should be asked to leave and they would find somebody else to do the cooking, but Nannie vetoed the suggestion.

"We might jump out of the frying-pan into the fire," said Nannie. "She's a good cook — I will say that — and I'm getting used to her."

"I don't know how you can bear it," declared Nell. "It takes me all my time to screw up my courage to go into the kitchen to order the meals."

"You can bear most things if they're temporary. I've told the gurrls that."

The "gurrls" were the two dailies who came up from Westkirk every morning on bicycles and worked in the house.

"Oh dear!" exclaimed Nell. "I hope she isn't being beastly to Winnie and Jean. They're not — upset — are they?"

"Och, there's no need to worry. They won't leave; they know which side their bread is buttered — and it's only temporary."

"She's so rude!"

"She's rude all right, but hard words break no bones — that's what I tell the gurrls — and there's something comic about it too."

"Comic!" exclaimed Nell in amazement.

"There's a comic side to it. She thinks she's a kind of duchess and she's nothing but a sumph. In fact," added Nannie confidentially, "in fact there's only one thing I can't bear about that woman and that's her religion."

"But — but she went to church on Sunday!"

228

"That's what I mean. She goes to church and she lets you know about it. She wouldn't miss going to church — but for all that she's no more of a Christian than a heathen Chinee."

"Oh, I see what you mean!"

"It puts people off," complained Nannie. "There's Winnie, for instance; I've been trying to get Winnie to go to church, and I'd almost got her round to it, but now she's off it for good and all. 'No church for me,' says Winnie, snorting. 'I'm a better Christian than Mrs. Corner for all I don't go to church.' And that's true, mind you," declared Nannie. "Winnie is a nice creature; you never get an unkind word from Winnie. If she thinks you're a bit tired she'll do things for you without being asked and she looks after that invalid sister and makes toys for the Children's Hospital in her spare time. So you see it's a pity Mrs. Corner goes to church."

"Perhaps it will do her good — in time," suggested Nell without much conviction.

"That it will not," retorted Nannie. "It runs off her like water off a duck's back. Och well, the work'll not get done with talking. I'd better go and shell the peas, or you'll get none for your dinners. It's beneath her to shell peas. Last time Mr. Gray brought in peas she threw the lot into the pig's pail — that's the sort of Christian she is."

CHAPTER
EIGHTEEN

1

Two days later Dennis received an answer to his important letter. It was a most satisfactory answer. Mrs. Weatherby was delighted to hear about Nell and was sure she was the right one for Den — she had absolute confidence in her son's judgment. All she wanted now was to see Den's Nell and make friends with her.

Mrs. Weatherby was not really very much surprised at Den's news for she had had a feeling that there was "something in the wind." The odd thing was that she had met some people at the Newtons' dinner-party — Sir Andrew and Lady Findlater — and they had been talking about Westkirk and the Ayrton family. They had mentioned Nell Ayrton, saying she was a great friend of their daughter's and a most delightful creature . . . and Lady Findlater had added that she could not think why Nell had never married. Naturally Mrs. Weatherby was wildly interested but she had been careful not to give anything away.

Certainly Den must stay on at Amberwell (continued Mrs. Weatherby). He must stay and help Nell in her troubles. He must stay as long as he could. It was a pity Nell looked upon him as a brother, but he must be patient and give her time. There were different ways of falling in love. To some people it came like a thunderbolt and to others it came gradually and almost imperceptibly. In Mrs. Weatherby's opinion the latter was the better and more lasting. Mrs. Weatherby thought Den was unduly fearful of putting his fate to the touch (it was difficult to believe that any girl would not love her son); she suggested that Den might ask Nell to come and stay at the new house for a little holiday. The house was now in good order and it would be lovely to have her. Perhaps here, on his own ground, Den would be able to summon up his courage. Mrs. Weatherby added that she would help all she could — he knew that, didn't he?

Dennis was relieved beyond words at his mother's reaction; his first thought was that the plan proposed by her was excellent. On second thoughts however he realised that it was impossible for Nell to leave Amberwell while Mrs. Duff was away. Nell was the hub upon which Amberwell revolved; she planned and directed everything and did a good deal of work with her own hands as well. Perhaps when Mrs. Duff returned from hospital he might be able to carry out his mother's idea, but meantime it was better not to mention it.

They were busy at Amberwell these days. Mrs. Corner did nothing but cook — and exude disapproval — and the rest of the work which should have been done by her was shared out between the other members of the household. In addition to these duties there was the duty of visiting Mrs. Duff and taking her eggs or flowers from the garden. Nell usually went herself but one day, when Nell could not go, Dennis took Nannie.

Dennis had not seen Mrs. Duff since the first day, when she had looked so frail and ill, and he was amazed at the improvement in her appearance. She was sitting up in bed and received her visitors cheerfully.

"Kate, you're looking fine!" exclaimed Nannie in delight.

"I'm feeling fine," replied Mrs. Duff smiling. "There's nothing the matter with me except my arm. If it wasn't for my arm, I could come home to Amberwell to-morrow."

"Could you not come?" asked Nannie eagerly.

"I'd be useless," said Mrs. Duff, shaking her head.

"But there'd be no need for you to do a hand's turn, with me and Winnie and Jean to do it for you! Och, Kate, come home for goodness' sake! I'm just about through with that Mrs. Corner."

Dennis felt it was time to chip in to the conversation; he pointed out that the doctor must be consulted — and Nell also — but Nannie was so excited at the prospect of Kate Duff's return to Amberwell that she refused to listen.

"We'll have you back in no time," declared Nannie. "It's just grand . . . I can hardly believe it. When I saw you taken away from the door in the ambulance I thought you'd be coming home feet first."

Mrs. Duff was in no way upset by this grim statement. She smiled complacently and replied that it took more than a wee tumble down the stairs to kill a Duff.

232

Mrs. Weatherby had advised Dennis to be patient, and he had been very patient indeed, but now his patience was beginning to wear thin. He had thought he was deeply in love with Nell before, but now he was very much more deeply in love with her. He had been quite happy at Amberwell, playing brother to Nell, but now he was no longer happy. The "Darby and Joan" evenings became a torture. Dennis was almost angry with Nell for sitting there so peacefully mending socks and chatting over the events of the day; talking about how lovely it would be when Mrs. Corner left and took her disagreeable atmosphere with her; how more than lovely it would be to have dear Duffy home again!

Dennis listened and fidgeted. He wondered what would happen if he took the plunge. What would Nell do — and say — if he suddenly broke into the conversation and told her that he loved her and wanted to marry her?

"You've been awfully good to me," said Nell, smiling at him in her usual friendly fashion. "I don't know what I should have done without you. If Roger had been here, himself, he couldn't have been kinder or more helpful."

This was the last straw. Dennis could not bear it a moment longer. He made some feeble excuse and went out into the garden.

It was a bright moonlit night, mild and pleasant, but Dennis was not in the mood to enjoy the beauties of nature. He wandered along the terrace and down the steps which led to the mermaid-fountain. I shall go home, thought Dennis. I shall wait until Monday when "dear Duffy" comes back to Amberwell and then I shall go. It's no use staying here — none whatever. Perhaps when I've gone she'll miss me — or perhaps not. She wouldn't miss me a bit if Roger were here to lock up the house at night and talk to the plumbers.

Dennis was making for the seat at the other side of the fountain, but as he approached he noticed that somebody was sitting there. It was Georgina Glassford.

"What a lovely night!" said Miss Glassford, rising and coming to meet him.

"Yes, isn't it?" agreed Dennis miserably.

Dennis had not seen much of Miss Glassford, for she had been away during the holidays and had just returned. He had been introduced to her at lunch, but had taken little interest in her; he had eyes for one person and one person only.

"Do come and sit down for a minute if you aren't too busy," said Miss Glassford.

Dennis sat down beside her on the seat. He could hardly say he was busy and he was so wretched that he did not care what he did.

"Did you hear the owl hooting?" asked Miss Glassford.

"No," replied Dennis.

"It's an eerie sound, isn't it? Some people are afraid of owls but I like them. Look, there he is, sitting up in that tree. Can you see him, Commander Weatherby?"

"Oh yes, I see him," replied Dennis a trifle more cheerfully. "He's a big chap, isn't he?"

234

The creature, disturbed by their voices, flew soundlessly across the garden and disappeared.

"How lovely!" exclaimed Miss Glassford rapturously.

There was a short silence and then Miss Glassford sighed. "Amberwell isn't a bit the same without Mrs. Duff, is it?"

"No, it certainly isn't."

"I wish Nell had written and told me about her accident. I could easily have come back and helped in the house — I'm very good at cooking — but of course I had no idea that anything had happened. I really feel very distressed about it," added Miss Glassford earnestly.

It was decent of her, thought Dennis. Aloud he said, "I expect Nell thought you needed a holiday."

"Well, it wasn't exactly a holiday. The fact is I'm very keen on running — perhaps Nell told you — and I've been staying with a friend and training seriously. I have a feeling that I've improved my time."

"How interesting!" said Dennis politely.

"Are you really interested?" asked Miss Glassford eagerly.

"Yes, of course," replied Dennis. What else could he say?

"That's splendid! I just hoped when I saw you at lunch that you might be interested, and I wondered if you would help me."

"Help you?"

"I expect you know how to use a stop-watch, don't you?"

"Yes," said Dennis reluctantly. "I've timed people at sports — and — and that sort of thing."

"That's splendid! It's most awfully kind of you, Commander Weatherby. I was almost afraid to ask you — but it really is so important to know what progress I'm making. I've got a mile marked out on the bowling-green. When would it suit you to come?"

Dennis had not said he would time Miss Glassford's mile but apparently she thought he had. He tried to wriggle free. "But look here," he said. "I've only done it for sports — and it was ages ago. I mean I wouldn't like to undertake it in case I made a mistake."

She smiled. "Oh, don't worry about that. I can easily show you how to do it — and we can have a few trials first. Would to-morrow morning suit you?"

"Not to-morrow. I promised Nell I would take Nannie over to the hospital to see Mrs. Duff."

"Oh, but I meant early — before breakfast — the children start their lessons at half-past nine."

"What about after tea?"

"The mornings are best."

Dennis was silent.

"You don't mind getting up early, do you?" asked Miss Glassford in persuasive tones. "It's such a beautiful time of day; so new and fresh and — and beautiful. I'm sure if you did it once you would want to do it again."

Dennis was sure he would not. He had "got up early" so often that the newness and freshness had worn off. He did not mind it particularly if he had to do it in the course of duty, but he was extremely

236

reluctant to do it when he was on leave . . . and Miss Glassford's last sentence held a threat that it would not be for one morning only."

"I'm always sleepy in the morning," said Dennis frankly. "I mean it would be no use depending upon me; I might say I would meet you at the bowling-green at seven — or whatever time you like — and not be there."

"Seven will be splendid," declared Miss Glassford. "It's very, very kind of you, Commander Weatherby. I'll waken you at half-past six." She rose as she spoke and flitted away to bed.

Dennis felt somewhat dazed. He had intended to say no, but Miss Glassford seemed to think he had said yes.

When Dennis went back to the morning-room he found that Nell had put away her mending-basket and gone upstairs to bed, so he locked the doors and snibbed the windows as usual. He felt even more miserable than before. Why had Nell gone to bed so early? It was only just after half-past nine. Why had she gone without saying good night to him?

As he went upstairs to his room he noticed a streak of light under Nell's door and hesitated for a few moments wondering whether he should tap on the door and say "Good night." Roger and Tom would have done so — in fact they would probably have gone in for their usual good night kiss! It seemed unfair to Dennis that he should have all the disadvantages of a brother but none of the advantages. The thought annoyed him and he decided he did not want to tap and say, "Good night."

Of course he was much too miserable to sleep, so when he had got into bed he proceeded to write to his mother, and it was just the sort of letter one would have expected a very miserable young man to write to a fond and understanding mother. This letter was quite different from his last, there was no carefulness about it, the pen flew over the paper almost of its own accord. When at last it was finished Dennis sealed it up and stamped it, and creeping down the stairs laid it on the hall-table with several other letters for the postman to collect in the morning when he delivered the Amberwell mail.

It was now nearly midnight and Dennis was surprised to see that there was still a thin streak of light beneath Nell's bedroom door. She must have gone to sleep with her light on, but it was far too late to tap. He got into bed and went off to sleep almost immediately.

3

Dennis was awakened by a loud and peremptory knocking on his door. It seemed to him that he had scarcely been asleep for ten minutes, but the room was bright with daylight so obviously it was morning. His first thought was that it was Nell; she had had bad news about Mrs. Duff — Mrs. Duff had had a relapse and the hospital had phoned for them!

"Come in!" shouted Dennis, bouncing up in bed.

The door opened and Miss Glassford appeared. "Oh, you're awake!" she exclaimed. "That's splendid! It's half-past six, Commander Weatherby."

238

"Half-past six!" echoed Dennis in amazement.

"It's a lovely morning," she told him. "Not sunny, of course, but — but it isn't raining. I'll wait for you in the hall. Don't bother to shave."

Dennis had forgotten all about Miss Glassford. "I say, look here —" he began.

"Don't bother to shave," repeated Miss Glassford — and was gone.

"Oh hell!" said Dennis aloud. "I suppose I'll have to."

He got up and shaved (he was damned if he was going out without shaving), and throwing on some clothes he went downstairs. Miss Glassford was waiting for him in the hall as she had promised. She was arrayed in her running-gear and a sweater and she looked fresh and eager — but this early morning freshness did not please Dennis, in fact it added to his annoyance. If one feels sleepy and jaded and tousled (having risen and dressed in a hurry) the sight of a radiant young woman with shining locks and sparkling eyes is not particularly pleasant.

They walked across the lawn together and through the orchard to the bowling-green, and as they went Miss Glassford prattled cheerfully about the beautiful freshness of the early morning and added that in her opinion people who lazed in bed until breakfast-time missed the best part of the day. She appeared not to notice the grumpiness of her companion.

When they reached the bowling-green she stooped and felt the grass.

"It's a little wet," she said, frowning.

"It often is in the early morning," Dennis pointed out.

"Oh well, never mind. I didn't intend to do the Real Test to-day."

"I thought that was the whole idea."

"No, I just want you to time some practice runs. I'll show you exactly what to do. Here's the stop-watch; this is how you set it —"

"I know how to set it," said Dennis, taking it out of her hand.

"But I thought you said —"

"I said I had done it before."

Miss Glassford looked at him doubtfully. "Yes, but I want an accurate timing. It's so important — but don't worry, you'll soon learn," she added kindly.

Dennis was obliged to admit that the young woman knew what she was doing: the course — or track — or whatever you liked to call it — was carefully laid out and clearly marked and she explained her plans with admirable lucidity. She then removed her sweater and began to prance up and down. She performed this exercise thoroughly and seriously, which made it rather comic. Dennis saw it was comic but did not feel inclined to smile.

"Now we're ready," declared Miss Glassford. "You must stand here, Commander Weatherby. Don't forget to wind the stop-watch."

"I've wound it," said Dennis.

They did some tests — practice ones of course — and Dennis timed them. He had not seen Miss Glassford running before and, like Roger, he was impressed by the apparently effortless speed of Atalanta, but unlike Roger it gave him no pleasure at all. I shan't do this again, thought Dennis, as he watched the long legs flying over the ground. I don't care what she says. I won't be dragged out again. She can get somebody else to time her blue-pencil mile. I'll be rude if necessary.

Having made this desperate decision Dennis felt more amiable (as this was the last time he might as well be decent and do his best for her) so he did his best and was commended for his efficiency.

"You're splendid," declared Miss Glassford a trifle breathlessly. "You've been a tremendous help. It's most awfully good of you."

"Not at all."

"Oh yes, it is," said Miss Glassford, nodding. "It's very kind indeed — but you've enjoyed it, haven't you, Dennis?"

"Er — well —"

"You don't mind me calling you Dennis, do you?"

"No, of course not," said Dennis without enthusiasm.

"I mean when people work together like this it forms a sort of bond between them, doesn't it?"

"Yes," said Dennis without conviction.

"And you'll call me Georgina, won't you?"

"Er — yes — if you want me to," said Dennis reluctantly.

The practice was over now so they walked back to the house together. Georgina, despite her activities, was still full of vim; when they reached the terrace she ran up the steps two at a time and waited for her companion at the top.

"Hurry up, Dennis!" she cried, waving her hand and smiling radiantly . . . but Dennis had had enough of Georgina. He decided to go round the house and enter by the back-door and so escape from her clutches — he waved to her in a perfunctory manner and walked away.

4

The back-door stood open and, as Dennis approached, Nell came out with a bucket in her hand and emptied it into the ash-bin.

"Hallo Nell, what are you doing?" asked Dennis in surprise.

"Cleaning out the stove," replied Nell shortly.

"But I thought Mrs. Corner did that."

"She isn't well."

Nell turned as she spoke and went into the kitchen.

Dennis followed her. "I wish you'd told me. I'd have done it for you. Here, give me that pail!"

"It's done. There's no need for you to bother."

There was something rather queer about Nell this morning. Dennis had never seen her like this before. He stood and watched while she went into the scullery and returned with a bowl of eggs. She did not speak.

"I say, is something the matter?" he inquired anxiously.

"I've told you. Mrs. Corner isn't well."

"But I mean — the matter with you?" Dennis explained. "You seem — a bit — worried."

242

"I'm not in the least worried." She put the bowl of eggs on the table and took a large frying-pan out of the cupboard in the corner.

"Let me help," said Dennis eagerly. "I'm awfully good at bacon and eggs."

"No, thank you. I can do it myself."

"Please let me. I'd like to."

Dennis tried to take the frying-pan from her hand but she clung to it like a limpet, so that without using brute force he could not wrest it from her grasp. There *was* something the matter, thought Dennis in alarm. There was something very wrong indeed. He abandoned the struggle for the frying-pan and, glancing at Nell's face, saw to his consternation that her eyes were brimming with tears.

"Nell, darling!" he cried. "Darling Nell, what is it? Tell me what's the matter — darling, darling Nell!"

The next moment she was in his arms, weeping upon his shoulder and Dennis was kissing the top of her head and patting her and making soothing sounds. The frying-pan clattered on to the floor unnoticed.

"Oh Dennis!" sobbed Nell. "Oh Dennis!"

"Don't cry, dearest love. Don't cry."

"I can't — help it —"

"Tell me what's the matter."

"Nothing," declared Nell, trying to control herself.

"But darling, there must be something. What is it, Nell?"

"Nothing — at least not now. It was just that I thought — but I was silly. Give me your hankie, Dennis."

He gave her his handkerchief and she mopped up her tears. "There, I'm better," she said.

Certainly she looked better — there was even a faint watery smile tilting the corners of her mouth — but he still was not satisfied. He drew her back into his arms and kissed her again. It was not a brotherly sort of kiss but Nell did not seem to object.

"Darling, is it all right?" asked Dennis anxiously. "I mean you *do* love me."

"Of course I love you."

"And you'll — you'll marry me, won't you?"

"Yes, of course," said Nell.

"Darling!" cried Dennis ecstatically. "Darling, beautiful Nell!"

Presently they remembered breakfast. The other members of Amberwell household would be coming downstairs expecting to find breakfast ready — and there would be no breakfast for anybody. Dennis picked up the frying-pan and Nell got out the bacon.

"There's no time for porridge, it will have to be flakes," said Nell.

"Have you made the coffee?" asked Dennis as he laid out the rashers of bacon in the pan.

"No," said Nell. "Oh yes, I have. I'd forgotten. Just see if there's enough water in the kettle for Mother's tea."

"Yes, there's enough."

"Dennis," said Nell in sudden alarm. "You won't want me to leave Amberwell, will you?"

Dennis had thought of this already and had realised that it would be useless to ask Nell to leave Amberwell

244

— at present. He realised also that Nell would be safer and happier carrying out her usual duties at Amberwell while he was away at sea. Later on if he got a post ashore, it would not be so good ... but Dennis was willing to let the future look after itself. "Of course you needn't leave Amberwell," he told her. "You must do just as you like — always."

"That's all right then," said Nell with a sigh of relief.

"Are you feeling quite well now?" asked Dennis in sudden anxiety.

"Of course I'm quite well!"

"You haven't told me what was the matter."

"Just silliness, that's all. Are you going to make the toast or shall I?"

"But you *must* tell me," said Dennis earnestly. "I mean we're going to tell each other everything. Aren't we?"

"You'll think it silly."

"No, I shan't."

"Well, it was just — I mean I thought — I thought you were beginning — to like — Georgina."

"Good lord, whatever made you think that!" exclaimed Dennis in amazement.

"I knew you would think it was silly."

"I don't," declared Dennis hastily. "But honestly —"

"Well, you went out and sat in the garden with her for ages — and you never even said good night to me!"

"But Nell, how could I say good night to you when you had gone upstairs to bed?"

"You could have — knocked on my door," said Nell, with a little catch in her breath. "You could have — called out to me. I waited — for ages —"

"But Nell —"

"You were sitting in the garden with — with Georgina!"

"But Nell —"

"So of course I thought you were beginning to — to —"

"I simply hate the sight of her," said Dennis fiercely.

"You hate the sight of her?"

"Absolutely."

"But you went out with her again this morning!"

"I know," admitted Dennis ruefully. "I can't think how it happened. She asked me to time her blue-pencil mile, and of course I meant to say no, but she misunderstood me or something, and —"

"Dennis, look out! The milk's boiling over."

"I just couldn't get out of it," said Dennis, shifting the pan. "And then of course the whole thing went out of my head until she knocked me up at half-past six."

"Half-past six!"

"Yes, she came in looking as fresh as a daisy."

"She's very pretty, isn't she?"

"I think she's like a horse," declared Dennis frankly.

Nell had thought this herself so naturally she was delighted to have her opinion confirmed. "Is the bacon nearly ready?" she inquired.

"Not quite. I like it crisp, don't you?"

246

Of course Nell liked it crisp — if Dennis did.

"She's a frightful woman," continued Dennis as he shook the sizzling pan. "She called me Dennis and she asked me to call her Georgina. Isn't it awful?"

"Why is it awful?"

"Because I shan't be able to. What's more I don't want to! That woman is positively — dangerous. I'm not going out with her again."

"Were you frightened of her?"

"Terrified."

"Poor darling Dennis!" said Nell with a little giggle of amusement.

Nell was passing Dennis as she spoke — she was on her way to the electric-toaster — so it was easy for him to waylay her and kiss her again.

"The toast will burn!" said Nell, trying to free herself.

"Let it burn! Who cares? Oh Nell, I do love you so frightfully!"

"Do you really?"

"Yes, I've loved you for three years. I loved you before I even saw you. I fell in love with your voice on the telephone . . . yes, honestly! When did you begin to love me?"

"I don't know, really. It was sort of gradual. It wasn't a bit like people who fall in love — in books. We've been friends for ages, haven't we? It was lovely having you as a friend . . . and then last night when I saw you sitting on the seat with Georgina —"

"But you understand about that now."

Nell drew back a little and looked up at him anxiously. She said, "You know, Dennis, I don't think I'm really in love with you."

"Not in love with me?" asked Dennis, with a sudden cold feeling in his heart.

"I just love you — frightfully. Does it matter?"

The cold feeling vanished. "Not a bit," declared Dennis with conviction. "It's perfect — absolutely perfect. Nothing could be better."

The toast was burning by this time but neither of them noticed. They noticed nothing until the door burst open and Nannie rushed in to find the kitchen full of acrid smoke and the cooks embracing fondly.

"I knew it!" cried Nannie joyfully, as she ran to turn off the toaster. "I knew it all along. I said to Kate Duff — it was the night before her accident — mark my words, I said, there'll be another marriage at Amberwell before we're much older!"

At that moment Winnie and Jean arrived and Stephen came in, looking for his breakfast; he was followed by Mrs. Ayrton. After that there was pandemonium in the kitchen, with everybody talking at once and exclaiming rapturously, while Nannie rushed hither and thither trying to save the food from being burnt to cinders.

Oddly enough nobody was surprised and there was no need to explain what had happened. Even Mrs. Ayrton, usually so vague, seemed to have expected this *dénouement*.

"You'll be married at St Stephen's, of course," said Mrs. Ayrton. "I must look out the veil. Connie was the

248

last to wear it; I think I must have put it in one of those boxes in the attic."

"You're pleased, Mother?" asked Nell.

"Yes, of course, dear," replied Mrs. Ayrton. "I thought Dennis was nice the first time I saw him. Of course I am pleased."

Georgina was the last member of the household to arrive upon the scene. She had changed out of her running-gear into slacks and a lemon pullover; she stood at the door gazing round in bewilderment.

"Aunt Nell is going to marry Uncle Dennis!" cried Stephen excitedly. "Then he'll be a real uncle — not just a pretend. Isn't it lovely, Miss Glassford? Isn't it *lovely?*"

"Yes, it's splendid," said Georgina in a tepid sort of voice.

Dennis went over and shook her by the hand. "Thank you very much, Georgina," said Dennis cordially.

"What for?" asked Georgina in surprised accents.

CHAPTER
NINETEEN

1

When breakfast was over and the excitement had died down a little, Dennis walked down to Westkirk to do the shopping and to send a telegram to his mother. The telegram was necessary because the new house was not yet on the telephone and the miserable letter was in the post. Dennis was ashamed of that letter and wished he had not written it. He tried to remember exactly what he had written, but without much success. He had written so much and so quickly and had sealed it up so hastily that he had not even read it over . . . and so many strange and important things had happened this morning that he could hardly believe it was less than twelve hours since he had sat up in bed and written that miserable wail.

It was a little difficult to decide what to say in the telegram. Dennis would have liked to let himself go and indulge in ecstasies, but he was far too shy to hand a message of this nature to the girl behind the counter in the post office, so he was obliged to control himself and make it cryptic. He spoilt several forms before he could find a satisfactory way of conveying the marvellous news to his mother.

YOU WERE RIGHT THE SKY IS CLOUDLESS PLEASE
IGNORE LETTER LOVE FROM DEN.

Yes, that would do, thought Dennis. She would
understand at once, but nobody else would have a clue
as to what it meant. (The fact that the weather was
deteriorating rapidly and it had actually begun to rain
was neither here nor there.) Dennis would have liked to
say, *please burn letter unread*, but he had too much
sense. Mrs. Weatherby was the soul of honour — as her
son very well knew — and if asked to burn the letter
unread she would do so, but being human she would
wonder what was in it and would imagine all sorts of
curious things.

Dennis handed in his telegram with a nonchalant air
and walked back to Amberwell in the rain — basking in
his own private sunshine.

The telegram arrived first of course and its recipient
had no difficulty in decoding it. She was full of joy at
the news, for the most important thing in the world to
Mrs. Weatherby was Den's happiness. She received the
letter next morning and (not having been told to burn
it unread, but merely to ignore it) she opened it with a
good deal of interest. It was a very long letter; there
were pages and pages of it. Mrs. Weatherby read it with
mixed emotions. In fact, if the truth be told, with a
mixture of tears and smiles; tears because it was a very
miserable letter and it was distressing to think that Den
had been so unhappy, smiles because the unhappiness
was past and the skies were cloudless. Somehow the
letter reminded Mrs. Weatherby of the first letter she

251

had ever received from Den when he had gone to his Prep. School. He had written to tell her that he *couldent bare it* and would she come and fetch him home to-morrow *becaus onnestly he couldent bare it.* Yes, it was very much the same sort of letter, thought Mrs. Weatherby as she wiped away her tears.

She had been told to ignore the letter which probably meant she was to destroy it (yes, she supposed she must) but she would keep it for a day or two because it was so very precious. It was precious because Den had turned to her in his trouble and opened his heart; precious because he would never write to her in quite the same way again. No, never, thought Mrs. Weatherby, never in quite the same way again . . . and then she sighed and put the letter in the fire and watched it burn . . . for of course that was what Den had wanted.

2

When Dennis returned from his expedition to Westkirk he found his future mother-in-law sitting in the morning-room and went in to chat to her. Mrs. Ayrton was always at her best with Dennis for he was kind and patient and took the trouble to speak to her slowly.

"Come in, Dennis," said Mrs. Ayrton. "We must make plans. It would be nice to have a Christmas Wedding. Connie and Gerald were married at Christmas-Time and the church was so pretty, all decorated with holly and white chrysanthemums."

252

"Yes," said Dennis. He only had a fortnight more leave before his posting to his new ship, which was in the Mediterranean, so he was neither surprised nor disappointed to hear that the wedding was to be at Christmas. What was three months when he had waited three years for his Nell?

"The Admiral is sure to give you leave at Christmas, isn't he?" continued Mrs. Ayrton, nodding complacently. "Everybody gets leave at Christmas."

Dennis did not contradict her nor point out that if "everybody" got leave at Christmas the Royal Navy would cease to function — he was too polite — he merely said that if the wedding was to take place at Christmas he would be there and all the Admirals in the Royal Navy would not prevent him.

"White satin and lace," murmured Mrs. Ayrton happily. "You will be in uniform of course, and the children in white, with gold sashes. We must keep it all white and gold. I wonder how many bridesmaids Nell will want."

Nell came in at that moment so her mother was able to ask her this important question. "There will be five children, of course," said Mrs. Ayrton. "Stephen and Emmie and Connie's three — but you will want some grown-up bridesmaids, won't you? I thought of Mary Findlater and Daphne Clayton."

"Oh, there won't be time," said Nell. "Besides we don't want a lot of fuss. I've just been telephoning to Roger."

"But Roger is in Germany!" exclaimed Mrs. Ayrton in surprise.

Nell laughed. "I know — but I just had to talk to him. I got through quite easily and his voice was perfectly clear. He didn't seem a bit surprised and he's coming over next week."

"Next week!" cried Dennis. "That's good. I shall see him before I go."

"He's coming over for the wedding," explained Nell.

"You mean — next week?" asked Dennis incredulously.

"Yes, it would be such a pity if Roger couldn't be here to give me away. He's the right person, isn't he? He can fly over on Monday and we can be married on Wednesday. Your mother will be able to come, won't she, Dennis?"

"Of course she'll come — any time!" exclaimed Dennis joyfully.

"A Christmas Wedding is so pretty," said Mrs. Ayrton, who had got left far behind. "And I can't think what you mean when you say there won't be time. We shall have three months to arrange everything and get your trousseau."

"Christmas? Oh no," said Nell. "There's no object in waiting until Christmas — unless Dennis would rather."

"No," cried Dennis. "No, please! I mean Wednesday is the day."

Nell smiled at him. She said, "We don't want a big party and a lot of fuss, do we?"

"The quieter the better!"

"That's what I think. Duffy will be here of course — she's coming home on Monday — so that will be all right."

"But Nell — your dress!" cried Mrs. Ayrton in dismay. "Your trousseau!"

"I don't want all that," said Nell earnestly. "I don't want to dress up and have a big party. I just want it to be quiet and peaceful so that we can think about what it really means."

Dennis nodded.

"I'm sorry you're disappointed, Mother," continued Nell. "I know you would like me to have a big wedding — like Connie's — with white satin and orange blossoms and all the rest of it, but I just couldn't bear it."

"I couldn't either," agreed Dennis. "At least I suppose I could bear it if I had to, but I'd much rather it was quiet and peaceful and — and solemn."

"Oh Dennis, you understand!"

Of course Dennis understood. He hoped and prayed he would always be able to understand Nell's feelings so quickly and easily.

"So we'll fix it for Wednesday," said Nell. "Then we shall have nearly a week before Dennis has to join his ship."

"We shall have a full week if I fly. Where shall we go for our honeymoon? Paris?"

"Oh, but I couldn't leave Amberwell —"

"You will leave Amberwell, my girl," said Dennis firmly. "Amberwell will have to look after itself for a week."

"But Dennis —"

"Amberwell can look after itself for a week."

Nell smiled. She said, "I suppose it can. Duffy will be here — and I've never been to Paris."

3

The wedding was to be quiet, but there was no reason why it should be dull. Nell's friends and relations decided that it should not be dull and acted accordingly. Mrs. Ayrton was incapable of organising anything and Nell seemed to be wandering in a dream, so Poppet Lambert was forced to take things into her own hands; she called a committee meeting consisting of Anne and Mary and Nannie to make the necessary arrangements. The meeting took place in the kitchen at Amberwell on Friday afternoon. Mrs. Corner always rested in the afternoon so they were free from interruption.

Although she was not a relation (unless you could count your son's sister-in-law a relation) Poppet Lambert had always been particularly fond of Nell. She explained this to the committee and the committee agreed unanimously that Mrs. Lambert was the right person to take charge and organise the affair. It was not easy to organise, for the bride and bridegroom took no interest in it. They merely said they intended to be married in St. Stephen's at half-past eleven on Wednesday morning so that they would have time to snatch a hasty lunch before driving to Renfrew to catch the London plane. When asked what their guests were supposed to do — whether to snatch hasty lunches or be sustained with wedding-cake — they replied that they did not want any guests.

The committee meeting opened with a discussion upon this matter.

"It's all very well for them to say that they don't want any guests," Anne declared. "But we can't send people home without giving them lunch. Roger wouldn't like it — I mean it's so inhospitable. We really must do something about it. Even if we don't have any outside guests there will be all of us and Connie and Gerald and their three children and there will be Mrs. Weatherby and Roger and the Maddons and Mr. Orme. Mr. Dalgleish, the lawyer, is coming and — and —" she paused and looked at Nannie in despair.

"We'll manage," said Nannie courageously. "I was thinking we'd keep Mrs. Corner till after the wedding — and of course Kate Duff will be here. She'll not be able to do much with her arm — but she'll be here anyway."

"Good idea," nodded the chairwoman.

"Cold chicken and ham, I was thinking," continued Nannie. "And jellies and ice-cream. It'll need to be all cold because Kate and I will be at the wedding and Mrs. Corner'll get in a rampage if there's nobody to help her. Maybe we could manage hot soup to start with, but everything else will need to be cold."

The committee saw the point and agreed upon the menu for lunch.

"There's no champagne in the cellar," said Nannie. "We used the last two bottles when the boys came home on leave."

"Johnnie can see to that," said Johnnie's wife, making a note of it. "He's going to Glasgow on Monday and he'll enjoy seeing his wine merchant and having a little chat about it. He can get a small wedding-cake as well."

"Flowers for the church?" asked Mary.

"I was thinking about that," said Anne. "I could do them if you like — and Mr. Gray would help. As a matter of fact I could ask Arnold too; he said he would do anything we wanted."

The committee agreed. It was a very agreeable committee.

"Are the children to be bridesmaids?" asked Nannie.

"No," said the chairwoman firmly. "We haven't time to bother with the children; they would just be a nuisance. One bridesmaid will be enough; it had better be you, Mary."

"Yes, you're the right person," nodded Anne.

"Nell hasn't asked me —"

"Nell isn't thinking about anything or anybody except that man. She isn't even thinking of what she's going to wear," declared Poppet Lambert.

"I know," agreed Anne. "I asked her about it and she said it didn't matter, but I think she means to wear that frock she got for the Claytons' garden-party and it doesn't suit her a bit. I do wish you could persuade her —"

"Don't worry, Anne. I'm taking her to Glasgow to-morrow to choose a new frock. She doesn't know yet, but that's what I'm doing."

"I doubt if she'll go," said Nannie.

"She'll go — if I have to bind her with ropes first," said the chairwoman defiantly.

The committee giggled.

"You must come with us, Mary."

"Me?"

"Yes. We can choose yours as well. Johnnie is giving it to you."

"Oh no! I mean it's frightfully kind of him, but —"

"It's fixed," declared the chairwoman. "Johnnie said he wanted to give it to you, and it will hurt his feelings if you refuse. You don't want to hurt Johnnie's feelings, do you?"

The committee settled these matters and others of less importance without any trouble at all, and the proceedings terminated with cups of tea brewed by Nannie and pieces of bread and butter and strawberry jam.

"If Kate had been here you'd have got scones and cake," said Nannie apologetically. "But that woman's scones are not worth eating —"

"Duffy will be home on Monday," Anne reminded her.

"Thanks be!" exclaimed Nannie. "The house will be different again once that woman's gone."

They had all heard about Mrs. Corner's delinquencies and were anxious to hear more, for if you did not have to bear with Mrs. Corner yourself her delinquencies were amusing.

"Tell us the latest, Nannie," said Mrs. Lambert, putting both her elbows upon the kitchen table and contriving to look elegant even in this inelegant attitude.

"Well now," said Nannie, nothing loath. "Well now, it was just to-day at dinner-time and she was holding forth about that husband of hers (What a time the poor unfortunate creature must have had! Small wonder he died young!) and she said, 'Corner was a great one for the girls.' Quite pleased about it she was," declared Nannie. "You'd wonder, wouldn't you? If I'd ever got married — which I could have if I'd wanted — I'd have seen to it that my man didn't look at anybody else."

"Quite right too," put in Mrs. Lambert approvingly.

"Well," said Nannie. "Well, this is what she told me . . ."

But what Mrs. Corner had divulged they never knew, for at this very moment, when Nannie's audience was anticipating a juicy piece of gossip, heavy footsteps were heard approaching along the passage outside the kitchen door.

"That's her!" exclaimed Nannie in alarm.

The party broke up immediately. Three of its members fled through the back-door and Nannie was left to face the gorgon alone.

4

Poppet got her way as usual and the expedition to Glasgow took place the following day; fortunately without the need for ropes but not without a great deal of persuasion. Frocks and hats and various other garments were chosen for the bride and the bridesmaid

— nor did Poppet forget to choose a fascinating outfit for herself — and on their return the car was so full of cardboard boxes that there was scarcely room for the passengers.

In Nell's opinion the expedition was a waste of time, for she had planned to pack a picnic lunch for herself and Dennis and to spend the day in his company, but she would not have been human if she had not been pleased and even a little excited by the contents of the cardboard boxes.

CHAPTER
TWENTY

1

Roger arrived at Amberwell on Monday in time for lunch. He had been told it was to be a very quiet wedding — and no fuss — so he was surprised to find the house in a state of upheaval. The big drawing-room was being prepared and the dining-room table had been lengthened. He was still more surprised when, on going into the pantry to look for Nannie, he discovered Mary Findlater cleaning the silver.

"Good heavens, what's happening?" exclaimed Roger.

"Oh, hallo Roger! We're just getting things ready," said Mary cheerfully as she laid down a glistening spoon and started to work upon a dull one.

"Where's Nell?"

"Trailing round the garden with Dennis, I expect. They're both quite mad . . . but Poppet is taking charge so everything will be all right. There's no need to worry."

"I thought it was to be quiet!"

"Yes, but you can't send people away hungry, can you? The bride and bridegroom may not want any food but other people will . . ." and she proceeded to give Roger an account of all that had been done and was being done by the wedding-committee, pointing out that they were really doing it on his behalf and for the honour of Amberwell.

"Yes, of course," agreed Roger. "It's awfully good of you to bother. Just tell me what I can do to help."

"Ask Poppet. She'll tell you," replied Mary.

Poppet was doing her best to organise the household but in spite of her efforts it was rather a muddle for there was so little time and Nell seemed incapable of putting her mind to anything practical. This was annoying, but Poppet found Marion even more annoying because she insisted on interfering. She was completely bewildered by the fuss and went about the house getting in everybody's way and declaring that they could not have the wedding on Wednesday.

"Christmas would be *so* much better," said Mrs. Ayrton in vexation. "I don't know why Nell is so stubborn about it. Connie was married at Christmas-Time and it was such a beautiful wedding. Everybody said so."

Poppet was sick and tired of hearing about Connie's beautiful wedding. It was Gerald's wedding too, of course, but Marion seemed to have forgotten that.

"What are you going to wear, Marion?" Poppet inquired.

"Oh dear, I don't know. I suppose I shall have to order a new dress."

"There isn't time. The wedding is the day after to-morrow. What have you got that you can wear?"

"Nothing!" exclaimed Mrs. Ayrton helplessly.

This meant another job for Poppet. She was forced to delve into Marion's wardrobe and find something fit for her to wear.

It was all the more difficult because Poppet was having guests at Merlewood. Gerald and Connie and the three children were all coming to the wedding and were staying two nights ... and although Poppet adored her son and was reasonably fond of her daughter-in-law she could have done without the company of her grandchildren very easily.

Unfortunately Connie had got hold of a book upon Child Psychology and had studied it with care. The book said that children should be allowed to express their ego; they should never be thwarted, never scolded and of course never punished. From their earliest days the Lambert children had been brought up in accordance with the book and as they were quite intelligent enough to realise that they could do exactly as they pleased without reproof they took full advantage of their licence.

Most of their friends and acquaintances were of the opinion that the Lambert children were intolerable little nuisances but their parents doted upon them and had no eyes nor ears for anybody else.

Poppet was not a child-lover at the best of times. She liked to be in the limelight herself. She liked to talk, not to listen to the inane chatter of the young. She hated her conversation to be interrupted. Poppet's house was beautiful and peaceful and ran on oiled wheels — but when Gerry and Joan and little Marion were there it was anything but peaceful. They were noisy and argumentative and took pleasure in practical jokes of a very annoying character . . . and they were so careless and untidy that their belongings were scattered about in every room.

The young Lamberts were not welcome visitors at Merlewood.

2

Luckily for all concerned Mrs. Duff returned to Amberwell on Monday and although she was unable to do much with her arm — as Nannie had foretold — she was able to use her head to good purpose. Her presence had a steadying effect upon the household. Even Mrs. Corner (who had got into a rampage at the sight of six large chickens and one enormous ham which she was expected to cook in preparation for Wednesday's luncheon) was subdued by the presence of Mrs. Duff. Duffy could be dignified when she chose and she had decided to be very dignified indeed in her behaviour to Mrs. Corner.

Mrs. Duff arrived at Amberwell in time for tea and began her campaign by settling herself firmly in her usual chair at the head of the kitchen table (which Mrs. Corner had occupied in her absence) and inviting Mrs. Corner to be seated upon her right as was due to an honoured guest. Nannie took the vacant seat and awaited developments. She had not long to wait.

"I hope you've found things comfortable here, Mrs. Corner," said Mrs. Duff in her best party manner. "I left in a hurry so maybe things were not just as neat and tidy as they might have been."

"Since you ask me they was not," declared Mrs. Corner.

"But they're worse now," said Mrs. Duff blandly. "I've never seen the kitchen in such a mess in all my life."

"I've been accustomed to a kitching-maid —"

"Me, too, Mrs. Corner. There were three of us in the kitchen at one time — before the war, that was — but I'm not sure we were any happier nor the kitchen better kept." She looked round at the clutter and added, "I've always been used to having things nice. That's the truth of it."

Mrs. Corner had become very red in the face. "I've been accustomed to the very best," she declared. "Nobody 'asn't 'ad better places than me. I was with Lady Seven for eighteen munce as cook-'ousekeeper with all the ord'ring — *and* the keys of the staw-cupboard. I 'ad a kitching-maid an' a woman for the rough — never 'ad to soil me 'ands! I wouldn't never 'ave come if I'd known Miss Hayrton would ask me peel pertaters! Lady Seven was a reel lady; — she 'ad two cars an' a stable with an 'orse in it for 'unting — very keen on 'unting she was. There was a butler — an' everything regardless."

"Why did you leave?" inquired Mrs. Duff with interest.

(Goodness! thought Nannie. Why did I never ask her that?)

266

It was obvious that Mrs. Corner did not like the question. She hesitated and then said, "I wanted a change. Oh, Lady Seven went down to me on 'er bended knee in a manner of speaking — but I wanted a change."

"Fancy that!" said Mrs. Duff in surprise. "If I'd got a place like that I'd have stayed on. Not that any place could be better than Amberwell nor any lady nicer to work for than Miss Ayrton."

"You 'aven't tried."

"I wouldn't leave Amberwell for anything."

"Not if you was offered a job at Buckingham Pallis, I s'pose," said Mrs. Corner with a nasty little laugh.

"I never was," admitted Mrs. Duff. "I was offered a job at Balmoral Castle, but I refused it."

Nannie gazed at her old friend with admiration. This was carrying the war into the enemy's country with a vengeance. It was perfectly true, of course. Kate Duff's cousin was one of the staff at Balmoral, and some years ago she had written to Kate asking if she would like her name put forward for a vacancy in the kitchen. Kate had not considered it for a moment; she had merely said that nothing would induce her to leave Amberwell, and that anyway she would rather be a big fish in a wee pond than a wee fish in a big one. It had seemed so unimportant at the time that Nannie had forgotten all about it. How lucky that Kate had remembered it! How clever of Kate to remember it just at the right moment and to mention it with a casual air, as if it were the most natural thing in the world to be offered a post in a royal residence — and to refuse it.

Mrs. Corner would have disbelieved the statement if she could, but she could not disbelieve it; nobody could be in Mrs. Duff's company for ten minutes without realising that here was a woman who scorned untruth.

Mrs. Corner was forced to believe it. She opened her mouth but no sound emerged, and it seemed to Nannie that her bulky form shrank visibly like a pricked balloon.

"Will you take a wee drop more tea?" asked Mrs. Duff politely. "There's no scones, I see. Maybe I'll manage a little baking to-morrow — though it'll not be very easy with one hand."

"Oh Kate!" exclaimed Nannie. "That'll be grand. I've not tasted a decent scone for weeks!"

Mrs. Corner was too deflated to resent the insult.

CHAPTER
TWENTY-ONE

1

Mrs. Weatherby had suggested that she should travel north on Tuesday, and that she and Den should spend the night at a hotel in Westkirk. (She pointed out that it was unconventional for a bride and bridegroom to spend the night before their wedding under the same roof.) Her suggestion was received with scorn, it was brushed aside as being not worth listening to, and as she was anxious to see as much of Den's future relations as possible she accepted the invitation to stay at Amberwell with a good grace.

She arrived on Tuesday afternoon and Dennis met her at Westkirk Station. He had wanted Nell to come with him, but Nell had a feeling that Mrs. Weatherby would like to be met by Dennis alone and have him to herself for a few minutes before her future daughter-in-law was presented to her.

Waiting in the hall and listening for the car was a nerve-racking experience for Nell. She walked to and fro like a caged tiger; she was almost sick with fright. Supposing Mrs. Weatherby did not like her? Dennis had assured her over and over again that his mother would love her — but would she? Nell felt certain that any mother with a son like Dennis would be very critical indeed of the girl he had chosen to be his wife. Nell knew that Dennis and his mother had been all in all to each other, that their relationship had been perfect, that they were not only mother and son but friends. Supposing Mrs. Weatherby thought her dull and stupid — not nearly good enough for Dennis!

Perhaps after all it would have been better to go to the station. Perhaps Mrs. Weatherby would think it was rude not to go to the station and meet her when she got off the train! But of course it was too late to think of that now.

Nell had already dressed very carefully for the important meeting but now, catching sight of herself in the hall-mirror, she suddenly decided that the frock she had chosen was a mistake. The blue one would be better. She fled upstairs and changed hastily, and was about to comb her disordered hair when she heard the car coming up the drive. Nell dropped the comb as if it were a hot potato and, rushing downstairs, arrived, flushed and breathless, in time to see the front-door open and the visitor being ushered into the hall.

"Nell, here's Mother!" exclaimed Dennis excitedly.

"I've been longing to meet you!" cried Mrs. Weatherby as she swept Nell into a loving embrace. "Ever since Den told me — and I should have known you anywhere from Den's description!"

Somehow Nell felt the same. This tall graceful woman with the friendly eyes did not seem like a stranger to Nell.

"I'm glad," she said simply. Her gladness was not an answer to what Mrs. Weatherby had said, but an expression of her feelings.

They went upstairs together, followed by Dennis with a suitcase in either hand. Mrs. Weatherby's room had been carefully prepared by Nell. It was the one practical duty she had undertaken. She had put out the best linen, polished the furniture with her own hands and filled the book-trough with her favourite books. Other things did not matter but Mrs. Weatherby's comfort was important.

"The house is in rather a muddle," said Nell apologetically. "It's my fault, of course. Mother wanted the wedding to be at Christmas. And it's my fault because I can't think about food and clothes and things like that. I didn't want all this fuss. I thought it would be lovely if Dennis and I could just walk down to the church together in our ordinary clothes, and be married — but they won't let us."

"No, they won't let us," agreed Dennis, putting down the suitcases and loosening the straps. "Apparently you can't be properly married in old clothes — and you must have flowers and fizz and fuss."

"Mr. Orme understood what we wanted, and he agreed —"

"But nobody else," said Dennis regretfully. "Everybody else wanted a beano — so there you are!"

"Well, we know the worst."

"You don't! There are new horrors in preparation."

"New horrors!"

271

"Yes, I heard Mrs. Lambert talking about confetti — and Arnold said something about an old shoe."

"Oh Dennis — no!" cried Nell in dismay.

Mrs. Weatherby could not help laughing. She laughed partly because it was really very funny and partly because she was relieved. To tell the truth Mrs. Weatherby had been nearly as frightened as Nell; she, too, had been "supposing." Of course Den had said there was no need to worry but supposing he was wrong? Supposing her new daughter-in-law did not like her or was the sort of girl she could not love? Supposing she was the sort of girl who would not make Den happy?

When Nell had not been there to meet her at the station Mrs. Weatherby had thought, *supposing she doesn't want to be friendly with me!*

But all these terrifying suppositions had taken flight. They had faded when she saw Nell flushed and breathless running down the stairs to meet her, and had vanished completely when she saw Den and Nell together and heard them discussing the preparations for their wedding. Mrs. Weatherby was now quite certain that everything was going to be all right, quite certain that if she had searched the whole country from Land's End to John o' Groats she could not have found a girl who would suit Den better.

Dennis watched his mother laughing. "It's all very well for you to laugh," he said ruefully. "You aren't being sacrificed to make a Roman holiday. And incidentally it's all your fault."

"My fault!"

"Your fault entirely," declared Dennis. "If it hadn't been for you Nell and I would have taken the plunge on Saturday when the Special Licence arrived and we saw the preparations beginning. I mean we'd just have walked down to the church together in our oldest clothes and got spliced then and there." He grinned and added, "It would have been fun, but we decided we couldn't get spliced without you."

"I'm glad you didn't," said Mrs. Weatherby smiling. "Perhaps it's selfish of me but I can't help feeling glad."

Arriving like this in the middle of a family party was somewhat bewildering for Mrs. Weatherby. When she came down to the big drawing-room it seemed full of people, and although Den had given her a short description of his future in-laws it was difficult to sort them out. Nell's brother was easy; he was tall and fair and extremely handsome and played the host to perfection, but it was some time before she discovered that the dainty, fairylike woman who seemed to be in charge of the proceedings was not her hostess. Den had told her about Stephen of course, but there were five children in the room — some of them rough and noisy — and there was a tall, fair young woman who looked as if she might be Nell's sister but had been introduced as "Mrs. Gerald Lambert." This puzzled Mrs. Weatherby considerably. She felt certain that Den had told her Nell's sister was Mrs. Selby. There were three other girls — none of them the least like Nell — and there were several men. Was the big, hearty, elderly man Nell's father? But what was she thinking of? Nell's father was dead — Den had said so! Altogether Mrs.

Weatherby was so bamboozled that she was glad to be rescued by Nell and told she must have a rest before dinner.

"Roger introduced you to everybody, didn't he?" said Nell as she conducted Mrs. Weatherby to her room.

"Yes, but I'm afraid —"

"Oh, it must be frightfully difficult for you!"

"I'm not very good at remembering people's names when I meet them for the first time."

"Neither am I," admitted Nell smiling. "Their names go in at one ear and out of the other."

"Which was your aunt?" asked Mrs. Weatherby, for having heard so much about the mysterious Aunt Beatrice she was anxious to identify her.

"My aunt? Oh, you mean Aunt Beatrice! We asked her but she didn't come. It was just as well, really, because there was a row and it might have been difficult. You never know with Aunt Beatrice."

"There was a thin man with very white hair —"

"Mr. Dalgleish," nodded Nell. "He's our lawyer. He's staying at the hotel in Westkirk, so he won't be here for dinner. Dinner will be quite peaceful."

"Peaceful?" asked Mrs. Weatherby in surprise.

"Yes, there will be just ourselves. The others will all go home. The Maddons aren't relations — just friends — and Connie and Gerald are staying with Poppet — and Mary as well — and the three children. Anne and Emmie live at the Rectory with Mr. Orme — and Georgina has dinner upstairs."

"Oh, I see," said Mrs. Weatherby untruthfully. The fact was that Nell's explanation — intended to be helpful — had added to Mrs. Weatherby's confusion.

"It must be frightfully difficult for you," repeated Nell sympathetically.

"It is — rather," admitted Mrs. Weatherby.

Nell wished she could stay and chat to Mrs. Weatherby, but Nannie was waiting to try on her frock.

"Nannie will be cross if I don't go," explained Nell. "So I think I had better. Roger and Dennis are going for a walk." She sighed and added, "Goodness, I wish it were all over! If I'd known it was going to be like that —"

"You wouldn't have agreed to marry Den?" suggested his mother.

"Oh well," said Nell, smiling reluctantly. "I expect I would — really — but we could have eloped."

2

Roger had suggested the walk as a means of escaping from the fuss, and Dennis (on finding that Nell had an engagement with Nannie) agreed to accompany him. They set off together directly after tea.

It was one of those still autumn afternoons, mild and misty, with the sun shining from behind a veil of thin white cloud. Coming suddenly from the drawing-room, noisy with chatter, the stillness and peacefulness of the outside world was sublime. The crack of a twig beneath Roger's foot sounded as loud as the report of a rifle. Dennis had expected to talk about plans for the future, but Roger was in no mood for talking so they strode along together in silence.

The leaves were beginning to fall. They fell reluctantly. They hovered in the air and drifted slowly sideways to the damp ground. You would wonder why, having survived days of wind and rain, they should detach themselves now, at this moment of peace. Did they part with the twigs voluntarily? Did they say, "Good-bye, we clung to you when the wind raged — but now our time has come"? Gently and slowly they drifted to the ground, making a carpet of brown and gold upon the grass.

It was not often that Roger was imaginative but this afternoon he was moved to see this gentle fall of leaves symbolic of his relationship with Nell. Together they had enjoyed sunshine and braved tempest but now Nell was gently detaching herself from the tree and drifting to an unknown bourne.

Roger was pleased of course. He had often said to himself that Nell ought to get married and have children of her own instead of expending all her mother-love upon Stephen. Nell was the sort of girl who ought to marry . . . and here was an exceedingly nice fellow who was going to marry her tomorrow. You could not find a better fellow if you searched for years — and they were devoted to each other. What could be more delightful? Naturally Roger was delighted . . . but somehow he did not feel as delighted as he should. There was a draught of air blowing about his heart. It was a queer cold sort of feeling.

Nell had always been a secure refuge. Yes, from the very earliest days of childhood. Looking back down the years Roger remembered her as a little girl in the nursery who had always had a special smile for him. He remembered a hundred adventures shared. Little things and big things shared with Nell. He remembered being sent to bed without his supper — as a punishment for some long-forgotten misdemeanour — and Nell pushing a piece of bread and a bar of chocolate beneath the locked door; he remembered sitting on her bed and trying to comfort her when Anne disappeared and could not be found; he remembered ringing her up and telling her that Clare had been killed; he remembered coming home to Amberwell after the war and Nell's rapturous greeting. All these things Roger remembered — and a hundred more — and now here was this stranger, who knew nothing of bygone days, and he was going to walk off with one of Roger's dearest possessions — Roger's favourite sister, precious beyond rubies!

For a few moment Roger almost hated Dennis, who was striding along beside him with a ridiculous grin on his face (for Dennis had given up his attempt to converse with Roger and was lost in his own private bliss). The silly owl, thought Roger, glancing at him sideways in contempt . . . and then he thought: but that's nonsense; of course he's happy. Who wouldn't be? I'm the silly owl — and selfish as well.

Having decided that he was a silly owl — and selfish as well — Roger shook himself free of old memories and present worries and began to talk to his companion. They talked about business matters, about Nell staying on and managing Amberwell in the meantime — at least until Dennis got a job ashore — and about the generous settlement which Roger intended to make his favourite sister.

"Perhaps you'll get married one of these days," suggested Dennis.

"Well — perhaps —" said Roger uncomfortably. "I mean — you never know — but I don't think so."

"You should," declared Dennis with conviction. "Marriage is a good thing."

"Only if you can get the right person."

"Oh, of course."

They walked on in silence for a little, and having come to the big mossy stone at the entrance to the woods, they paused and looked back.

"This is one of my favourite haunts," said Roger. "You can see the whole of Amberwell from here. It's almost like seeing it from the air."

"I came here one morning with Tom," replied Dennis. "It was before I went to Burma." He hesitated. It had been on the tip of his tongue to tell Roger that he had sat here beside Tom and written a poem to Nell and then torn it up and buried the fragments . . . but Roger would think it silly.

"Pity Tom can't be here to-morrow," Roger said.

Dennis agreed.

They leant against the stone (it was too damp to sit down) and watched the sun declining towards the western horizon. There were banks of cloud fringed

278

with gold over the sea. Soon the sun would disappear behind them and the light would fade.

"Look here, Dennis," said Roger suddenly. "Don't say anything about what I told you — I mean that I might perhaps get married — not even to Nell. There isn't any chance."

"Are you sure?"

Roger was silent.

"Perhaps I'm interfering," said Dennis.

"No, of course not. I'd rather like to talk about it," Roger replied. He would not have liked to talk about it to anybody else — but Dennis was sound. When they had met in Rome Dennis had given him sound advice so he was willing to take more advice from the same quarter. "Go on," added Roger. "What were you going to say?"

"Not much — really. Just that girls are funny. You never know what they're thinking. At least that's my experience . . . not that I've had much experience," added Dennis hastily, in case his future brother-in-law should fall into the error of thinking him a Gay Lothario. "I mean that was my experience with Nell. I thought there wasn't any chance at all."

"Really?" asked Roger in surprise. "But I thought you and Nell had been friends for years."

"Friends — yes — but I wanted more than friendship and I was scared stiff of putting it to the touch in case I lost everything."

"'He either fears his fate too much,'" suggested Roger.

"Exactly. I feared my fate so much that I was on the point of going home, and then suddenly I found it was all right. It was like pushing against a door that you expect to be shut and discovering it was open."

Roger saw what he meant. "But my problem is difficult. You see I don't really know my own mind."

"Oh, if you're doubtful —"

"I don't mean it like that," declared Roger. "I just mean I can't understand myself. I thought all that sort of thing was over for me. I was married before. You know what happened, don't you?"

"But that was when Stephen was a baby — eight years ago, wasn't it?"

"Yes, eight years ago — but all the same . . ." Roger hesitated and then added, "I'm all mixed up. I can't explain, because I don't understand it myself. I still love Clare. I haven't forgotten her. For years I was utterly and absolutely miserable, but now it seems as if it had all happened in another life — or as if it had happened in a dream."

Dennis nodded. "I think I can understand. But life is real, isn't it? We can't go on living in dreams. Look here, Roger, supposing you'd been killed in the war would you have wanted Clare to go on being miserable all her life?"

"Goodness, no! What a horrible idea!" exclaimed Roger. Then he saw what Dennis had in mind. "Oh, I see," he said slowly. "I never thought of it that way."

They began to walk home together down the hill. The sun had slipped behind the banks of cloud and there was a queer diffused glow upon the western sea.

The light was failing rapidly. It was the ideal time for confidences.

"That's how my mother thinks of things," continued Dennis. "We talked about it once, long ago. I've never forgotten the conversation. She said she wouldn't want people she was very fond of to grieve for her and be unhappy. She meant me, of course, but it applies to — to other people."

"Yes, I see that. I've been a bit blind."

They walked on for quite a while without speaking and then Roger sighed. He said, "Yes, I've been blind. Clare wouldn't want me to be unhappy. The only thing is Clare and — and this girl were friends. I mean I've talked to her about Clare — told her I could never forget Clare — and all that. She might think it queer."

"You could explain."

"Difficult to explain."

"Not really," said Dennis earnestly. "I've understood the whole thing quite easily."

"Yes, I know, but —"

"And women are much better at understanding these sort of things than we are."

By this time they had almost reached the door of Amberwell and they stopped with one accord for the conversation was too important to be broken off.

"I don't want to interfere," Dennis declared. "I'm only talking in a vague sort of way and I may be quite wrong. I don't know who the girl is — or anything — but it seems a pity to miss the chance of being happy."

"You think I should 'put it to the touch'?"

Dennis nodded. "If I were you I'd have a bash at it," he said.

CHAPTER
TWENTY-TWO

1

The day of Nell's wedding was bright and fair and the bells of St. Stephen's were ringing merrily when Roger drove the bride to the church. The Ayrton family and their immediate friends had seemed a large crowd in Amberwell drawing-room but they only filled the three front pews. The fourth pew contained Nannie and Mrs. Duff and Mr. and Mrs. Gray; behind them sat Winnie and Jean and Bob Grainger — all in their Sunday clothes.

If it had been in the afternoon half Westkirk would have been present to see the Ayrton wedding, but eleven-thirty in the morning was an impossible hour for business people and their wives. There was a sprinkling of townsfolk at the back of the church and some women with babies in prams waiting outside the door, but that was all.

Mary decided that it had been a mistake; they should either have had a big crowd with all the usual trimmings or nobody at all. There is nothing so depressing as a half-empty church.

Perhaps Mary felt this more than the rest of the party for she was "dressed up" and yet had no real part to play. The dress (which Poppet had chosen and Johnnie had paid for) was very pretty and becoming but it was much too smart for this sort of occasion — or so Mary felt. The empty pews seemed to gape at Mary as she followed Nell and Roger up the aisle, and the music of the organ went echoing round the rafters in an eerie sort of way. There was no choir (how could there be at this hour, with the boys all at school, and the butcher and the stationmaster and other well-tried vocalists busy at their jobs?) so in spite of the fact that the wedding committee had chosen hymns that everybody knew the singing was lamentably thin. The flowers were beautiful — Anne had seen to that. Chrysanthemums from Amberwell gardens, lilies from the greenhouses all banked up with autumn leaves, filled the air with their heady perfume.

There was nothing wrong with the flowers and most certainly there was nothing wrong with the bride and bride-groom; they were not bothering whether the church was full or empty. They had eyes for nobody but each other and ears for nothing except the low clear voice of Mr. Orme.

"I require and charge you both as ye will answer at the dreadful day of judgment when the secrets of all hearts shall be disclosed that if either of you know of any impediment why ye may not be lawfully joined together . . ."

It was a frightful warning, thought Mary. She had attended a great many weddings, often as bridesmaid, and this reminder of "the dreadful day of judgment" had always given her a sort of shock. Marriage was not just flowers and fuss; it was serious and rather terrifying

. . . and one always suffered a momentary qualm in case one or other of the principal actors would suddenly remember an "impediment." Nobody ever did, of course, and certainly there was not much chance of it to-day. Mr. Orme scarcely hesitated for a moment before going on to the next part of the service and uniting Dennis and Nell for better for worse for richer for poorer, in sickness and in health . . .

Mary had often officiated as bridesmaid, but never alone — there had always been other girls standing beside her — and she had not realised how trying it would be to stand in the aisle by herself. As the marriage went on she began to feel a little queer. Perhaps it was because she was partly responsible for the arrangements and was not very happy about them, or perhaps it was the scent of the flowers. She told herself it was nonsense — she had never fainted in her life — but unfortunately it was not nonsense. Mr. Orme's voice seemed to come from a long way off and everything began to waver before her eyes in a very odd kind of way . . . at that moment Mary felt a firm grip on her arm and Roger drew her into the pew beside him.

"Are you all right?" whispered Roger. "Would you like to go out?"

She was all right now. Things were steadying down. Mary was even able to smile at her rescuer — though a trifle wanly.

"Sure you're all right?"

Mary nodded. She was feeling better every moment and was very much annoyed with herself for being such a fool — nearly swooning like a heroine in an early Victorian melodrama! What on earth had been the matter with her?

The sun was still shining brightly when the wedding-party came out of church. Several cars were waiting to take them to Amberwell but it was such a fine morning that some of them decided to walk back through the gardens to the house. Roger chose to walk; he set off with Mrs. Weatherby and Stephen and was followed by Gerald and Mr. Dalgleish. Mary did not feel like walking so she got into a car with Nannie and Mrs. Duff.

Mary wondered whether they — or anybody else — had noticed her peculiar behaviour, but apparently they had not.

"You're the bridesmaid, Miss Mary," said Nannie. "You ought to be in the other car — not with us."

"It doesn't matter," said Mary. There were so many unconventional things about this wedding that one more or less did not matter at all, and to tell the truth Mary had chosen her companions deliberately. She was still feeling slightly vague and unfit for bright conversation. Nannie and Mrs. Duff were comfortable.

"I'm glad it's fine," said Mrs. Duff.

"Happy is the bride the sun shines on," agreed Nannie. "And mind you there's a lot of truth in it. When my niece was married it was a thick fog — just like pea soup it was — and she's had one trouble after another ever since."

There was a short silence, broken by Mrs. Duff. "It was a nice wedding," she declared.

"The singing was poor," objected Nannie.

"Well, what could you expect? I think it was a nice wedding. Maybe not so cheery as Miss Connie's, but Miss Nell was beautiful — and so happy — it made me want to cry."

"There's nothing to cry about. She's got a good man."

"You were weeping yourself."

"I was not."

Mary thought it was time to change the subject. "I hope Mrs. Corner has managed all right," she said.

"Managed!" exclaimed Mrs. Duff in surprise. "There was nothing left for her to do but heat the soup. Surely to goodness she's capable of that!"

"You don't know her like I do, Kate," said Nannie pessimistically. "Oh, I don't say but what she isn't quite a good cook when she likes — but will she like? That's the question."

"What could she do? There's nothing but the soup —"

"If she gets into a rampage there's no knowing what she'll do. Did I tell you about her throwing a whole basket of new peas into the pigs' pail?"

Nannie had, of course. She had told everybody about it.

"Well then," said Nannie. "If she could do that she could do anything. Maybe we'll find she's poured the soup down the drain."

"Maircy!" exclaimed Mrs. Duff in horrified tones.

The dire supposition put an end to further conversation and nothing more was said until they

arrived at Amberwell. All three of them immediately
made a rush for the kitchen where they discovered,
much to their relief, that Mrs. Corner was not in a
rampage but was perfectly calm and collected. The
soup was being heated and everything was under
control.

2

The wedding-committee had tried to decide where
everybody was to sit at the long luncheon table but
there were so many conflicting personalities in the
Ayrton family that they had given up the attempt in
despair, so except for the seat upon Roger's right which
was reserved for Mrs. Weatherby and two seats at the
other end of the table for the bride and bridegroom, the
places were unmarked.

"People can sit where they like," Poppet had
declared.

This sounded all right (and incidentally relieved the
wedding-committee of all responsibility in the matter)
but it did not work out well. Unless people are told
where to sit they are liable to settle in the nearest chair
and late-comers are obliged to fill the gaps. Thus it was
that Mary found herself sitting between Arnold and
Georgina Glassford. She liked Arnold but not Georgina
— and she was aware that Georgina disliked her. Other
people were even less fortunate; Poppet, coming in late,
discovered that the only vacant seat was between her
two younger grandchildren. She hesitated — but only
for a moment — and then, moving little Marion to the

chair next to Joan, she sat down in Marion's place beside Dr. Maddon.

"But I don't WANT to sit next Joan!" cried Marion in her shrill clear voice.

"But I want to sit next to Dr. Maddon," said Poppet calmly.

Everybody laughed (or nearly everybody) for it was well-known in Westkirk that Dr. Maddon and Poppet Lambert were as thick as thieves.

Connie did not laugh. "I think somebody had better sit between the children," said Connie with a worried frown. "If Arnold wouldn't mind changing places with Joanie —"

"But Arnold would mind," said Arnold frankly. "Arnold would rather sit next to Mary. Will they bite each other or what?"

"Of course they won't bite each other," declared their mother indignantly. She looked round and added, "As a matter of fact we've arranged ourselves very badly; nearly all the men are on this side of the table. Gerald, why don't you change places with little Marion?"

"Oh, I think we're all right," said Gerald, who was comfortably situated between Anne and Emmie and could not be bothered to move.

"Ow, Joanie has pinched my arm! I knew she would!" wailed little Marion.

"I'll change places with Joan," said Georgina in a self-sacrificing tone of voice.

"How kind of you!" exclaimed Connie.

Mary was amused. The change of seats placed Georgina next to Arnold — and Arnold had told Mary that the girl was a menace.

"Talk to me for pity's sake!" said Arnold to Mary out of the corner of his mouth.

The table was still badly arranged but that could not be helped:

Roger

Mrs. Weatherby	Stephen
Dr. Maddon	Connie
Poppet	Mr. Dalgleish
Little Marion	Mr. Lambert
Georgina	Young Gerry
Arnold	Anne
Mary	Gerald
Joan	Emmie
Mrs. Ayrton	Mr. Orme

Dennis Nell

Having seen that everybody's glass was filled Mr. Lambert rose to his feet and proposed the health of the bride and bridegroom.

"I've known Nell all her life," declared Mr. Lambert. "She's one of the best and her husband is a lucky fellow. Everybody here knows Nell so I don't need to sing her praises (and that's a good thing because I've got a voice like a crow). From what I've seen of Dennis — and heard about him — I should say he's just about good enough for Nell. Can't think of any higher praise at the moment. Marriage is a good idea — at least I think so. Poppet wouldn't like it if I told you how long we've been married, but it's quite a long time, and if Nell and Dennis are as happy as Poppet and I they won't do badly. Can't think of any better wish for them. So now I'll ask you all to drink to the health and happiness of Nell and Dennis."

They all stood up and drank the health — all except young Gerry who sat and gazed before him open-mouthed.

"Stand up and drink, you ass!" said his grandfather, nudging him.

Thus adjured young Gerry stood up and, taking a large gulp of champagne, choked and spluttered in a thoroughly disgusting manner. "Ugh, it's nasty!" he exclaimed.

Fortunately nobody except his immediate neighbours heard him or took any notice for the bridegroom had risen and was saying his piece and doing it very nicely indeed. After that the soup was served and luncheon began in earnest.

It was a good lunch, thought Mary, as she chatted to Arnold. The wedding was not such a "flop" after all. Everybody was talking now (or nearly everybody). They were talking and laughing and eating. They were drinking the excellent champagne chosen by Johnnie for the occasion. Roger and Mrs. Weatherby seemed to be getting on like a house on fire — she wondered what they were saying. Stephen was listening eagerly.

Stephen had been clever and had chosen his place at the table carefully, sitting down beside his father with the sublime disregard for everybody else which is possible only when you are very young. Stephen was happy — and beautifully behaved. It was a pity Connie and Gerald had not taught their children to behave properly. Poor Connie was not enjoying herself at all. She was watching her children with that anxious frown which had become habitual and would soon make a wrinkle in her smooth forehead if she did not take care. Connie had been so beautiful — the prettiest of them all — but she was beginning to look a little haggard.

Mr. Dalgleish and Johnnie, who certainly should not have been sitting together, were quite contented in each other's company. Mary caught a word here and there. "They've gone up three points since Monday," Mr. Dalgleish was saying. Johnnie nodded and replied, "Those stockbroker fellows don't know any more than we do."

"So we've finally decided to send him to Summerhills," Gerald was saying to Anne. Poppet was laughing merrily at some story of the doctor's. "Goodness!" cried Poppet. "You mean there was nothing the matter with her after all!"

Dennis and Nell were doing their duty to their neighbours: Nell was chatting to Mr. Orme. Dennis was listening to Mrs. Ayrton.

"You'll enjoy it," declared Mrs. Ayrton. "The last time we were there we stayed at a very nice hotel — I can't remember its name. The lift was painted gold like a bird-cage and when we were half-way up it stuck and a French lady had hysterics. William was very cross about it," added Mrs. Ayrton. (Mary wondered whether

292

"William" had been cross about the lift or with the French lady for having hysterics. In either case it seemed sad that Mrs. Ayrton's memories of Paris should be so unprofitable.)

Listening to all these snippets of conversation Mary had omitted to talk to Arnold, so Georgina had got him. "Breathing is very important," she was saying earnestly. "Deep breaths every morning at an open window . . . and foot exercises of course. Raising yourself on your toes —"

"Excellent — if you happen to have toes," agreed Arnold brightly.

This silenced the unfortunate girl and Arnold was able to reopen the conversation with his right-hand neighbour.

"Not very kind," Mary told him.

"I know," said Arnold regretfully. "I ought to be thicker skinned by this time. Fact is when people tread on my toes I bite instinctively — and then I'm sorry. Shall I apologise or would that make it worse?"

"It would make it worse," replied Mary without hesitation.

It seemed to Mary that the meal lasted a long time, for although she liked Arnold she had not much in common with him — except Summerhills of course — and when she had inquired after her bow-window and had been given a good report upon its progress there was not much more to say. But all things come to an end and at last lunch was over; even young Gerry could not eat any more.

The bride and bridegroom had left the table earlier and now appeared in their travelling garments to say good-bye, and as they were in a hurry to get away to catch their plane at Renfrew the whole party rose and followed them on to the steps.

Nell had said good-bye to so many people on the steps of Amberwell. She had stood there and waved them away — often with a very heavy heart — but to-day she was the one who was leaving and the others were staying behind. She was coming back, of course, but it would not be quite the same. For a moment Nell's heart failed her . . . and then she looked at Dennis and saw his encouraging smile. Dennis understood, and everything was all right.

"Where's Duffy?" cried Nell. "Where's Nannie? I can't go away without saying good-bye to them."

Mrs. Duff and Nannie were fetched and said good-bye tearfully, several times over — as if Nell were going to Timbuctoo for a year instead of to Paris for an exceedingly short honeymoon — but at last Dennis was able to get his wife into the car and away they went in a shower of confetti with the old shoe bumping after them down the drive.

"Well, that's that," said Roger, gazing after the car rather sadly.

There was cake and coffee in the drawing-room, but somehow it seemed rather pointless to eat chunks of wedding-cake when there was no bride in white satin and orange blossom to cut it — besides everybody had already partaken of an excellent lunch — so the party soon broke up. The guests went home and Mrs.

Weatherby went up to her room and had a little weep.

CHAPTER
TWENTY-THREE

1

The young Lamberts and their children had been staying at Merlewood for two nights only, but they had spread themselves over the whole house in a most extraordinary way, so it was quite a lengthy business getting their belongings gathered together and packed into the car.

"I don't understand it," declared Connie helplessly. "We seem to have more things than when we came — but we haven't."

"Are you sure you've got everything?" asked Gerald, who knew his family only too well.

"I think so," said Connie.

"Better have another look round."

They had not got everything (Mary discovered a drawer full of garments which had been overlooked, and Joan's galoshes were found in the linen-cupboard) but eventually the job was completed; the last bulging handbag was wedged securely between Joan and little Marion — so that they should not pinch each other — and the Lamberts were ready to depart. Gerald settled himself at the wheel and the car moved off down the drive.

Poppet and Johnnie and Mary stood upon the doorstep of Merlewood and waved until the car disappeared from view; then Poppet rushed back into her desecrated house and proceeded to put it in order. She beat up the cushions in the drawing-room and pushed the chairs into their rightful places (the whole house was clamouring for her attention but the drawing-room came first). Mary helped of course but Johnnie stood on the rug in front of the fire and chuckled.

"You didn't laugh when Gerry put salt in your shaving-cream," said Poppet crossly. "You didn't laugh when Joan dropped your keys into the cistern and put out her tongue at the postman, or when Marion tore some pages out of that silly old book."

"That wasn't funny," said Johnnie.

"Neither is this," Poppet declared. "It isn't a bit funny to destroy things and you don't like it any more than I do."

"I can bear it for two days."

"That's a nice thing to say!"

"It's true. I can bear it for two days — but then I'm not jealous of my grandchildren!" said Johnnie in a teasing voice.

"Jealous!" cried Poppet indignantly.

"She's jealous, isn't she, Mary?"

Mary was obliged to hide a smile.

"I don't know what you mean," declared Poppet. "I'm sorry for them! I'm ashamed of them! Did you see Mrs. Weatherby looking at them yesterday when we were having tea at Amberwell — and thinking how frightful they were! And they were frightful to-day at lunch — simply frightful! Gerry is an absolute boor and the girls are intolerable little nuisances. If that's how you like your grandchildren to behave I DON'T," cried Poppet, seizing a cushion which had fallen on to the floor, and shaking it viciously.

"Ha, ha, that's dear little Marion!" exclaimed Johnnie.

"I wish it were!" cried Poppet.

Mary said nothing of course. Her host and hostess amused her vastly and she had been staying with them for so long that she had become more like a daughter than a guest. At first their little tiffs had alarmed her, but very soon she had discovered that there was no cause for alarm; Johnnie and Poppet were so fond of each other and understood each other so well that their little tiffs were perfectly harmless and merely added a spice to their dish of life.

As she went up to her room to dress for dinner Mary suddenly found that she was very tired and slightly depressed. The tiredness was natural for she had done a great deal in the last few days but the depression was less easy to account for. Perhaps it was due to reaction after all the excitement of the wedding or perhaps to the feeling that the wedding had not been a great success. There was nothing wrong with the bride and bridegroom — they were blissfully happy — but the organisation had been at fault. Nell's wedding had been neither one thing nor the other.

Weddings were curious ceremonies, Mary decided. Even savages gathered the whole tribe together and celebrated their marriages with traditional rites handed down from one generation to another, with singing and dancing and feasting. Civilised people had traditional rites as well and ought to observe them. It was no use trying to pick and choose; saying you would have marriage-bells and flowers but not all the other trimmings. You should either creep away quietly and be married without any fuss (as Nell had wanted) or else gather the whole tribe and have everything.

Mary wondered if anybody else had felt the same about Nell's wedding — perhaps Roger! Roger had seemed in a queer sort of mood, not like himself at all. He had been kind to her in church, dragging her into the pew beside him (rescuing her from making a fool of herself by fainting in the aisle), but afterwards he had avoided her and when she had spoken to him in the drawing-room he had scarcely replied. He had had a long conversation with Poppet; in fact he had chatted to everybody in the room — except Mary. She wondered why. Perhaps he was annoyed with her for being so foolish, but if so she could not help it . . . and what did it matter? Mary decided that it did not matter at all.

At dinner they talked about the wedding and Mary discovered that in the eyes of Poppet and Johnnie it had "gone off" very well indeed, so she kept her own feelings to herself and agreed with Poppet that the bride looked beautiful and with Johnnie that the "fizz" was delicious.

"You won't mind if Johnnie and I go out to-night, will you?" asked Poppet. "I promised the Claytons we'd go along after dinner and tell them all about it."

"You're too tired, Poppet," said Johnnie. "Better ring up and wash it out."

"I'm not tired a bit," declared Poppet. "I'd like to go, if Mary doesn't mind being left alone."

Mary said she did not mind at all, though this was not quite true for in her depressed condition the cheerful company of her host and hostess would have been pleasant. "I'll go to bed early and read," said Mary. "Don't worry about me."

But apparently Poppet was worrying. "There's a lovely fire in the drawing-room," said Poppet. "Much better sit there and read. We shan't stay long at the Claytons'. I wouldn't go out and leave you but I think Alison Clayton is a tiny bit hurt because they weren't asked to the wedding."

"We only asked relations," Mary pointed out.

"The Maddons aren't relations. Neither are you."

This was true of course.

"We should have had everybody," added Poppet with a sigh. "Once you begin to pick and choose it always leads to trouble."

Mary was still inclined to go to bed and read — reading in bed was a luxury she enjoyed — but for some reason Poppet was against it.

"Why not let the girl do what she wants?" asked Johnnie reasonably.

"She'll be much more comfortable in the drawing-room," replied Poppet, and before Mary could make any more objections she found herself settled upon the drawing-room sofa with her feet up and a rug over her knees. The lamp was placed conveniently, a book was provided and the fire made up with logs.

"There," said Poppet. "You'll be all right now, won't you? Don't go to bed until we come home — and you might listen for the door-bell and answer it if anybody comes. Janet is out."

"Are you expecting somebody?" Mary inquired.

Poppet was tying a scarf over her head and arranging it becomingly — she did not seem to hear. "We shan't be very long," she said. "You see I promised Alison Clayton we'd go over and tell her how the wedding went off. Are you ready, Johnnie?"

"I've been ready for the last ten minutes," Johnnie replied in resigned tones. He sighed and added, "But I can't think why you want to —"

"Because I promised Alison."

"But why? I mean we'd be much more comfortable —"

"Darling Johnnie, don't be a bear!"

"All right — all right —"

They went off together. Their voices died away and the front door closed with a thud.

2

Mary settled down to read. She was very comfortable indeed, and the book was a new one by her favourite author, so she should have been perfectly happy, but she was not. The book failed to hold her attention and presently she put it down and abandoned herself to gloom. It was unusual for Mary to feel gloomy without a good reason — and there was no reason at all for her to feel gloomy to-night — but all the same she felt depressed and out of temper. Everything was "stale, flat and unprofitable" — yes everything. She was cross with Poppet. Why should Poppet always get her own way? It did not matter whether it was a big thing or a small thing Poppet got her own way. Everybody always did what Poppet told them.

I'm tired of it, thought Mary. That's what's the matter with me. That's why I feel so depressed. I'm tired of being here and doing what Poppet tells me. I'm tired of Summerhills. (Yes, she was sick and tired of Summerhills. She had been bored stiff with Arnold talking about it at lunch. Even the name, which had seemed attractive, sounded a stupid sort of name.) I'll go home, thought Mary. At least I can't go home because I haven't got a home any more — but I can go back to the parents.

Mary was still brooding mournfully when the front-door bell rang. Poppet had told her that she was to answer it because Janet was out! For a few moments she hesitated and then she sighed and got up and went to the door.

The visitor was Roger.

"Poppet and Johnnie are out," said Mary inhospitably. "They've gone over to the Clayton's'. I don't know when they'll be back."

"I know they're out," replied Roger. "As a matter of fact I told Poppet I wanted to talk to you."

"You told Poppet —"

"Yes, she said you'd be here alone."

By this time Roger had taken off his Burberry and thrown it on to a chair, so Mary had no option but to lead him into the drawing-room and invite him to sit down.

"I suppose you want to talk about Summerhills," she said. "Have you had time to go and look at the bow-window? Arnold says they're getting on with it quite well, and there's no doubt —"

"No," said Roger. "I haven't had time — and anyway I didn't come to talk about that. First of all are you feeling all right, Mary?"

She nodded. "It was frightfully silly, wasn't it? I very nearly fainted. I can't think what was the matter with me."

"It wasn't silly at all. It was perfectly natural. Nobody can stand for ages all by themselves in the middle of a space. Even trained soldiers find it trying. I wouldn't like to do it myself."

"Really?" asked Mary in surprise.

"I told Poppet she shouldn't have let you do it," added Roger rather crossly.

"Did you!" exclaimed Mary, even more surprised; people did not often take Poppet to task for her actions — and it was not really Poppet's fault.

Roger nodded. "Yes, I told her. Oh, she was quite decent about it — said she was sorry and all that."

This sounded so unlike Poppet that Mary was speechless.

"But as long as you're none the worse it's all right," added Roger.

There was a short silence and then Mary said, "Was that what you came about, Roger?"

"Not really," he replied. "I really came to talk about — something else."

Roger had sat down in Johnnie's chair and Mary had returned to the sofa. The room was softly lighted by the standard lamp. It was a beautiful room, quiet and peaceful, but Mary did not feel peaceful; she was beginning to feel afraid. Roger looked grave and serious and his hands were clasped so tightly upon the arms of the chair that his knuckles had whitened.

"About — something — else?" asked Mary uncertainly.

"About me," he told her. "Perhaps it's a funny thing to do, but I thought it was the best thing. I mean I want you to know the whole story. At first I thought of writing to you — it would have been easier — but then I thought I wouldn't. People sometimes misunderstand letters, don't they?"

"Yes — I suppose they do — sometimes." Mary found difficulty in breathing.

"We've talked about Clare," continued Roger. "You know what I felt about her, don't you? When Clare was killed I felt as if my life was over. I felt like chucking myself into the sea. There was no happiness left. There was no pleasure in anything. That went on for years and years."

"Oh Roger, I know —"

"Please wait," he said. "If you don't mind I'd like to tell you all about it. Then you'll understand — at least I hope so. It's difficult to explain because I'm not one of

304

those fellows who think a lot about their own feelings — there always seems to be things to do and it's better to be busy. For instance there was Summerhills; it's been good fun planning Summerhills, getting all the alterations fixed up and getting them done in the best possible way. Ever since I came home on leave in June I've been happier — I've felt quite different and more alive — and I thought it was because of Summerhills."

"I expect it was —" began Mary.

"But it wasn't, it was you."

Mary gazed at him. She could not utter a sound.

"Yes, it was you, Mary. That very first morning, when I was talking to Gray in the garden and I saw you come in at the gate, I thought, 'What fun, here's Mary — and she hasn't changed a bit!' I looked at you and I saw you." He hesitated for a moment and then went on. "You'll think that's a crazy thing to say, but I hadn't really seen a girl for years and years. I hadn't bothered to look at girls; they didn't interest me in the least. Nobody interested me except Stephen — and Nell. That's what I mean when I say I looked at you and saw you. Of course I didn't realise it at the time, I just felt happy to be with you, that's all.

"We walked up through the woods," continued Roger. "We talked about Stark Place — and other things — about Clare and Ian and what fun we used to have when we were little. Perhaps you don't remember —" He paused and looked at her.

"Yes, I remember," said Mary in a low voice.

"There were two cuckoos in the woods, calling to each other. It was a lovely morning. I didn't want to leave you and go home."

Mary was silent. She had not wanted to go home either. She had wanted Time to stand still so that she could go on talking to Roger — but Time never stood still.

"Then I saw you again," said Roger. "We met at Stark Place before I flew out to Rome . . . and when I went back to Germany you wrote to me. I loved getting your letters. All this time I thought it was the school that made me happy and gave me an interest in life. It wasn't until later that I realised your letters gave me pleasure because they were full of you. I might have gone on like that for ages — not knowing the truth. It sounds quite mad, I know, but as I said before I don't really think about myself very much. I just — carry on — and do things."

Roger paused for a few moments. He leaned forward and gazed at the fire. "Sorry to — to bore you with all this," he declared. "But I want you to understand everything. It was a silly little incident that shook me up and gave me the clue — quite silly and not worth mentioning except that I'm telling you everything. It was the day we arranged to meet at Summerhills and you told me about your idea for the bow-window. I had said I would go and watch Georgina running and time her with a stop-watch. She had asked me to do it and I was such an idiot that I couldn't refuse. Well, I expect you remember that I rang her up and put her off. Georgina was furious, she was frightfully rude and —

306

and unreasonable. She — she said — things," declared Roger uncomfortably. "She said — well, it doesn't matter what she said but it made me angry. It sort of — shook me up. I began to realise what an awful ass I had been.

"It all seemed — pretty hopeless," continued Roger in a lower voice. "The more I thought about it the more hopeless it seemed. I was sure you didn't care about me, except in a friendly sort of way for old times' sake — and even in those days it was Tom who was your special friend and not me at all. Besides, there was Clare. I was all mixed up in my mind about Clare. I felt it was wrong to love somebody else — and be happy. It wasn't until afterwards that I realised I was looking at it in a cock-eyed sort of way. I've got it clear now because somebody said — something. You see I still love Clare — but it's all like a dream — as if it had happened in another life — not my life at all. I don't know whether you can understand that — or not — but it's true. Well, anyhow, I was so mixed up and so miserable that I felt like going back to Germany the next day, and I believe I would have done just that if it hadn't been for Poppet's party. She was having the party especially for me so I couldn't very well back out of it. I wasn't feeling like a party — anything but! At first the party was awful, and then I saw you. You were so lovely, Mary. There was nobody else in the room except you — nobody at all. You were wearing a rose-coloured dress and two real roses — not artificial ones — and you were just like a rose yourself. I watched you all the time, going about and talking to people and smiling at them. I was watching you when Poppet spoke to me and sent me to give you a message. It was queer, really, because I had made up my mind that I wouldn't talk to you — I felt quite hopeless — but I couldn't refuse to give you Poppet's message. How could I refuse? Besides everybody does what Poppet tells them . . . and then suddenly I thought I would talk to you and see — and see if there was any hope at all. We sat on the veranda and talked. I told you I liked your letters because they were full of you, and you understood. You said my letters were full of me. It wasn't much but it was better than nothing. There seemed to be a tiny glimmer of hope.

"That's all, really," said Roger. "I've told you — everything — and if you think — I mean if you think you could possibly — like me at all — some day —" He paused and looked at her anxiously.

Could she like him — some day? What a silly question! Mary had loved him for months, ever since that day in June — that lovely summer day when they had walked through the woods together and leant on the gate and heard the cuckoos calling!

"Mary, could you — possibly?" repeated Roger.

"I think — I could —" said Mary in a shaky voice.

"Mary!" he cried. "Oh Mary —"

"Wait, Roger," said Mary, holding out her hand to stop him. "Wait a minute. You've told me things — and I want to tell you something. It's about Clare. I'm awfully glad you told me — all that — about Clare."

"You understand?" he asked, leaning forward and looking at her.

"Yes, of course."

"And you don't mind?"

"Oh Roger — no! How could I mind? We both loved Clare, didn't we? There was nobody like her. I'm glad you haven't forgotten her. She's still — in your heart."

"Like a dream," said Roger earnestly. "It's all — like a dream. You're real, Mary."

"Clare wouldn't mind either," Mary told him. "She would want you to be happy — and I think I could — make you happy." She raised her eyes and looked at Roger as she spoke. Her eyes were dewy with tears but there was a radiance behind the tears. "If love can make you happy," she added in a whisper.

ENVOI

The headmaster of Summerhills decided to hold the Sports on the last Saturday in June, for if there is any time of year when you can depend upon good weather (which of course there is not) you can depend upon the end of June. Also by this time the headmaster hoped that all the alterations would be finished and the last workman would have gone. In this hope the headmaster was a little too optimistic. Certainly all the major alterations were completed: the bow-window was ready (making his small, dull sitting-room into a fine, cheerful, bright room which was much admired by visiting parents); the hatch was ready and in constant use; the partition-wall in the large dormitory had vanished; the door into the changing-room had been made and the baths and showers and other toilet equipment were all installed ... but there were still a few workmen wandering about the house with their bags of tools, and the joiner was still putting up extra shelves in the linen cupboard and screwing in extra hooks. These last lingering workmen were a source of pleasure to the boys (who dogged their steps whenever possible, pestered them with questions and hindered them in their work), but they were a source of irritation to the headmaster.

The morning of the last Saturday in June was cloudy and rather chilly, with a strong breeze from the west, but by afternoon the clouds had vanished and the sun was shining in a bright blue sky. It shone down upon the fine old house — all spick and span in its new paint — and upon the noble trees and the green expanse of playing-fields which were already laid out for the Sports. It shone with positively blinding brightness upon the white marquee which had been erected for the occasion, and upon the twenty little boys in white shorts and blue blazers who were waiting for the Sports to begin. They were chattering in shrill voices, ragging each other and rolling about on the grass like excited puppies.

"Look out!" they shouted. "Do stop it, you ass! What d'you mean by kicking me on the head!" "I say, have you seen the prizes? They're super!" "You won't win any!" "Yes, I shall." "No, you won't!" "I'm going to win the sack-race!" "Bet you tuppence you don't."

They were getting a little out of hand, thought the headmaster, but he did not call them to order for it was better that they should let off steam before the serious business of the afternoon began.

The guests were arriving now. They walked about and talked to each other or found chairs and sat down. There were quite a number of guests; some of them were people living in the neighbourhood who had come out of curiosity to see the new school; others were friends of the headmaster who had come to back him up; most important of all were the "parents" who had come to see their sons win the prizes and cover themselves with glory.

Twenty excited little boys running round in circles (pushing and shoving and shouting in high-pitched voices) can make quite a stir, so the headmaster was not really surprised when one of the parents remarked, "What a lot of boys you've got already, Mr. Maddon! There must be thirty at least."

"Not quite," replied Mr. Maddon smiling. "But we're coming along nicely. If we go on at this rate we shall soon be full."

Yes, Arnold was pleased with the start they had made; he would have been even better pleased if all the parents had been paying the standard fees for the education of their sons — but that was not his business. His business was to run the school. He was doing it to the best of his ability assisted by a very young Oxford graduate (who did not look much older than his elder pupils) and by a comfortable, motherly sort of woman who had been recommended for the post of matron by Mrs. Lambert. There was also an elderly Frenchman who could speak and teach several languages besides his own.

The domestic staff was adequate, it was headed by young Lumsden who had been engaged as janitor but had taken over a great many other duties in addition. He was a hero to the twenty little boys; he was their guide, philosopher and friend; he was at once their nursemaid and the headmaster's right-hand man. Young Lumsden was worth his weight in gold to Summerhills.

By this time all the guests had arrived and been greeted by the headmaster. He had chatted to all the parents, giving and receiving information about his boys and incidentally obtaining quite a number of new boys for the school.

"Alec looks so fit and happy," said Alec's mother. "We're thinking of sending you Ian as well. He is very young, of course —"

"Better book him," said his father. "Ian isn't doing any good at that potty little day-school."

"We'd like to have him," declared the headmaster. "We like to catch them young — and if he's like his brother he'll do well. Alec has settled down splendidly."

"I was wondering about my nephew," said another parent. "He's at a big school in the South of England but he isn't getting on very well. You see he's shy and rather delicate. My sister thinks he would get on better at a smaller school and I was telling her about Summerhills. She said I was to ask you . . ."

"Yes, of course," agreed the headmaster. "It's much easier to give a boy individual attention at a small school."

"Oh Mr. Maddon," said another parent. "Some friends of ours are going abroad after Christmas. They've got twin boys. It says on your prospectus that you make special arrangements for looking after boys during the holidays."

"That's right," said the headmaster. "We've got several boys whose parents are abroad. Perhaps your friends would like to come and see the school, would they?"

"I'll tell them to ring up and make an appointment."

"No need to make an appointment. They can see the school any time — and me too," added the headmaster, smiling.

"Do you mean you're always here?" asked Mr. Cartwright in surprise."

"Yes," replied the headmaster. "As a matter of fact this is a twenty-four-hours-a-day job. Later on I hope to get hold of a fellow I know — a responsible middle-aged fellow — but meantime I prefer to be here myself. Poulton is much too young to be left in charge."

Mr. Cartwright was impressed. He went off to spread the news that the headmaster was on duty morning, noon and night.

It was now three o'clock and young Lumsden was blowing his whistle to collect the runners for the first race of the afternoon. There were no non-starters. Twenty little boys rushed madly across the field to take up their positions on the line. Lumsden was waiting to arrange them. Poulton and Monsieur Dubois were waiting at the finish to pick out the winners.

Seeing that all was in order the headmaster decided he could spare a few minutes to speak to his own particular friends and began to make his way to the huge oak-tree at the end of the field where a group of people had gathered.

The sun was hot by this time and the spreading branches of the oak-tree made a pleasant shade. The little group of people looked comfortable and relaxed. They all knew each other so well that they could talk or be silent as the spirit moved them. Dr. Maddon was

314

here, sitting upon a deck-chair with his old friend Mr. Orme beside him.

"Pity Roger couldn't come," Dr. Maddon was saying. "Arnold was hoping he would manage it, but he couldn't get away. He's in London now — at the War Office — but you know that, of course."

"Yes, Anne hears from Mary occasionally," replied Mr. Orme. "They've got a flat. They asked Anne to go and stay with them for a few days."

"Do her good," grunted the doctor.

"I know, but she won't go. Anne doesn't like London . . ."

The Lamberts were here in full force — three generations of them — for Gerry Lambert was one of the twenty little boys who were being educated at Summerhills (and incidentally young Gerry was more trouble to the headmaster than all the others put together). Johnnie Lambert was talking to his son, who had motored down from Glasgow that morning. Poppet was not talking to anybody; she was sitting on a rug with her back against the tree and observing her fellow creatures. They looked happy, thought Poppet, and so they should, for it was a happy occasion. Poppet had been a little dubious about this venture of Roger's, but she was no longer dubious. Summerhills had got off to a good start. She, too, wished that Roger could have been here this afternoon.

Nell was here but not Dennis (Dennis had had his leave at Easter and had spent it at Amberwell); but in spite of his absence Nell did not look sad. She sat a little apart from the others, half in the shade of the tree and half in the sunshine, and there was an air of quiet contentment about her. Poppet, who had always loved Nell, thought her more beautiful than ever, and quite suddenly she guessed the reason for Nell's new loveliness . . . but there will be plenty of time to knit a Shetland shawl, thought Poppet, smiling to herself.

Connie was the only one of the little group who was not enjoying the afternoon. She was sitting between her two daughters, trying to keep them quiet, and the anxious frown was puckering her forehead. For years Connie had thought her children perfect, but just lately she had begun to have doubts — and this afternoon she would have given a good deal if Joanie and Marion had been a little different. Why couldn't they behave like Emmie who was sitting beside her mother looking quite happy and peaceful? Why must they be always squabbling and fidgeting? Quite suddenly Connie made up her mind that Joanie and little Marion were not perfect — nor Gerry either. It was a horrible moment.

Connie's frown deepened. "Sit still," she said sharply. "If you can't sit still and behave properly I shall take you straight home and put you to bed. You're just being a nuisance."

Her daughters were speechless with amazement.

Arnold was now approaching the tree. He saw Anne first, of course, and Anne looked up from the rug where she was sitting and smiled at him in her usual friendly way. They were still friends — no more and no less. Arnold had very nearly abandoned hope of a closer tie but he found great satisfaction in Anne's friendship. It was only sometimes at odd moments that he felt a little

316

sad and the world seemed bleak and lonely; sometimes in the evening when the curtains were drawn and he settled down in solitary seclusion beside his comfortable fire.

Arnold was about to greet his friends when the report of a revolver rang out sharply and every head turned to watch the race . . . twenty little boys scampering over the meadow as fast as they could go! The twenty started in a long line carefully spaced by young Lumsden and instructed by him to run straight and keep well spaced-out, but the excitement was too intense for them to remember their instructions and after a few yards they bunched and ran like a flock of sheep. Then two boys emerged from the ruck and took the lead: one was the biggest boy in the school (a tall sturdy lad of eleven years old), the other was very nearly the smallest. These two were neck-and-neck for three-quarters of the race and then the smaller one increased his pace, striding out manfully, head up, elbows to his sides, running so lightly and easily that his feet seemed scarcely to touch the ground.

"Stephen!" shrieked Emmie, leaping up in excitement. "Go it, Stephen! Hurrah, hurrah, he's winning! He's winning easily!"

Yes, Stephen won easily. His only serious rival was ten yards behind.

It was sad that Georgina Glassford could not have seen the results of her coaching, but Georgina had left Amberwell in the spring. She had passed like a ship in the night and was almost forgotten. Perhaps it was a little ungrateful of the Ayrtons to have forgotten her so soon — she had done a good deal for them one way and another — but it is doubtful whether any of them realised how much she had done. Stephen was the only one who thought about Miss Glassford this afternoon. He thought about her as he arrived, somewhat breathless, at the finish of the race — and even his thought was not so much gratitude as a wish that she could have been present to see his triumph.

The little group beneath the oak-tree had been watching the race so intently that they had not noticed two new arrivals who were walking across the field to join them. Now, when the tension was over and they could breathe again, the new arrivals were quite near.

"Goodness, here's Roger and Mary!" exclaimed Arnold in surprise.

"We managed to come after all," said Roger, smiling.

"Roger got a few days' leave unexpectedly," Mary explained.

"It's grand!" cried Arnold, laughing with pleasure. "It makes everything perfect — you being here! There was something wanting before. This just rounds off the occasion."

There was a chorus of agreement (everybody had felt the same) and the new arrivals were welcomed warmly. They settled down together in the shade of "Ian's tree" and prepared to watch the races.

Roger had changed in the last few months; he had put on a little weight, and the slight air of sadness (which Poppet had found so appealing) was replaced by an air of happiness not quite so romantic but much more pleasing to his wife. Their marriage had taken place shortly after Nell's, and had been a nine days' wonder, for the secret had been well kept and nobody except Poppet and Johnnie Lambert had the slightest idea they were engaged.

"All or nothing," Mary had said firmly. "Either a slap-up wedding, with all the tribe and all the traditional rites, or else a *really* quiet wedding with nobody but our own two selves — and Poppet and Johnnie to sign the book."

They had talked it over. Poppet thought it would be lovely to have a traditional wedding (and was eager to hold the reception at Merlewood) but Roger thought not, and as it was impossible to have "a really quiet wedding" at St. Stephen's they had been married in Germany. Sir Andrew and Lady Findlater knew and approved, but nobody else, and the secret was not divulged until Poppet and Johnnie Lambert returned from a short holiday with the news that they had flown over to Germany with Mary and seen her safely married to Roger by the Regimental Padre. The news was so unexpected that it was almost incredible, and at first their friends and relations were somewhat annoyed (in fact all Westkirk felt cheated, for an Ayrton-Findlater alliance was an important event and should have been celebrated with the pomp and circumstance befitting the occasion); but Roger and Mary were hundreds of miles away so the fuss did not worry them at all and by the time they came home to Amberwell for Christmas leave their "hole-and-corner wedding" was forgiven.

"Roger," said Nell, "were you and Mary here in time to see Stephen win the race?"

"We watched from the terrace," replied Roger. "It was a good show, wasn't it? In fact it was splendid," he added with a chuckle.

Nell met his eye and smiled.

"Stephen doesn't know you're here, does he?" asked Anne.

"No, it's a surprise. We'll talk to him in the tea interval. He's much too busy to talk to us now — too busy to see us."

"They're all too busy to notice an earthquake," said Arnold, glancing at his charges with affectionate amusement.

The headmaster's statement was no exaggeration, for arrangements were now being made for the egg-and-spoon race and again the whole school was competing for the prize. Twenty little boys with spoons clasped tightly in their hands were awaiting the report of Lumsden's revolver. The "eggs" were represented by potatoes which had been placed before them in a long straight line. Suddenly the report rang out, the boys picked up their "eggs" and off they went . . .

There is not much difficulty in carrying a potato upon a spoon and if they had heeded Lumsden's warning to "go slow" they could have managed it easily, but they were much too eager to go slow. Three of them ran ahead; the others, unwilling to be left behind, quickened their paces. The leader dropped his potato and stooped to pick it up; two other boys fell over him and their potatoes flew in all directions. By this time another competitor had taken the lead, but instead of hastening on he looked over his shoulder and stumbled. The course was now a jumble of boys, some rolling on the ground, others squatting and endeavouring to pick up their potatoes with hands which trembled with excitement.

There was one competitor — the last to start — who took no notice of his companions. He was a small, fat, stolid individual in spectacles. Carefully he picked up his potato, slowly and cautiously he walked from start to finish. He placed his potato upon the white line and then stood up and looked round.

"Gosh, have I won?" he exclaimed in surprise.

There was a roar of laughter from the onlookers.

"That's Cartwright all over," said the headmaster of Summerhills. "Slow and sure is his motto. He takes no notice of anybody but goes on doggedly to the end."

"Cartwright?" asked Roger in surprise. "He's Stephen's friend, isn't he?"

Arnold nodded. "Yes. They're buddies. It's strange how often boys choose their opposites to be friends with. I've seen it happen over and over again."

"Good for them both," declared Dr. Maddon.

"Gerry was third," said Connie, who naturally enough had been watching her own child. "He would have been second if that other boy hadn't upset him."

"How is Gerry getting on?" asked Gerry's father.

Arnold hesitated for a moment and then replied, "Well, if you really want to know, I'm hoping that in time young Gerry Lambert will become fairly tolerable. I've thrashed him twice and it's done him a lot of good."

There was a breathless silence.

"Take him away if you like," added Arnold, smiling.

"Take him away!"

"Yes, if you don't approve of my methods."

"Oh dear," exclaimed Connie. "It seems — dreadful, but perhaps — perhaps if you don't do it too hard . . ."

Young Gerry's other relations breathed again. It was a pleasant thought that in time he might become "fairly tolerable" and there was a firmness behind the smile of his headmaster which told of an intention to deal with him faithfully.

Roger did not ask for news of his son; there was no need, for he had received several letters from Arnold since the beginning of the term saying that Stephen was well and happy. He had also received a letter from Stephen which corroborated the headmaster's report. Roger had smiled over Stephen's letter and had put it away safely amongst his private papers. Some day, in the distant future, Stephen would smile over it himself:

Dear Daddy

School is nice. Lumsden has a meddle like you. It is the D.C.M. He has a fawlse hand but he can do things with it. I am being a pebbel on the beech like you said. Cartwright is my speshal friend. He is super. He is coming to tea at Amberwell on Sunday. Aunt Nell said I could. It is a pitty you cant come to the sports.

Your loving

Stephen

There was no need to worry about Stephen, he was "being a pebbel on the beech" and liking it. Later Roger would have a talk with his headmaster, but it would be a private talk. He did not intend to discuss his son in front of all his friends and relations.

The boys were jumping now, and as this was not so interesting to the spectators a babble of conversation had broken out. Roger took advantage of the chatter to speak quietly to his wife.

"You're feeling sad, Mary," he said in a low voice.

"Perhaps — just a tiny bit," she admitted.

"We shouldn't have come."

"No, Roger, that's silly! I'm glad we came. It's just that I can't help thinking of the old days."

"I know."

"But we shouldn't," declared Mary. "It's no good thinking about the past. The old days have gone — Stark Place has gone. Summerhills is looking ahead to the future ... all those little boys growing up into men!"

"In these beautiful surroundings," put in Roger. "They'll remember Summerhills all their lives."

Mary nodded thoughtfully. "Yes, and it belongs to us, Roger. Summerhills belongs to you and me — your vision and my dear old home! I think we've made something valuable and — and lasting, something really worth while."

"That's exactly what I've been thinking," said Roger gravely. "Summerhills is a good thing for us to have made."

Also available in ISIS Large Print:

Amberwell

D. E. Stevenson

Five young Ayrtons all grew up at Amberwell, playing in the gardens and preparing themselves to venture out into the world. To each of these children, Amberwell meant something different, but common to all of them was the idea that Amberwell was more than just where they lived, it was part of them.

Amberwell drove one of its children into a reckless marriage and healed another of his wounds . . . and there was one child who stayed at home and gave up her life to keep things running smoothly.

ISBN 0-7531-7373-5 (hb)
ISBN 0-7531-7374-3 (pb)

The Marigold Field

Diane Pearson

Through the vibrant years of the early part of the century — from 1896 to 1919 — lived the Whitmans, the Pritchards and the Dances, whose lives were destined to be intertwined . . .

Jonathan Whitman, his cousin Myra, Anne Louise Pritchard and the enormous Pritchard clan to which she belonged, saw the changing era and the incredible events of a passing age — an age of great poverty and great wealth, of the Boer War and social reform, of straw boaters, feather boas and the music hall.

Throughout all of this is the story if one woman's consuming love and of a jealous obsession that threatened to destroy the very man she adored. . .

ISBN 0-7531-7331-X (hb)
ISBN 0-7531-7332-8 (pb)

ISIS publish a wide range of books in large print, from fiction to biography. Any suggestions for books you would like to see in large print or audio are always welcome. Please send to the Editorial Department at:

ISIS Publishing Limited
7 Centremead
Osney Mead
Oxford OX2 0ES

A full list of titles is available free of charge from:

Ulverscroft Large Print Books Limited

(UK)
The Green
Bradgate Road, Anstey
Leicester LE7 7FU
Tel: (0116) 236 4325

(Australia)
P.O. Box 314
St Leonards
NSW 1590
Tel: (02) 9436 2622

(USA)
P.O. Box 1230
West Seneca
N.Y. 14224-1230
Tel: (716) 674 4270

(Canada)
P.O. Box 80038
Burlington
Ontario L7L 6B1
Tel: (905) 637 8734

(New Zealand)
P.O. Box 456
Feilding
Tel: (06) 323 6828

Details of **ISIS** complete and unabridged audio books are also available from these offices. Alternatively, contact your local library for details of their collection of **ISIS** large print and unabridged audio books.

... make our books in large print and
... biography. Are suggestions for books you
would like to see in large print or audio are always
... ome. Please send to the Editorial Department at:

Isis Publishing Limited
7 Centremead
Osney Mead
Oxford OX2 0ES

A full list of titles is available free of charge from:

Ulverscroft Large Print Books Limited

(Australia)
P.O. Box 314
St Leonards
NSW 1590
Tel: (02) 9436 2622

(Canada)
P.O. Box 80038
Burlington
Ontario L7L 6B1
Tel: (905) 637 8734

(New Zealand)
P.O. Box 456
...
Tel: (09) 521 6859

... Isis Complete and Unabridged audio ...
... available from these offices. All ...
... for details of their collection of ...
... unabridged audio books.